Cath Staincliffe is the author of the acclaimed Sal Kilkenny mysteries as well as being creator of ITV's hit police series, *Blue Murder*, starring Caroline Quentin as DCI Janine Lewis. Cath was shortlisted for the CWA Dagger in the Library award in 2006. She lives in Manchester with her partner and their three children.

Praise for Cath Staincliffe:

'A painfully honest exploration of an ordinary family under stress . . . a stunning piece of work.' Anne Cleeves

'Modest, compassionate . . . a solid, ingenious plotter with a sharp eye for domestic detail.' *Literary Review*

'An engrossing read.' *Sunday Telegraph*

'About as good as the British private-eye novel gets.' *Time Out*

'Complex and satisfying.' *Sunday Times*

'It's always exciting to see a writer get better and better, and Cath Staincliffe is doing just that.' Val McDermid

D0474604

C800492391

Also by Cath Staincliffe

The Kindest Thing
Witness

SPLIT SECOND

Cath Staincliffe

ROBINSON

Constable & Robinson Ltd
55–56 Russell Square
London WC1B 4HP
www.constablerobinson.com

First published in the UK by Constable,
an imprint of Constable & Robinson Ltd., 2012

Published in this paperback edition by Robinson,
an imprint of Constable & Robinson Ltd., 2012

A copy of the British Library Cataloguing in
Publication data is available from the British Library

ISBN 978-1-84901-346-8 (paperback)
ISBN 978-1-78033-556-8 (ebook)

Typeset by TW Typesetting, Plymouth, Devon

Printed and bound by CPI Group (UK) Ltd, Croydon, CR0 4YY

1 3 5 7 9 10 8 6 4 2

For Daniel, Ellie and Kit.
With thanks to writer Martin Baggoley
for advice on court procedure.

CHAPTER ONE

Emma

They burst on to the bus shoving and yelling; all energy and an edge of menace. Emma felt her stomach cramp, and along with that came a wash of resentment at the likelihood of disruption, the prospect that the rest of her journey home would be ruined by the chavs. Three of them. A girl: pretty, flawless milky skin and dark eye make-up, her white hooded jacket trimmed with fake fur; and two lads, a runty-looking one with thin lips and a tattoo like barbed wire on the side of his neck, and a bigger lad, red hair visible as he swiped his hood back, shaking the snow off. He had freckles and round baby-blue eyes.

The trio swung past the stairs and swayed along the central aisle, led by the big one telling some story at the top of his voice, swearing. The foul language, a sally of ammunition, fell through the air, hitting the passengers, who shrank and tensed. The girl was giggling and echoing half-phrases in a high-pitched squeal.

The teenagers scoured the passengers, waiting for anyone fool enough to make eye contact. Emma prayed none of them would sit next to her. The bus was almost half full, maybe ten people on the lower deck; the back seats just behind her were free. Would they sit there?

They didn't even pay, she thought. And none of them showed a travel card. What was the driver playing at? Why let them on? Couldn't he see they were trouble? He could have just closed the doors and driven on.

Emma tried to think about something else, shifted the bags of Christmas shopping at her feet. Nearly all done; got the ones to take home for Mum and Dad and the rest of the family in Birmingham, just need a couple for the girls at work.

'Shit!' The redhead broke off his tale and crowed at the top of his voice. 'Look who's here – Pukey Luke!'

He homed in on a mixed-race boy sitting a couple of rows in front of Emma on the other side. Short curly dark hair, skin the colour of toffee. There was a muttered curse by way of reply, then the clap and rustle of scuffling as the boy tried to get up.

'Going nowhere, pal,' the big guy said, and shoved him back down then knelt on the seat beside him. The girl and the weedy one flanked him. Now the cornered lad was looking away from the chavs out of the steamed-up window.

The bus clattered to a halt; an old couple got off and a woman with a baby in a buggy got on, wheeling the pram to the space opposite the bottom of the stairway.

'You ignoring me, wog boy?'

The word hung in the air, resounded around the space. Emma bit her tongue, felt her face heat up. The bus seemed to hesitate, to wait shivering, its panels rattling by the roadside, and Emma wondered if the driver was going to chuck the troublemakers off. But then with a defeated sigh the doors closed and the bus shuddered into motion.

It probably looks worse than it is, she thought. They obviously knew the boy – Luke, presumably. Could just be mucking about; they do that, don't they, play-fighting and next minute they're all friends. She didn't really know what was going on.

'Talking to you, dickhead.'

'Tell him, Gazza,' the girl giggled, egging her friend on. 'Black bastard.'

2

Ahead of her, Emma could see the latest arrival bending her head to focus on her sleeping child, an expression of dismay and the tug of anxiety in the way she bit her lip.

Emma's stomach hurt and she felt thirsty, a bit dizzy. Maybe she should say something. But no one else was doing anything. If it really was serious, someone else would say something, wouldn't they? What about the really big bloke sitting near the front, looking like a rugby player? He'd not done anything and he'd got size on his side. Or the group of studenty types, four of them, with long hair and funky clothes. They were just huddled together ignoring it.

What could she say, though? *Stop it.* Something friendlier? *Please leave him alone.* The words sounded pathetic in her head, weedy. She'd look ridiculous. Let alone the fact that the group might turn on her, she could get attacked. People did. What if she asked them to stop; then the boy, the ringleader, she could imagine him swivelling his gaze at her, those big marble eyes set off among his freckles, pushing himself away from the seat, homing in on her. 'You talking to me?' Then calling her names: 'Fat slag, stupid cow, keep your nose out.'

And what about the driver? He'd done nothing. This was his bus, his job; if anyone had a responsibility to do something, it was him.

She could ring the police, report the abuse. But if she did it now, everyone would hear. Besides, they'd probably snatch her phone as soon as they noticed. If the lad kept on ignoring his tormentors, maybe they'd lose interest. No one else was saying anything. Perhaps they knew it wasn't worth it, or that it was just chavs messing about, bored, maybe on drugs too.

'He's shitting himself,' the runty one cackled.

There were two women in front of Emma: middle-aged, dressed up well against the weather. Now she saw them exchange a glance, share a tiny shake of the head, caught the muscle in one woman's jaw tighten with disapproval. Shocking, dreadful, but what can you do?

There was a sharp crack and a tremor through the floor as the one called Gazza kicked the seat next to his quarry. Emma startled.

'Hah,' yelled Gazza. Another thump. 'You want a kicking? That'll sort you out,' he shouted at the boy at the window. 'You dirty nigger.'

The woman in the aisle seat in front of Emma pressed the bell, and she and her friend got to their feet, made their way to the front, standing near the driver as they waited for the lights to change. The large windscreen wiper was pushing slushy snowflakes in an arc across the glass. One of the women peered at the driver, but the man, grey hair, grey complexion, stared steadfastly ahead. She coughed; the driver glanced into his offside wing mirror and drove the bus across the junction, drawing in to the kerb with a whoosh of brakes. The doors folded back, letting in the cold air and a swirl of snow as the women got off. The bus moved on.

'I'll do you,' the bully said, his tone intense with pent-up rage. 'I'll have you. I've got a knife. Tell him.'

'He has,' barked the runty one. 'He'll shank you.'

'He'll cut you,' threatened the girl.

The air hummed with tension, the prospect of danger. Emma felt her neck burning, a band of pain around her head. They're just boasting, she thought, winding each other up. It'll all fizzle out in a minute. Just playing macho, aren't they? The passengers were mute, the atmosphere thick with shame and fear. They all sat cocooned, eyes cast down or out of the window.

The girl giggled. 'He's shaking, Gazza. Look at him.'

The bell dinged and the red bus-stopping sign illuminated. A lad stomped down from the upper deck, hair down to his shoulders, zipping up his olive-green parka, one of those bright woolly hats on with ear flaps.

'Knobhead.' Gazza slapped Luke; the boy's head banged into the glass.

The lad in the hat saw it; he flushed, moved down the bus. 'Leave him alone.'

Gazza turned. 'Or else? Fuck off.'

But the young man wasn't cowed; his face darkened with outrage, 'Just leave it.'

With a malicious snort, Gazza swivelled out of the seat and lunged at him, pushing him back and on to the lap of an old Asian man with bags of shopping.

Luke seized the distraction to leap into the aisle and run to the doors as the bus drew in to the stop.

'Get him!' Gazza roared, and the three of them scrambled after Luke. Pandemonium. Shouts of outrage and curses as they spilled off the bus.

The lad in the hat righted himself and followed at speed.

Emma felt sick. The doors closed, and she saw the woman with the baby shake her head at an old man on the disabled seats at the other side. But still no one spoke.

Emma looked out of the window as the bus drove away, tyres hissing on the wet tarmac, and saw Luke trip and recover and dart into a garden. The kids were close on his heels and the one in the hat behind them. It was the first house with lights on and there was a car parked at the side. Luke would be able to knock on the door, get help.

Should she ring the police now? And say what? There were some youths on the bus shouting abuse and making threats and now they're chasing this lad? It

5

would be hard to make the call on the bus with all the noise and people earwigging, and by the time she got home there wouldn't really be any point. And they'd probably tell her they'd look into it but it wasn't like anything definite had really happened. Well – one slap and the insults. It wasn't up to her, really; perhaps the driver would report it when he reached the terminus. Maybe he'd not done anything because he knew it wasn't actually worth reporting.

The bus trundled on and she sat, just like the rest of them, isolated and dumb, wanting to be anywhere but there.

Louise

'Brilliant!' Louise clapped as her daughter's voice faded along with the backing track. 'Dead good!'

Ruby was flushed, her brown eyes glittering, a sheen on her face from the exertion making her coppery skin glisten.

'Yer nan'd be proud of you.' Louise got up from the sofa, ready for a cup of tea.

'You always say that.' Ruby switched off the sound system.

''Cos it's true.' Louise had spent half her childhood applauding her mother, who'd made a living as a singer, fronting a twelve-piece band and crooning ballads or belting out show tunes. She'd spent the other half of it pining for the woman off criss-crossing the ocean singing for her supper on the cruise ships. Now she was here cheering on her daughter; the musical gene, the exhibitionist gene, had skipped a generation.

'Did Dad sing?' Ruby asked quietly.

Louise paused in the doorway to the kitchen. It had

been ages since Ruby had spoken about her dad Eddie, who'd died suddenly at the wheel of his taxi when Ruby was only four years old. Heart attack.

'Yeah, he did, he loved it. Couldn't hold a tune for toffee, though.'

Ruby grinned.

Louise went on, 'He'd sing hymns and football songs. Didn't matter to him which. He'd sing to you – d'you remember?'

Ruby shook her head, disappointed. Four was so young to lose him, Louise thought, so few memories to cling to.

'What did he sing to me?'

'Hymns and football songs,' Louise said wryly.

Ruby laughed, then swung round to face the mirror on the wall. 'What about my hair?' Her voice now leaking frustration. In the gene stakes, she had won her dad's Caribbean features: dark brown eyes, a wide nose and full mouth and tightly crinkled hair that she regarded as a total nightmare. They spent a small fortune on hair products: relaxing treatments, straighteners and the like. Louise, of Irish descent, with blue-white skin, wore her own wavy dark brown hair scooped back in a barrette. She saw little of herself in either of her children. Though they both had her fingers, thin and spidery, and her large feet.

'You could get it plaited, cornrows, like before.'

'Then I'd be stuck with it.'

And we'd be sixty quid worse off, Louise thought. But she didn't want to play that card now. Ruby was auditioning for stage school. She had wanted to act, to sing and dance all her life. Every spare penny, the precious few they had, went on ballet and tap and modern dance lessons, leotards and pumps. Now fourteen, Ruby was stunning, slender and gamine, with Eddie's high cheekbones, her teeth naturally white and straight. She moaned about being flat-chested, but all Louise saw was her beauty. And her drive, the ambition that Louise supported to the hilt.

'In a bun, then? Like it is but higher?' Louise suggested.

'A chignon?'

'Whatever they call it. Or wear something over it.'

'A paper bag,' Ruby slung back, and they both cracked up laughing.

'One of those . . .' Louise put her hand above her head, waggled her fingers.

'A fascinator.' Ruby curled her lip.

'You'll have to decide soon,' her mother cautioned. 'First week of January – and if you do want it styling, some places will be closed over the holidays. Now – I need a cuppa.'

'Get us a hot chocolate?'

Louise raised an eyebrow.

'Please.' Ruby curtsied. She began to practise one of her dance steps, the furniture around the edge of the room juddering as the floor shook.

'Watch the china,' Louise said.

'Cheek. Where's Luke?'

'Out,' Louise answered as she walked into the kitchen.

'Where?'

'God knows,' she called out. 'I told him to be back by eleven.' She filled the kettle. She peered through the window. It was snowing. Maybe they'd have a white Christmas.

'I don't know why you bother.' Ruby came into the kitchen.

Louise didn't reply. She switched the kettle on. 'When we get the tree up, you'll have to practise upstairs.'

'My room's too small.'

'Use mine, then.'

'Cool. When are we getting it?'

'Tomorrow,' Louise said. 'Carl's bringing one down.'

'Is it big?'

'Big enough.' She got the drinking chocolate out.

'That means it's titchy.'

'Wait and see.' Louise smiled. She'd paid for a six-footer. It would look great. And she was off Christmas Day.

Carl was at the agency with her, home help, social care. Closest thing she had to a boyfriend, but she kept it casual. She liked the company, someone to share a meal or a laugh or a bed with, but nothing more serious. He was a nice bloke, a bit dim, but well-meaning, sociable. Polish. The agency work was crap money really, but for Carl it was way more than he could make back home. The job itself was okay: cleaning, shopping, feeding, changing, a lot of listening. Some of the people Louise had been calling on for years, knew more about them than their own families did. But the agency was always trying to screw as much as they could from you.

Louise looked back out at the garden. Some of the snow had settled, on the grass and the shed roof, but the path was gleaming wet. Be nice if it did stay. Course, it caused problems, people falling and fractures and buses not running, but it looked lovely.

'Or a wig?' Ruby said. 'Like a dead bright colour, yeah? Red, like my shoes.'

Andrew

He thought he heard something over the noise of the shower. Banging? Perhaps Jason had forgotten his key. More than likely. Andrew tipped his head back, let the water play on his face. In fact it was unusual for Jason to remember his key. A dreamer. It drove Val round the bend, her son's lack of focus, his apparent ineptitude.

'Is it a boy thing?' she'd demanded of Andrew one day when Jason was about six. Still struggling to tie his shoelaces, still forgetting his book bag, his games kit, his permission slip, to brush his teeth, to turn the television off.

'He's just made like that, I guess,' Andrew said.

'All I do is nag,' she complained. 'And if I don't, nothing happens.'

'He's only little.' Andrew pulled her to him, kissed her. 'D'you want me to nag?'

She shook her head, still exasperated.

'Maybe he'll never be the world's most organized person, but he's bound to get a bit better.'

'You think?'

'I hope.'

But Jason's absent-mindedness had persisted; his relationship to the practical, physical world had never become one of mastery or precision, though he was skilled in other areas. He could play any instrument he picked up, despite never having had a lesson in his life; he'd overcome his moderate dyslexia to get four A levels and a place to study geography at Durham.

'Geography!' Val had exclaimed when Andrew told her Jason had been talking about it. 'He can barely find his way home from school without a sat nav. He's no sense of direction – in either sense of the word.'

'He loves geography, though,' Andrew had said. 'Remember all those maps we used to make?' Pieces of lining paper scrawled on with felt pens: islands littered with treasure troves and hazards; sharks and sinking sands, whirlpools and stingrays. Staining the paper with used tea bags, singeing the edges with the kitchen matches and setting the smoke alarm off, rolling them into scrolls, tied with broken shoelaces.

'He liked maps because you did,' Val said.

'Maybe. Does it matter? It's good to know there's something he wants to do – and his marks have been great.'

'Yes.' She softened, gave a rueful smile. 'I just worry about him, that's all,' apologizing, acknowledging the tension she brought to the discussion, that for all his charms, her child's flaws still irritated her, made her feel impatient and then guilty.

Jason had seen it through, taken the offer from Durham, got his grades and moved into halls twelve weeks ago. The house had been deadly without him, ghostly without the trail of debris, the piles of laundry, the racket as he moved about the place, heavy-footed, clumsy, big-boned. Now he was back home for Christmas. He'd gone to the pub tonight, to catch up with his mates from school, the group scattered to universities around the country.

Andrew turned, let the jets of water drum on his back, inched the temperature control up a notch. He bent for the shower gel.

'Andrew! Andrew!' Val braying at the bathroom door. Was there a leak? The shower flooding into the kitchen below? Her voice frantic, furious. For a moment he wondered if he had done something wrong, or failed to do something, but what would merit such fury? He stopped the shower. 'Get out here!' she yelled. 'There's a fight outside. Jason's there!'

He almost slipped stepping out of the shower, swiped a towel down his front and across his back, pulled on clothes from the floor, his jeans and pullover, the wool itchy against his skin. He hurried downstairs, where he could see the front door open, Val just inside, the phone in hand, her voice urgent, shaky as she gave their address and then shouted to Jason.

Andrew went past her on to the front lawn. Jason was tussling with a boy, dragging at his sleeve; on the grass beside them lay a figure, curled small. Two people waited at the gate, yelling: a girl in a white coat and another bigger lad in a hoodie, popping-out eyes. Andrew ran forward, yelling too. The boy wrenched himself free from Jason, leapt over the prone figure and ran. Andrew went after them, screaming, his heart thumping fiercely in his chest, fury red at the edges of his eyes. He lost his footing on the slippery pavement, he had no shoes on, and went over, his shoulder and hip hitting the ground hard. He scrambled up but the trio were already near the junction and he saw them veer off. He'd never catch them now.

He ran back to the house, the ground cold and wet and gritty beneath his feet. The crystals of snow on the grass squeaking as he went to his son. Jason was bent over, hands on knees, breathless, panting. He swung his head, saw Andrew. 'Dad, call an ambulance.' He was close to tears. 'I think they've killed him.'

'Oh God!' Andrew's phone was upstairs. But Val was already . . . 'I think your mum . . .'

'Call a fucking ambulance,' Jason screamed at him.

Tears started in his eyes, at his son's anguish, at the pathos of the scene. He ran upstairs, grabbed his phone and punched in 999. He hurried back down and the operator answered on the second ring and transferred him to the ambulance service. Val was still talking. 'Three of them, a girl and two boys, they've only just gone.'

Outside, Andrew hunkered down. The boy on the floor was still; his face was bloody and swollen. Andrew's stomach flooded with acid; his heart was still pounding, and he was trembling. He followed what the voice on the phone said, tried to answer their questions as best he could.

'I think he's dead,' Jason gasped. 'He was jerking, like a fit.'

Andrew repeated the information for the operator, and listened to her instructions.

'They're coming,' he said.

'We should do something.' Jason's voice was wild with panic. He was batting his fists together. The boy was still; by his head, the snow was pink, like sorbet with raspberry sauce. Flecks of snow landed and melted on his hair, on his poor, poor face.

'I need to check if he's breathing,' Andrew said.

Jason began to cry.

'Hey.' Andrew straightened up, folded him into his arms. Felt a tremor ripple through his son. And another. 'You're freezing, go in.'

Val came out. 'Jason.'

'Mum.'

'Take him inside,' Andrew urged. He heard sirens howling in the distance. Coming here, he prayed.

'No, I'm not—' Jason began to protest, but Andrew shushed him.

'Come inside, Jason,' Val said.

'I think he's in shock,' Andrew told her. 'He must have seen it all.'

'Oh, Mum. Mum.'

'Come on, love. Dad'll look after him.' Jason went with her.

Andrew crouched down closer to the boy. He could smell the blood raw on the night air; it made his gorge rise. He put his hand gently on the boy's chest and felt movement, a slight rise and fall. Yes! Oh, thank God. He scrambled to his feet and ran to meet the ambulance, aware that neighbours were coming to their gates and others pulling their curtains back, peering out through snowy stencils, their faces illuminated by twinkling fairy lights and the garish pulse of flashier outdoor decorations.

The paramedics wanted Andrew to move away while they assessed the victim, and a police officer asked for Val. Andrew took him inside. Val was coming downstairs with a blanket for Jason. 'He's still shivering,' she told Andrew.

'Sugar,' he said. 'I'll make him a drink. The police want you.'

The officer nodded and introduced himself and asked Val if she could tell him what had happened. He followed her into the front room. Andrew looked in. Jason was white as a sheet; he looked awful, just like he used to before he was sick as a child after an unwise fairground ride, or a long car journey. 'Jason?'

'Dad.' His voice was thick, gluey. Val glanced over, stopped talking. Andrew felt it in the room, a current, electric, biting at the back of his neck, crackling up his spine. He moved towards his son. 'I feel—' Jason slumped forward, his legs skittering on the carpet. There was a dark stain on the back of the armchair, wet, deep vivid red. The same on his parka.

'Oh my God!' Val dropped the blanket and ran to him.

'Jason!' They were both beside him. Then there was blood coming from his nose. Andrew grasped his shoulders, tried to straighten him up. His mind screaming: *What do I do? What do I do? Help, please help.* Sounds colliding around him, shouts, and a paramedic pulling his arms away from Jason. Jason on the floor, on his side, Val weeping. Someone pulling them back, getting between them and their son. *Stab wound.* Who

14

said it? *Stab wound.* Panic rearing inside him like waves, higher and higher, and he couldn't stay still. Val biting her fist, shaking her head, strands of her blonde hair stuck to her face. Then they were moving him and someone would take them to the hospital. Did they have their house keys? Phones?

Outside it was snowing again, fat flakes pirouetting in the street lights, settling and turning red on the front lawn.

CHAPTER TWO

Louise

W hen her phone went, Louise didn't recognize the number. She wondered if it was someone from the agency. It was late, but not impossible: some of the work was respite care, staying with people whose regular carers needed a break, most often elderly people with dementia, and on rare occasions the agency worker allocated would have a problem and need replacing.

'Hello?'

Ruby came downstairs in her pyjamas.

'Who am I speaking to, please?' a woman asked.

Louise was suspicious, some sort of spam call maybe, but she replied anyway, watching Ruby put her homework back in her school bag. 'Louise Murray.'

'You're related to Luke Murray?'

Her blood ran cold. 'Yes. His mum.'

'This is Manchester Royal Infirmary. Luke was involved in an incident earlier this evening.' Louise felt the slap of shock, a thump in her guts that forced her to step back, murmuring, 'Oh no, no.'

She saw Ruby turn and freeze, alarm enlarging her eyes.

Luke! Oh, God. 'Is he all right?' Dread flared through her.

'He's stable,' the woman said, and went on to give her instructions as the pressure built in Louise's chest, making it hard to breathe, hard to concentrate.

'I'll come now, yes.' She ended the call, her hand shaking. Panic fluttering at her back like wings.

'Mum?'

'It's the hospital. Luke's there. Get your coat.' Ruby nodded, fled.

'Please,' Louise prayed, 'please, please let him be all right.'

The car door was frozen, the key wouldn't turn.

The de-icer was inside the car, so she hurried to fetch the kettle and ran hot water over the lock. The metal made a chinking sound.

It worked, and she got the de-icer and the plastic scraper and scoured away at the ice on the windscreen, her breath great puffs of mist. Beneath her feet the grass verge was lumpy, unyielding. Everything was frozen solid, brilliant and brittle.

They drove through the snow. The middle of the main road was clear, but everything else, the pavements, hedges, roofs and trees, was smothered in a layer of white. Smudging the edges.

Ruby spoke. 'What happened?'

'They didn't say, just that he was stable.'

'Maybe there was an accident? Like a crash?'

Incident, Louise thought, they said *incident*. 'I don't know, love.' Thinking only that he was hurt, whatever it was, he was hurt. Alcoholic poisoning? Drinking himself stupid. Would that be an incident? Or if he'd been messing with drugs. Something else reckless? Trespassing on the railway line. He wasn't a bad kid, not nasty, just daft at times, taking risks. Better lately, though, much better. That didn't matter, not now. All that mattered was getting there. Make him better, make it better. She wouldn't let herself imagine how he might be injured, fought against the pictures rearing up inside

17

her head. Not going there. Just do this, just get through this.

He'd always been a handful; the number of times she'd been summoned into school: Luke giving cheek, Luke not showing up. He was bright and bored. He couldn't wait to leave. She'd been the same at that age. She had tried talking to him about A levels or doing a BTEC. Something to give him a chance of a decent job, not end up like her in the poverty trap, no qualifications, everything a struggle.

'No way,' he'd said. And she knew there was no shifting him. Stubborn as a mule, never knew when to back down or back off. Could be a good quality at times, that persistence, but at others he'd back himself into a corner and brick it up.

Days later he came in from town, put a pizza in the oven and announced that he wanted to join the army.

Over my dead body, Louise swore to herself. She hadn't spent sixteen years raising him to have him go off and get blown to bits by a roadside bomb in a godforsaken desert. 'Thought you didn't like people bossing you about,' she'd said. 'That's all you get in the army: rules and regulations.'

'So?'

'C'mon, Luke, you're not exactly hot on authority, are you?'

'What you saying?' He was truculent, ready for an argument. 'Someone's got to fight for their country.'

She stifled a sigh, didn't want to alienate him, wondered where the sudden interest in soldiering had come from. 'What's the attraction?'

'Best training in the world, isn't it?'

Then what? Kill people, be killed. Eight years ago, Louise had dragged him on the anti-Iraq war march, him and Ruby both. He'd loved it, shouted himself

18

hoarse, enjoying the novelty of mass protest, the whiff of disobedience, transgression, marching down the middle of the road between the police lines, waving the flag he'd made. Ruby had cried, fearful that planes would come and bomb them any minute. Not understanding that this was a war where only the children of the 'enemy' would lose life and limb. An unequal and illegal war fought for duplicitous reasons.

'Grandad was in the army,' he said. Meaning Louise's grandad, his great-grandad.

'That was different, he was called up. He'd not have wanted you fighting in Afghanistan. He was a communist, I've told you that. He'd have known exactly what it was down to: oil and economics.'

While Louise's mother had been roaming the world entertaining passengers in her glittery gowns and long black gloves, Louise and her dad Phil had lived with her grandparents. Grandad was a docker, a union man and a lifelong Party member. The only paper that came into the house was the *Morning Star*. Louise's dad was a liberal, if pressed. Wishy-washy, according to Grandad. The house rang with political arguments and debates. Louise got dragged along to fund-raisers for Cuba and Angola, or commandeered by her grandad to give out leaflets for pickets during the miners' strike, but once grown, she'd never joined a party or got involved. Her political activity ran to voting every election, paying union dues, even though the agency wasn't unionized, attending the occasional demonstration and peeling racist stickers off lamp posts.

Maybe the army thing was a reaction against her and her views. Luke rebelling, thinking of something to put her back up. She decided not to give him any more ammunition. 'Okay,' she said steadily, 'how about this – you still want to join up in a year's time and you can go.'

19

He frowned at her, wary. 'Why wait?'

'You're only sixteen, you'll need my consent if you're under eighteen, but I'd like you to give something else a go first.'

'Such as?' He leaned back on the chair, rocking it on its back legs, arms folded.

'A trade – you choose.'

'Not college,' he insisted.

'An apprenticeship. You'd be earning. There's usually day release.'

'What?'

'You do a day a week at college, the rest on the job.'

'You just don't want me to join the army,' he objected.

'No, I don't.' She kept her voice level. 'But I can't stop you, once you're old enough. People die, Luke, they get injured, lose limbs; or they get stressed out, can't settle again. Why would I want that for you?'

'I won't change my mind,' he said, his eyes fixing on hers. His lovely fine brown eyes

She nodded. 'But give it till your next birthday. I'll ask around, see if anyone knows anyone.' She waited, tense. Hoping to God she could find an opening. Half the kids in Manchester were on the dole, a lost generation, they were saying. What would Grandad make of this? Cameron and cronies finishing Thatcher's job. Privatizing everything that moved, dismantling the public services, the NHS, crushing the north, where no one ever voted Tory, penalizing the poor.

''Kay.' He let the chair fall back in place, got to his feet. 'Not doing plumbing, though – skanky, man.'

Emma

Her flat was across the other side of the dual carriage-way, next to the railway station. She was on the second floor, her windows level with the platforms. Sometimes she got the train to work, though if she did, she had a fifteen-minute walk across town at the other end.

Emma liked being near the line; the sound of the trains was reassuring, somehow, telling her that there were all those people out there going places, coming back. Growing up in Brum, the railway had run at the end of their terraced street, so it was probably in her blood.

She fed the fish and went into the kitchen. She hadn't had anything to eat since lunch, but with all that bother on the bus, she felt queasy still. Maybe something light? She opened the fridge and got out the Philadelphia cream cheese, put bread in the toaster and went to change out of her office clothes.

She settled in front of the telly with her plate and a mug of cappuccino. She kept flicking the channels, but there was nothing that held her attention. There was a repeat of *A Place in the Sun: Home or Away* on, but it was one she'd seen first time round. The couples were so choosy, and didn't ever seem to actually settle on a place. They never liked the places that Emma did.

Sometimes Emma thought about working abroad. The sort of job she had, working in the claims office of an insurance company, meant she had quite a lot of transferable skills, for other office work at least, but she didn't speak any other languages. 'Barely speaks English,' her dad would say. 'Don't mumble, girl.'

He'd always been impatient with her, impatient and disappointed. Because she got tongue-tied, because she was shy, he decided she was stupid. She sometimes

21

wondered when it had started: had he been critical even when she was a baby? Because she was chubby (in other words fat), because she slept a lot and didn't walk until she was eighteen months old, and because when she talked, her speech was whispered, hesitant. Had she been born like that, or grown to match his expectations: someone with no guts, no gumption, no wit? Feeble, worthless.

Emma texted her mum as she did every night, told her that work had been busy and town had been frantic. She paused, thinking about the bus: the hard face on the lad who hit the mixed-race boy, the girl's thin giggle, that awful feeling, tight and sick, making you want to close your eyes and block your ears. She couldn't have done anything, could she? She thought about telling her mum, but then her dad would want to talk to her, and she couldn't face him now. She shook away thoughts of the bus; she was home, it was done with. She typed that it was snowing and sent the text.

Unable to settle, she turned off the lamp and pulled the curtains open. That way the velvet blue light from the aquarium cast a glow in the room. Outside, she could see the snow falling: rhythmic cascades of flakes, quick and quiet. The roof of the ticket office was cushioned in snow, as was the fence and the platform. Everything looked softer and cleaner somehow with the white covering.

Watching the fish usually helped her relax. Hypnotic or something. She didn't know how it worked, but following them as they drifted to and fro would calm her down. The stripy green discus fish darted and turned swiftly in the tank, and the shoal of little neon tetras, sparkling blue and silver and red, wove in harmony through the weed. Emma stared for long enough, but her stomach was all knotted up. Maybe she was just too tired tonight. She'd feel better after a good long sleep. And it was Saturday tomorrow – a lie-in.

Andrew

Andrew and Val sat in the waiting area for close to an hour. The place was quiet, just the faint background shush of air-conditioning, and now and then the squeak of footsteps as someone in scrubs or overalls wandered past along the corridor. The lights were harsh, recessed behind shiny silver grids in the low ceiling. At either end of the space, cheap foil banners proclaimed *Merry Christmas*, and someone had taped a sprig of plastic holly above the big round clock.

Andrew was thirsty; his tongue felt rough and too large for his mouth, his throat ached, peppery, but he would not move to go and find a drink. Someone would come. They must wait here.

Every few minutes Val spoke to him, often repeating herself. 'They must have had a knife but he didn't know. He didn't even know he'd been hurt. He walked inside, you saw him. He was so worried about the one they'd set upon, he didn't even think about himself. Why didn't he ring the police instead of charging in like that?' They weren't questions to be answered, just asked over and over like penance, a chant of angry disbelief flung to the Fates or the Gods, falling on stone-deaf ears.

In the silences between, Andrew watched the long, slim black hand on the clock edge past the minutes. He got up and walked to the double doors, left ajar, and stared at the map of the hospital on the wall. The garish blocks of colour indicating different wards, a bewildering key below organized alphabetically by complaint rather than numerically by ward, starting with the emergency department: adult emergency. They were somewhere there.

He'd done some sessions in the rehabilitation unit here for one of his placements when he'd been training. He still did some NHS work alongside his private practice, but almost all of it at Wythenshawe Hospital, a few miles south, on the edge of the city. That had been a tough time – his training. He'd left his job in the local authority planning department after six months on sick leave with work-related stress. Val, also at the town hall, working in training, had wanted him to sue for constructive dismissal, furious at the insidious bullying by his manager, but Andrew hadn't had the energy or the emotional wherewithal to do anything more than limp away. He was close to cracking up completely, and just the thought of confronting his manager, of statements and meetings and tribunals, made him panic. His health was more precious than winning the argument.

Training in speech therapy had been a random choice really, prompted by a radio documentary. It meant two years as a student on a bursary then a not very good income afterwards. Certainly less than he'd have made climbing up the civic ladder. But Val, now a team leader, was on a good salary, and with only one child, they were reasonably well off.

'Andrew?' She'd been repeating his name.

'Sorry,' he turned from the map, 'what?'

'Do you think we should go and find someone? Find out what's going on?'

Who? Where? He felt completely inadequate. Before he had a chance to frame a response, a man appeared, his scrubs rumpled, his head covered with a patterned hat. Val stood up and quickly crossed to join Andrew. Her jaw was trembling.

'Mr and Mrs Barnes?'

Andrew nodded. Val said, 'Yes.'

Andrew watched the man close his eyes, a slow blink before he spoke, his lips parting, an intake of air.

That was all it took, and Andrew knew.

They could not go home. The police officer apologized, but the house had been sealed for examination. It was a crime scene. They could be taken to a hotel and a family liaison officer would meet them there. After tonight, perhaps they would rather stay with family?

Stupefied, they let themselves be shepherded from the room where Jason lay and along to the exit. The officer kept talking, a meaningless burble. Andrew wondered if he was doing it to comfort himself, like a child whistling in the dark, or if he thought it might help them.

As they reached the automatic doors, Val stopped and turned to Andrew. Her face contorted and tears spilled down her cheeks. 'Not on his own.' She shook her head, her voice thick.

It was half past four. They had sat with their son in the anteroom in the bereavement suite since ten past midnight. Andrew had held Jason's hand, tracing the lines on his palm, lines of destiny now met, rubbing the calluses on his fingers made by the guitar strings, noticing the fine golden hairs on the back of his wrist.

The policeman stopped and cleared his throat. 'If you need a bit longer . . .'

A bit? How about another fifty years?

'. . . but the pathologist—'

'Start work at four in the morning, do they?' Val snapped, and shivered.

Andrew took her arm and led her back, along to the lifts, up to the room.

At quarter past eight the sun rose crimson over the snow-covered city and the pathologist came for Jason.

Louise

Louise held Ruby's hand; her daughter's touch was warm, the skin smooth and soft, unlike her own, roughened from chores and her habit of biting the skin around her nails.

The doctor was young, Oriental-looking, Chinese or Japanese, maybe Korean. Dr Liu. She spoke softly and Louise had to crane her neck to hear her above the white noise spitting in her head.

'Luke is still unconscious,' the doctor said. 'There's a fracture to the skull so we want to do a scan to check on that; there is a chance we will need to operate, to reduce any swelling and alleviate the pressure on the brain.'

Louise felt her nose burn, bit her cheek; the tang of blood made her mouth water.

'He's breathing on his own, which is a good sign,' the doctor went on, 'and there is nothing to signify damage to any other internal organs.'

'Will he be all right?' Louise asked, the words sounding brittle and dusty. Broken leaves.

'We'll know more when we have the scan results.'

Which was no answer at all really.

'Can't you wake him up?' Ruby asked.

'The body can better repair itself in the unconscious state. It's best if he wakes up naturally. He is being hydrated with a drip. You can go in to see him before we take him up. It looks bad.' Her eyes held Louise's, black like jet beads. 'It may be a big shock.' She glanced sideways at Ruby, then to Louise, an unspoken question.

'Rube, if you—' Louise began.

'I wanna see him.'

Oh God. Louise barely knew him. His face was misshapen, swollen and still bloody. A lump the size of an orange on his left cheek and his right eyelid torn, the lashes, his long curling lashes, gummy with blood. His lips cracked, slightly parted, his front teeth at the top missing. The ferocity of it ripped through her in a wash of terror and rage. Oh my poor lamb. How frightened he must have been.

'Oh God,' Ruby breathed.

That he should suffer so. Someone had done this to him, her blessed, troubled boy. Louise turned away, her hand shielding her eyes, her chest aflame. Ruby was crying quietly, sniffling. Louise hugged her, murmured words of solace, then stepped away, studied her son. She wanted to scoop him up, cradle him on her knee and sing to him, comfort him. Or shake him awake, force him to his feet, clean his wounds. She wanted to kiss him, stroke his hair, but his head was so raw, so exposed, she was fearful she might hurt him. His hands lay at his sides, the drip going into his left arm; she picked up his right hand, hot and limp, pressed her mouth against his palm, tasted salt there, smelt iron. She tried to replace the bloated face with his usual profile, that of his father Roland. The Nigerian student who had spent a summer working in the care home where Louise had her first job. Roland, who broke her heart. Wooed her with his flirting and his patter, promised her the earth, then when she fell pregnant told her he was engaged to a girl back home and he'd be marrying his intended as soon as he graduated. Roland the rat, sleek and smooth.

'He'll be going up for the scan in a moment,' Dr Liu

said. A knock on the door made them all turn. It was the police.

He took them into a side room. Louise hated leaving Luke, but the police officer said it would only be for a few minutes.

'What happened?' She had agreed to tell the officer anything she could to help, but she was also frantic to know how it had come to this.

'He was attacked by three youths earlier this evening,' the man said.

A sea of fury swelled inside, the waves smashing against the rock of her heart. 'Where? Why?'

'Kingsway. We don't know why yet.'

'Because he's black?' Louise said. Pity and grief and hurt swirling through her. Laced with guilt too, because her first thoughts had been that Luke had done something silly and got himself hurt. But someone had done this to him. Deliberately battered him.

'We'll be looking into that as a possibility.' The man had his notebook open; he twisted his wrist and read his watch, jotted down the time. 'I just need all the formal details out of the way: name, address, date of birth and so on.'

She gave him those, then he asked her when she'd last seen Luke.

'Tea time. Half six. Then he went out.'

'Where was he going? Did he say?'

'He's a teenager; "out" is all I get. Sometimes he goes into town with his mates, but he wasn't dressed up or anything.'

'Where else?'

Round Declan's getting stoned, she thought, or in the park. But in this weather? Mind, they didn't feel the cold, did they, kids; image was more important. 'Perhaps just with his mates.'

'I'll need their details.'

She nodded. 'The people that did this. Who are they?'

'We've not identified them yet.'

'Do you think they knew him?' She was desperate for answers, for meaning, for sense.

He took a breath, scratched his head. 'I don't think anything; I'm just asking the questions we need to ask. Has Luke been in any trouble recently?'

'No,' she said. He had settled on an apprenticeship as an electrician. One of Carl's mates had taken him on. He didn't like the college part, but he'd gone along each week so far. And he'd wired some outside lights for Christmas. Rigging them up in the sycamore tree at the corner of the garden. It looked great – big, soft white globes, way better than the tacky flashing Santas and cartoon reindeers on the house opposite. She'd been so proud of him, and excited at the prospect that he might find his footing working in the trade. Make a good living. Settle into his own skin and forget about the army.

'Any history of trouble in the past?' the policeman asked her.

She sighed, worried that her answer would influence how he thought of Luke and what effort they'd put into catching his attackers. 'A couple of cautions for antisocial behaviour and criminal damage.'

The officer waited, his pen poised. 'Why was that, then?' Did she imagine it, or had his tone changed, the warmth leaking away?

'Messing with fireworks,' she said, 'and some graffiti.' He could find out anyway – she didn't want to appear uncooperative and add to any impression he might have that her family was a bad lot. 'But he's turned things around now,' she said as brightly as she could manage. 'He's got an apprenticeship, as an electrician.'

He wrote it down. 'Anything else you can tell me?'

'He said he'd be back about eleven.'

'Ruby?' The man shifted his attention to her. 'Anything else?'

She shook her head.

Louise swallowed. Sat up in her seat, determined to keep on top of it all, to just do what had to be done. To fight the impulse to withdraw into sorrow and shut down.

'There was another victim,' the policeman said. 'Jason Barnes, do you know him?'

Louise shook her head.

'He didn't make it.'

'What!' She tried to untangle what he was saying. Saw the resignation in his eyes. 'Oh my God. Oh no.' She couldn't stop trembling. Thinking that could have been Luke. Dead. Killed.

'I'm sorry,' she managed to respond. 'Can we go now?' she asked, rising. Her head spinning, her knees weak as straw. She had to get back to him. Dread pooling in her belly, between her shoulder blades. 'Please?' She had to be there, watch over him, keep him safe.

He nodded, and she held on to Ruby's arm for support and numbly retraced her steps.

Andrew

The light on the snow was blinding, Andrew winced and narrowed his eyes. Two men were clearing the paths; the clang of shovels on the stone rang loud in the air. The snow muffled the other sounds, shushing the city.

He had moved the car in the middle of the night,

30

sweeping clods of snow from the windscreen, the frosty air stinging his nostrils and nipping at his ankles; he had pulled on shoes but not socks in the race to get to the hospital.

Now they walked to the car park. 'You'd better ring your parents,' Val said.

This could kill Dad, he thought, already battling high blood pressure and angina. 'I'll tell Colin.' His older brother lived close to the family home. 'He can go round there.' He pulled out his phone.

'In the car.' Val frowned.

He didn't understand.

'Less noise,' she said dully. There was nothing for him in her expression, no affection, no compassion. She was exhausted.

Colin answered. 'Andrew, hi. How you doing?' Upbeat, bright.

Andrew closed his eyes, cleared his throat, a noise like a whimper.

'What's wrong?' Alarm now, and Andrew felt the hair on his neck stand up and the bottomless swirl in his guts.

'It's . . .'

'Andrew?'

He forced the words past his tongue, through his teeth. Into the air, in the car, in the car park, let them loose to fly across the glittering roofs, up amid the skyscrapers and towers and bridges, across the city to the whole wide world. 'Jason was stabbed last night, a fight on the street.' He heard Colin gasp at the other end but he kept going. 'They took him to hospital, they couldn't bring him back. Can you tell Mum and Dad?'

Colin was saying things, *shock, can't believe, sorry*, and Andrew clung on, his fingers a vice around his phone, answering the questions while he watched the

31

city sparkle and wondered if they had the old sledge and if Jason might fancy a go.

'Andrew.' His father was in the kitchen doorway, his face whey-coloured, eyes wounded. 'There's someone here from the police.'

Andrew dipped his head. Three people came in; two men and a woman. His parents had knocked their kitchen through years ago, combining the old scullery with the bigger room and creating space for the family to eat in. Introductions were made, condolences given, and the man doing the talking asked for Val.

'She's upstairs with my mother,' Andrew told them.

'She witnessed the fight?' the man asked.

'Yes.' The word rustled in his throat. He'd drunk a cup of tea, but it hadn't touched the dryness when he swallowed. The man turned to Leonard, Andrew's father, still hovering in the doorway. 'Is there somewhere we could talk to Mrs Barnes?'

'The living room.'

'We need to get a statement from each of you,' he explained to Andrew.

There was no rushing any of it, as people were rearranged and notebooks and forms produced. They must know, he thought, that we can't function any faster, that everything is slow motion, gravity's shifted. All at sea, unable to resist the current. A container ship had shed a load of plastic ducks a long time ago, in the Atlantic; years later, bleached and blinded by sun and salt, they were still washing up, teaching climatologists about the currents.

'Mr Barnes?'

'Sorry.' He laid his arms on the table, tried to clear his head. His back ached, the whole of his spine, as though the snow had got in there too, crystals of ice

32

fusing the bones and burning the nerve endings. He felt a jolt of surprise when he saw an outlined plan of their house and garden, the houses either side, the dual carriageway. He recalled filling in car claim forms after a bump when Jason had been a toddler. The diagrams: X marks the spot. Jason's maps, 'Why is it X, Dad?'

The questions came at him and he replied as best he could: Jason was home from uni, back two days, gone out to meet friends for a drink. Andrew was in the shower when . . . Jason was so concerned about the other boy . . . No, they didn't know him . . . No, they didn't know them either . . .

'Is there anything else you can tell me?'

What? he thought. That he was a lovely young man, he was frightened of heights and moths. He wouldn't get on an aeroplane or learn to drive because of global warming. He fell off his bunk bed and broke his wrist when he was ten. He hates jazz. The only thing he can cook is bacon and egg. He's ticklish. He is dead. He is dead and cold and I will never hear him laugh again. He has a tattoo of a dragon on his shoulder. He can't change a plug or build a shelf but he plays music like an angel.

Andrew shook his head and put his face in his hands.

The woman was their family liaison officer, Martine. She told them it would be a couple more days before they would be able to return home, and they might want to consider staying on at Leonard and Jean's anyway. There would be a great deal of media interest in the case. The police would work in partnership with the media, but it was important that the family didn't talk to anyone without running it past Martine, who would check things with the press office.

'It's already in the lunchtime edition.' She laid the *Manchester Evening News* on the table.

Val grabbed at it, her lips moving round the words of the headline. *Have-a-Go Hero Stabbed to Death. Teen victim fights for life.* 'How did they get his picture?'

Andrew stared at his son, a recent image, his hair tangled, muddy blond, almost shoulder-length. He'd grown it over the summer. 'YouTube,' he told her. He felt sick. The doorbell went, and then his brother was there, with his wife and the kids. Everyone was there. Everyone except Jason.

CHAPTER THREE

Louise

The operation had been a success, the surgeon told them. They had removed the fluid that had built up and hoped that the swelling would now subside. Luke would be kept sedated and given respiratory assistance for the next seventy-two hours. This should give the best possible chance for the brain to heal.

Louise ran her hands over her head, bone-tired. Hollow but for the burr of anxiety. 'He will get better, wake up?'

The surgeon pursed his lips. 'That's certainly our aim. No two patients are alike, and to be honest we still don't understand why some patients make a full recovery while others don't.'

'He's young.' She stumbled over the words, a prayer more than anything.

'Yes, and otherwise strong and healthy. We're moving him into the ICU now.'

There was a dressing on his head, drips in his arm and a breathing tube over his nose. The nurse said it was just a little extra help, to boost his oxygen. His face, the bruises, the swellings, looked even worse. The nurse chatted to them in a brisk whisper, gave them a leaflet about the unit. Louise and Ruby sat down either side of Luke's bed.

'Can he hear us?'

'I don't think so – the sedation, it's like he's fast

asleep.' Louise saw that Ruby was wiped out, her eyes bleary, head drooping. 'We'll go home for a bit.'

Ruby glanced up and across at her, alarm furrowing her brow.

'He's just resting, love. We should too. We'll come back later. You've not eaten anything.'

Ruby looked at her brother.

'It'll be all right,' Louise reassured her. 'Come on.'

Louise bent over Luke, close to his ear. 'Luke, we're popping home for a bit, we'll come and see you later. Love you.'

'Mum.' Ruby in tears again.

Her own eyes stung in response, but she fought against it; she had to be strong, pull them all through this. 'Hey.' She moved round the bed. Held her daughter.

'It's not fair,' Ruby blurted out. 'It's so awful.'

'Shush, hush now.'

When Ruby had calmed down, she too said goodbye to Luke, and then they followed the winding corridors out.

The freezing air hurt Louise's lungs, the same sensation she remembered after she'd had the kids each time, when she'd been awake for hours on end, using all the reserves her body had. She pulled her scarf over her nose and mouth. She switched her phone on and felt it buzz. A stack of messages: Ruby's school, Carl, the agency. People to tell.

At home, Luke's lights were still on in the sycamore tree, sparkling on the frost that limned the branches. Glittering on the snow.

Ruby had some cereal and went to lie down, while Louise sat and rang round. Her mind looping back again and again to Luke in the hospital bed, his poor ruined face, his broken teeth. Listening to people's expressions of horror as she outlined what had happened.

When she went into the kitchen, she saw a dark shape against the back window. The tree that Carl had dropped off, bound in a nylon sheath and propped up, out of sight of the road and anyone with light fingers. She flung open the back door and went round to the garden. She grabbed the tree, the needles piercing her hands, and shoved it over, kicked at it, almost losing her footing on the slippery snow. Furious, repeating over and over as she swung her foot, 'Stupid bloody tree, bloody stupid bloody tree.' Until she was spent and sobbing in the keen night air.

She couldn't sleep; her body was too far gone, her nerves tight as cheese wire. She sat unseeing at the table for long enough, then went round to her neighbours, desperate for a ciggie. She'd given up almost three years ago, but now the craving was extreme.

'Oh, Louise, how is he?' Angie was shaking her head. She was housebound, diabetic and extremely obese. Answering the door rendered her breathless. She lived in her sitting room, slept in a reclining chair. Her daughter Sian looked after her.

Louise gave her the low-down. 'You got a spare ciggie?'

'Course.' Angie walked slowly back to her chair, picked the packet up from the side table and passed it to Louise. 'Lighter's inside.'

Grateful, Louise pulled out a fag, fired it up. Felt dizzy, her eyes doing funny patterns like a kaleidoscope. Took another drag.

Angie nodded at the coffee table. 'The paper's there, you seen it?'

Louise picked it up, sat on the settee. *Student Stabbed*

to Death. She studied the photograph. She felt dull, her wits blunted by the trauma. She wondered if the boy was a friend of Luke's, but she couldn't recall him knowing any Jasons, and she didn't recognize the lad in the paper. The attack had been outside this Jason's house. They hadn't given Luke's name.

'The police didn't tell us much,' she said. 'I don't know what he was doing there.'

Angie tutted at the paper. 'They all carry knives these days,' she said, wheezing as she spoke. 'Terrible.'

Did Luke? Louise didn't think so, but she couldn't be completely sure. He wouldn't be that daft, would he? 'Can I take another?' She held up the packet.

'Take a twenty.' Angie nodded to the corner cupboard. 'In there. I've plenty more. Sian got 'em duty free.'

'You're sure?'

'Go on, before I change my mind.'

Louise nodded. Took a packet. 'I'll pay you back.'

'You will not,' Angie scolded. 'Don't you bloody dare.'

Louise wanted her grandad. Times like these it was him she missed, more than her mother or father or grandma. He'd been proud as a peacock when Luke was born, insisted on taking him in his pram to the CND meeting at the Labour club, promising to be only an hour. By then her mum had died. Just keeled over one day in Asda. When they did the post-mortem, they found she had a hole in her heart. It had been there all along and no one had ever known.

They had a party for Louise's mum after the funeral, and her friends from the ships came, those that were in between trips. They sang all her repertoire. One man brought along a cardboard cut-out of her mother in a wine-coloured evening gown and long gloves, her hair in a Doris Day, pearls round her neck, something that had been used to advertise a forties night on board. Teenager Louise hated them, all these people who knew her mother well, who'd had the best of her. Coming up and insisting on talking about the larks they'd had and how Louise's mum had been a good friend in times of trouble.

'Why did they have to come?' she complained to Grandad.

'They mean well.' He'd looked at her a while, his eyes soft. 'She had itchy feet, always had. Hard on you.'

She felt a flash of hatred for him then too. Why did he always have to be so bloody understanding? 'I'm fine!' she retorted. She downed her drink too quickly, making her throat burn, and flounced off.

The police had kept Luke's phone, but the staff at the hospital had given her his wallet and gold chain and his ear stud. All in a plastic bag, 'Patient's Valuables and Clothing' written on it. The chain was grimy, mud she thought, but when she washed it, the water turned pink. She braced her arms on the edge of the sink, let her head hang down, taking a moment.

Louise knew his friends should be told what was happening, but she only had a few numbers and the thought of calling each of them was overwhelming. She decided to ring Declan and ask him to spread the word. He should be up by now. Declan had no work, no education; he signed on and sponged off his mum, who was on incapacity benefit with mental health problems. When Louise called, he answered with a suspicious 'Hello?' then wary recognition followed by fractured disbelief as she told him: *ICU . . . sedation . . . they just don't know . . . police.*

'Did you see him last night?' Louise said.

'No, not since Wednesday.'

'Do you know where he was?'

'Some Christmas do, from college. A meal, I think,' he told her.

'He never said.' And I fed him bangers and mash at six. 'He say where?'

'A tapas place – near Deansgate.'

'This lad, Jason Barnes,' she asked, 'did you know him? Did Luke?'

'No, no, never heard of him.'

She promised to let him know about visiting, thinking it shouldn't be like this, sixteen-year-olds having to deal with hospital visits. One minute they were invincible, full of life and cheek, and then bam! Parallel universe.

A meal in town after a tea at home. Typical. He could eat like a horse and not put on an ounce; he had that sort of metabolism. Live wire, her grandad had called him. Wick, Grandma said, which Louise didn't under-stand at first. A Yorkshire word apparently; meant he was quick and lively. Grandma had a cleft palate; people who didn't know her found it hard to follow her. Even at home she was sparing with her words. Her husband made up for that.

Luke, live wire. Walking at nine months, climbing like a little mountain goat too, and then prone to running off. Louise took him to the park every day for a kick-about and a clamber on the playground, or to the meadows where he could run himself ragged. Sometimes she thought he was born in the wrong century, that he'd have been better living somewhere outside, wild and unfettered, where physical activity was a way to make a living, not just a valve for letting off steam. They'd done what they could, getting him on

40

to the five-a-side team, sending him to Woodcraft Folk, where he could go camping and the like without all that 'royalist authoritarian scouts crap', as Grandad put it. Most of the other kids were better off, middle class, big houses, went skiing in the winter and the like, but that was okay. Their house always had a weird mix of people passing through: dockers and welders rubbing shoulders with university lecturers and doctors – shared ideals, loyalty to the cause, the Party bringing them together. They kept the local branch banner at Grandad's. Louise had helped to make it. Winter nights when she was thirteen or so, cutting out silk and embroidering round canvas letters. Listening to the conversation, which ranged far and wide but included a great deal about the struggle and feminism and housework and the best way to advance women's liberation.

Grandma and one of the other women had done the design: a frieze of figures along the bottom, holding symbols: flowers, sheaves of wheat, paintbrushes, a kite, tools. The words *unity*, *freedom*, *peace* repeated around the edges of the cloth, and in the centre the name of the branch, each dot above the 'i' a small hammer and sickle. Along the bottom they had sewn thick, gold-coloured upholstery fringing. Carried on dark wooden curtain poles up either side, the banner was so heavy when it was done that they needed harnesses to strap round the waists of the bearers. It was beautiful.

Louise carried on sewing for a few years. Her grandma had always done it; even Louise's mother, who couldn't boil an egg, could turn her hand to alter a dress, tart it up with a nip and a tuck and a sprig of lace or fresh buttons. Louise made cot quilts each time she was pregnant. She didn't bother with sewing now, not beyond a bit of mending or the odd costume for

Ruby's school plays and fancy-dress parties, though she still had the rag-bags shoved in the roof space and the old Singer taking up space in the under-stairs cupboard. Nowadays it cost more to dress-make than getting something new. Clothes were that cheap. Unless you recycled stuff. She quite liked the idea. Some people made a living doing it, creating unique clothes, but Ruby wouldn't wear anything second-hand.

She got to her feet and the floor pitched, her head swam; she used the furniture to balance until the vertigo eased. They should get back to the hospital. She went to wake Ruby and put some bread in the toaster. The smell made her mouth flood with saliva and she thought she'd retch, but she breathed carefully, resisting the impulse. She buttered a slice for herself; she had to eat something. She'd be no use to anyone half starved.

Andrew

They lay on the twin beds, which were pushed together in the guest room. Almost as large as the master bedroom, it had been Colin's room when they were kids. Andrew, as the youngest, had the box room next to Colin's.

In the intervening years it had been repapered and spruced up, the old sash windows replaced, a new carpet fitted. A few remnants of childhood stood on the alcove shelves, amusement for visiting grandchildren: dominoes and a game of Mousetrap, a set of Russian stacking dolls (who on earth had bought them?) and a box of Dinky cars and tanks and lorries.

The curtains were drawn, the radiator ticking. The room was airless, hot and stuffy. Andrew could smell food cooking downstairs. They lay on top of the covers, like spoons, her back to him, his arm across her side, holding her wrist.

'The other boy's been in surgery,' Val said. 'Head injury.'

'Oh God!' Andrew felt a gout of shame; he hadn't thought to ask the police about him – presumably that was how Val knew.

'He's still unconscious so he's not been able to tell them anything. It's a miracle he survived, the way they—' She broke off.

Andrew exhaled. 'You don't have to.'

'It's important I remember,' she carried on, withdrawing her arm. 'I heard shouting. I went to the window first; I could see there were people, but not what was going on, not clearly. I think I knew it was a fight. I went to the front door. It was all so quick. One of them was on the ground and the others were kicking him.' Her voice shook. 'They were all doing it, even the girl.'

Andrew gave a ragged sigh.

'And Jason was coming in the gate, he was shouting, he was frantic. I just wanted him to come inside, to get away. That awful feeling, you know, when you see that sort of violence, like we're animals, just animals. All the instincts kicking in. I was so scared, I was shouting, there was so much noise. Then he pulled one of them off, the biggest one, grabbed at his shoulders. The boy just pushed him over.'

Andrew felt his own limbs rigid with apprehension.

'Jason grabbed the lantern stand; you know the cast-iron one near the snowberry bush. He went for the same boy, hit his back; that's when I ran in for the phone. Went upstairs to get you. I never saw a knife. Oh God,' she wept, and Andrew felt the tremors deep in his own belly. He smelt her hair, faint traces of shampoo and a hint of the perfume she always wore.

43

'He was so brave,' she said, her voice clotted with tears. 'Why did he have to be so bloody brave?'

Andrew was running, sliding, skittering, ice underfoot. He woke sweaty, breathless, after the dream. The shapes of it dissolving, drifting as he tried to clutch at them. The story of it lost, but a sour, squalid residue in the pit of his stomach.

Jason! For a moment, a delicious, delirious moment, he willed that the loss of Jason was a dream too, that any time now he would open his eyes for a second time to his own bedroom and the sound of his son crossing the landing and all the bright possibilities, the glorious mundanities of a normal day. But the hope shrivelled, the edges of the picture flaring and charred. Ashes and blood.

He felt overloaded; the weight was crushing him, compacting his bones and the marrow within, compressing his vital organs, lungs, liver, heart.

Val was there, and the family liaison officer, Martine. Andrew's mother offered toast and tea. Tea, he agreed, and pulled out a chair. Val had a pad of paper in front of her, a laptop open.

'How are you?' his mother asked.

Andrew shrugged, rubbed at his face. He hadn't shaved, hadn't washed.

Martine explained apologetically that the investigating team needed statements from them both. She knew it was a terrible time, but it was crucial to do it as soon after the incident as possible. She could take them to the station and bring them back. Was that okay?

Outside the station, Andrew was appalled to see Jason's photo, the one from YouTube, and the word MURDER in dense black capitals. He wanted to run, to scuttle off and burrow somewhere. He squeezed Val's hand. The place was deserted. Martine pressed an intercom and gave her name to gain entrance, and then they all waited by the empty front desk until someone appeared. Andrew sat and watched the screen fixed high on the wall as it switched between views of the car park, which must be behind the building, the outside approach to the main entrance and the reception area itself. Showing them on the camera: Val, preoccupied, quiet, one hand supporting her head, eyes half closed; Martine, smart and trim and alert; and himself, unfamiliar, nondescript. A bloke, just some bloke.

'Mr Barnes? Mrs Barnes?' Introductions, handshakes, then Martine and Val went one way and a policeman called Neville Long settled Andrew in a meeting room. It was kitted out with sofas and easy chairs, rugs and coffee tables. No posters on the walls; just prints, wispy landscapes.

Neville Long was a bulky man with a full beard and large plump hands, tiny feet, Andrew noticed, really small. Small as Val's? Jason was a 12, bigger than Andrew, who took size 10.

'Mr Barnes.'

'Sorry.' Had he missed something? 'My concentration . . .'

'When did you last eat?' the man asked him.

'I'm not hungry.'

'Have some tea.'

'I don't . . .'

'Try.'

He went off and came back carrying a tray with two mugs of tea and a plate of mince pies.

'Please help yourself.' Neville Long took a mince pie, prised it out of the foil case and bit into it. Pastry crumbs scattered on the coffee table. He adjusted a file on his knee. 'I want to take a formal witness statement, get all this down in writing. Yes?'

Andrew nodded.

'Then we'll look at what you can give us in the way of detailed descriptions. Perhaps you can start by telling me in your own words exactly what you saw.'

'I was in the shower,' he began. He felt the lump in his throat, the band tighten on his Adam's apple. He shifted, coughed and dragged the sounds out, every sinew in his body stretched taut, his muscles rigid. His account was halting, trying to convert the slideshow in his head into phrases and sentences. 'And then?' the detective kept prompting. And then? And then? And then? Until he had forced Andrew out into the snow and that ghastly mess on the ground, down the street after them and back to Jason's anguish, *I think he's dead*, and into the living room and Jason pale, swaying, Andrew knowing he was ill, Jason falling, blood on his coat, all the way to the quiet hospital room where his son's body was laid out.

Neville Long asked him to describe the three attackers and he did as best as he could: their clothing, height and build, colouring, features, but what he could recall seemed pitifully little.

After that he was taken through to a small office to work with the technician on the e-fit. The man navigated through the software, constantly asking Andrew to choose between different options, everything from the arc of the eyebrows to the cast of the complexion, the width of the chin to the shape of the nostrils.

Each time the technician would drag items on to the face in the centre of the screen: 'Like this?' he'd ask. 'Or better like this?' and click and drag an alternative. It reminded Andrew of the eye test at the optician's, and like that, he often found it hard to judge which was the best version.

'I didn't get a very clear look,' he kept saying, or 'It was just a glimpse' and 'I honestly can't remember.' His head ached with the effort of concentration and there was a sickening pulse of pain in his temples and behind his eyes.

When they had finished, he was unsure whether the three pictures were a true likeness of any of the youths. The boys felt like caricatures: the round eyes of the one who'd been by the gate too bulbous, the peaky, feral face of the one he'd seen Jason shove just a lazy shorthand for his impression of the scrappy-looking lad (poor and wild), and the girl, he could barely remember anything of her beyond the coat, he didn't even know what colour her hair was. She looked like any of a million teenage girls and the e-fit of her was as bland as a Barbie doll.

He hoped Val could remember more.

Would their parents recognize them, their friends? With dismay or disbelief or fury? He tried to imagine what that might feel like: to have a child gone so wrong, a child you were appalled by, ashamed of. All the hopes you had for them strangled, their actions violent and ugly and now made public.

Violence breeds violence. He knew that and understood that kids who ended up in serious trouble invariably had very dysfunctional backgrounds. There had been a baby in the neonatal ICU when Jason was born, in the next ventilator. No one seemed to visit the little girl, and Val heard the staff talking and pieced together the story. The father had beaten his wife so badly that she'd gone into premature labour. The baby, should she survive, was also deemed to be at risk. The abusive relationship had lasted many years; another child was already in care. The mother was being given support, but unless she agreed to leave the father, the baby would be taken into care with a view to adoption.

Val and Andrew had taken Jason home, one precious day after eight long, long weeks, and never known the baby's fate. Such cases made the news. And now we are the news, he thought.

He looked at the e-fits. You killed my son, he accused them. And a swell of rage beat inside him, running over an ocean of sadness.

CHAPTER FOUR

Emma

Emma couldn't believe what had happened. The man in the parka, who was a student, had tried to help and they'd stabbed him. Killed him! Just think if she had said something . . . And the other one, Luke, he might not make it. The police wanted people to give information, but all she saw was what happened on the bus and a bit after, and they had CCTV on the buses so they'd know all that. And they could talk to the driver, couldn't they?

She worried about it all Saturday night and finally rang the number on the Sunday morning. She had to repeat herself three times before she was transferred to a second person. She walked about as she waited, to the window and back, the window and back. Alongside the station, trees feathered the sky, stark as woodcuts. She watched the frost steam in the pale sunshine.

She had to give her name and address and date of birth.

'And you're ringing in connection with the Jason Barnes inquiry?'

'Yes,' she said. 'I saw him on the bus.'

'Can you speak up?' said the man.

'Sorry.' She tried to talk more loudly, her hand gripping the phone hard, still walking to and fro. 'He was on the bus when I was coming home, on Friday.'

'Jason Barnes was?'

'Yes. And these boys, and this girl, they were causing

trouble . . . erm. Ganging up on this other boy, and Jason told them to stop.'

'How many of them were there?'

'Two boys and a girl.' She remembered the girl, how pretty she was, and the big one's round blue eyes. 'Then they all got off.'

There was a pause; Emma wondered what to say. She felt a bit dizzy.

'Did you see anything after that?'

'Just them running after the other boy and Jason following them.'

He asked her how old they were and what they looked like and what they were wearing. She guessed they were seventeen or eighteen, a few years younger than her, and did her best to describe them.

'Thanks. Can you hold for a minute?'

There was no on-hold music like they had at work when staff had to check records or refer to the handbook or get a supervisor for help. At work they played some classical instrumental music, quite perky. The sort of stuff that people dance to in costume dramas. Emma thought it would drive you bonkers while you were fretting about the flood damage or the boiler repair or your mother's jade and gold necklace that had gone in the robbery and hearing this prancy music skip on and on.

All she could hear now while she waited were bits of conversation and a phone ringing and someone with a shocking cough. Then the man came back on.

'Emma, thanks for calling. We'd like to arrange to come and get a full statement from you; we can do that at your house.'

'I'm going away the day after tomorrow,' Emma explained, 'for Christmas.'

'How about tomorrow?'

'Yes, erm . . . it'd have to be after work.'

'Fine, what time will you get home?'

'About six.'

'Shall we say six thirty?'

'Yes.'

He thanked her again and she said goodbye and rang off. He hadn't asked her the questions she'd been waiting for: the ones that kept buzzing in her head like fat bluebottles. *Why didn't you say anything? Why didn't you do anything? Why did you just sit there and let it all happen?*

'That's near you, isn't it? Kingsway.' Laura at work raised the tabloid so Emma could see the headline: *Samaritan Student Slain. Coma Boy Fights On.*

Emma picked her coffee up, nodded. Felt something tighten inside. Tried to swallow. Laura looked at her. 'What?'

Emma felt wobbly. *The Jelly*, that's what they'd called her at school, the whole of Year 9. *Smelly Jelly.* She tried to ignore it because people said if you reacted it would get worse, but she couldn't help it when she blushed or was unable to talk because the girls who kept slagging her off were all staring at her. Luke had tried to ignore them; he'd looked away out of the window, but they wouldn't let him be.

Both the Kims were in the staff lounge on break, too, and they waded in. 'There was a girl with them, joining in. That is really sick,' said Little Kim.

'Girls are the worst,' Laura said. 'They egg them on.'

'What was it about?' Blonde Kim asked.

'Doesn't say.' Laura was studying the paper.

'Probably a mugging,' said Blonde Kim.

'I was mugged,' said Little Kim. 'Walking home one night when I worked at the bar. Scared the life out of me. He had a knife.'

Blonde Kim gazed at her, biscuit poised. Laura looked up.

'He said "Give us yer phone and yer money."'

'Was he a druggie?' Laura asked her.

'Dunno,' said Little Kim. 'I just gave him it and he ran off. I was crying, I could hardly walk, I was shaking that bad. It was horrible.'

'I saw them,' Emma managed to say, her face heating up.

'You what?' Blonde Kim gawped.

'Before the stabbing.'

'Oh. My. God.' Little Kim clutched her hands to her chest theatrically.

'Where? What? Spit it out!' said Laura.

Spit it out, Emma, I haven't got all day. One of her dad's phrases.

'They got on my bus. I've got to give a statement to the police.'

'The police!' Little Kim shrieked. 'Will you have to go to court and everything?'

Emma shrugged.

'It must have been horrible,' Laura said. 'What did they do?'

'Just kicking off, you know. Threatening this boy, the one who's in hospital.'

'Oh, Emma,' breathed Little Kim.

She didn't want them going on about it, she didn't like it. She set her cup down, still half full, and put her bag back in her locker.

'Someone's keen.' Laura glanced at the clock. Another four minutes.

'We're not all slackers,' Emma tried to joke, but she sounded weird, sort of bitter, and she saw the Kims raise eyebrows at each other.

They could be very cliquey and it had taken her a

while to make friends here. She didn't want to mess it up, but she couldn't think of what to say now to put it right. Her face glowed; she hated blushing. 'See you in a bit,' was all she managed.

As she left and closed the door, she heard them laughing and her eyes stung. Two more days and she'd be off home for the holidays. It would all blow over and things would get back to normal.

Back at her desk, she began work. The forms and the figures, the policy numbers and dates and exclusions were a relief, a place to get lost.

Andrew

Time lost meaning, hours morphed into days, minutes hung slow, poised, paused. Andrew felt there was a membrane between himself and the world. Translucent, invisible. A caul. And any real understanding, any comprehension as to what had happened was there on the other side with everyone else.

They had been to register the death – he knew that, though recalling the event clearly was impossible, like trying to make out writing that had blurred and run in the rain. Rorschach blots staining the paper where letters once processed.

He hadn't driven, he knew that much; they wouldn't let him drive, so Colin had taken them.

The woman studied the medical certificate from the hospital and checked the facts with them and then made out the entry in the register in her small neat italic writing. The ink was sooty black.

Andrew felt like he was underwater; everyone's words took an inordinate amount of time to reach him and half of what they said was incomprehensible. He kept losing his place, as though the co-ordinates had been shifted, the land rippling beneath him and leaving him on a different contour line with no way-marks.

Colin must have driven home too, Val carrying the death certificate and the one for burial, though he had no memory of it.

'Dad?'

He was on the stairs carrying holdalls up, when he heard Jason. Someone had been to the house, got clean clothes for them, toiletries. His heart burst, soared with joy, and he whirled round, seeking his son, waiting for further proof that this had just been some awful, dreadful mistake. His body hungry to hug his boy, to tell him how they had all been knocked sideways but here he was. Here he was and his life was golden and green and wide with potential.

He stood and waited, holding his breath, his head inclined to catch the faintest echo, eyes shut the better to smell Jason's approach – a mix of sugar and mint from the gum he was always chewing and the cologne his mother had bought him last birthday. A better option than the Lynx body spray he'd favoured for years.

Andrew's father found him on the stairs. 'You need a hand with those?'

Andrew looked down, bewildered at the bags in his hands, felt the ache in his fingers and wrists, the numb pain across his back. He tried to remember what was in the luggage and where he was meant to be taking it.

'There's a site for Jason,' Val said, her eyes glittering painfully, 'on Facebook. Look.' She pushed the laptop along the table. He turned away.

'All his friends,' she said, 'and people who never even met him. Thirteen thousand already,' she added.

Andrew stared down at the table. People jumping on the bandwagon, pseudo-grief, trite platitudes from strangers.

'There are some lovely messages,' Val went on, pulling the laptop back. 'And photographs.'

The anger came without warning, a bolt of it, driving him to his feet, pushing him away from the table, roaring in his ears, drowning out the murmurs of shock and concern.

He bowled out into the conservatory and wrenched at the patio doors, locked of course. Beat at them with his fists. The garden beyond draped in snow, a splash of yellow on the witch-hazel, frilly flowers like shredded crêpe paper, the old stone bird table and footsteps leading to and back, the shocked flight of robins and magpies as he shook the doors.

'Andrew.' She was behind him, tears in her voice. Her hand on his shoulder, her head on his back. 'We have to do this,' she said. 'We weren't the only ones who loved him. And there are things we have to do: the arrangements, the funeral, work out what he'd have liked.'

What he'd have liked? Christ, the preposterous notion made him choke back a laugh. What he'd have liked! He'd have liked to live, he'd have liked to get a degree and drink too much with his mates and play the field, he'd have liked to grow up and get hitched and maybe have kids himself, see something of this world and smell the fucking daisies.

Andrew shifted, turned to her.

'We'll do it together,' she said. She was always so strong, so sure. She put her hands to his face, kissed him.

* * *

Martine had information for them. The police were releasing the name of the victim – the one Jason had gone to help. Luke Murray.

Andrew felt a spike of anger, a needle inside, hot and piercing. 'Why would they do this? Beat up this Luke and then take a knife . . .' he demanded. 'Why?' He had to stand up. Move.

'We don't know,' Martine said. 'Once we've identified them—'

He spoke over her. 'There must be a reason.'

'Once we've apprehended the suspects, we might have more information.'

'Was it a racist attack?'

'That's one avenue we are exploring. I understand it must be very frustrating for you both,' Martine said.

'It doesn't matter why,' Val said. 'There probably isn't any good reason. But they'll pay for it.' Her lips trembled.

Andrew's anger drained away. He sat back down. Val took his hand. As Martine talked about the investigation and how it was going, Andrew was back in the garden, his feet cold and wet on the snow, seeing the lurid stain against the white, the ruin of Luke Murray's face, watching Jason screaming for him to call the ambulance, seeing the smallest boy flailing and then running to the gate, his accomplices, their faces contorted as they screamed. He felt his throat spasm, mouth water, then a convulsion in his abdomen. He made it to the downstairs toilet and puked until he was spent. He gazed bleary-eyed at the face in the mirror, wiped the string of drool from his chin, his fingers white and bloodless. There was something odd; he stared, puzzled over it, then realized that he hadn't shaved, his face was shadowed with thick stubble.

Someone came to find him eventually, someone always came after him even though he wanted to be left alone.

Their house was pictured on the news again, police tape fluttering in the slight breeze, which snatched the lightest dusting of snow and blew it round in a fine spiral. Outside their fence, bouquets of flowers and cards and candles. The photograph of Jason, and then two images of Luke Murray. The second one showing his horrific injuries. Val murmured in shock and Andrew groaned. The bare facts of the case were narrated, then the man leading the inquiry appealed for information.

When the next item came on, Val muted the sound. Turned to Martine. 'When can we go home?'

'I'd suggest leaving it for a few more days,' Martine said. 'You'd be likely to be besieged by the press if you went back now.'

'But you can't stop us?' There was grit in her tone.

'Maybe we're better here,' Andrew ventured.

Val turned to him. 'I want to be closer to Jason. I want to be where he was.'

He swallowed.

'Let me check how things stand.' Martine got up. 'I'll make a call.'

Andrew reached out a hand, covered Val's. It was the best he could offer by way of support, but the prospect of returning home filled him with cold dread.

'I need some air,' he said to Val later. 'I need to get out.'

'Want company?'

Oh God. His heart contracted; he felt a pulse quicken in the roof of his mouth. He hesitated. He didn't want to hurt her, but he felt trapped.

She understood. She let him go.

Andrew walked towards town, avoiding the centre of the pavement where the snow had been compacted to treacherous ice, stepping instead on the edges, on the untouched white. The snow creaking underfoot.

He could see his breath, milky smoke.

Dragon's breath! Jason chortling, six years old and his head full of dinosaurs and pirates.

The sun was hidden; clouds mottled pearly grey blanketed the sky. The bushes, each twig and leaf, were laced with frost. He walked north towards Withington. On the eighteenth-century maps, this was a toll road from Manchester to Oxford; Withington was where one of the turnpikes had been, a village surrounded by farmland before it had grown and fused with others to form the city. The route south was dotted with coaching inns every few miles, forerunners of the railway stations. He glimpsed a snowman on a side road, squat and plain, eyes but no other features, no hat or scarf. He passed the milestone outside the fire station: *4 miles to Manchester, to Centre of Saint Ann's* on one face, *8 ¼ miles to Wilmslow* on the other.

He walked on; let his eyes roam over the buildings, shops and houses, apartment blocks. All this now charted in the A–Z, captured on Google Earth, in aerial or street view. He and Jason had looked up their house when they first downloaded the software; they had worked out when the photograph must have been taken, because it showed the old greenhouse, which had been wrecked by spring storms and had been taken down by Andrew shortly after and replaced with a polytunnel.

He reached Rusholme. The streets were chock-a-block here, the shops and Indian restaurants brightly lit and buzzing with people even though it was daytime.

The traffic was loud, buses lumbering along the bus lane and taxis and cars snarled up in the narrow road. Someone sounded a horn repeatedly. People were shouting to each other, walking too close to Andrew; they were staring at him. A fine sweat broke out over the whole of his body and his heart hammered painfully.

He took the first turning right, away from the main thoroughfare. Soon he was on quiet streets, halls of residence empty for the holidays. Had anyone told Durham about Jason? Val would know; she was keeping a list, an A4 pad to help them stay on track. On track to where? Destination unknown. How could they know the right route? No one else had made this journey, not this exact same journey. Even if others had lost a child, they hadn't lost Jason. Andrew didn't want to be forced along any particular path. He wanted to wander in the wilderness. Yes, like some deranged prophet, grow a beard and rent his clothes and live on honey and locusts. Hah! The image, the pathetic self-pity, made him bark a laugh, and a woman across the street looked over in alarm.

He reached another arterial road, where the tall buildings on either side funnelled air into a wind. The pavements here had been treated, the brown grit mixed with slush, fudge coloured.

He felt cold, his back tense, shoulders raised. His nose was running but he had no tissues. He sniffed, and when that didn't help, resorted to wiping his nose on the back of his glove.

He went in through the A&E entrance. They'd brought Jason here. He wasn't here now; he was in the funeral parlour. Andrew's eyes ached at the thought. Couldn't bear it. He checked the hospital map and found the location he sought, then navigated his way among the visitors and staff, the walking wounded and the patients pushed in wheelchairs and on trolleys.

There was a buzzer entry system at the Intensive Care Unit. Andrew hesitated, then pressed the button. He could see through the glass to the reception desk. One of the nurses stretched out an arm, pressed the release for the door.

The phone was ringing inside the unit. Andrew's eyes roamed over the chart behind the desk. The list of names and bed numbers, initials for consultants and care. He found the right name and felt an eddy of apprehension.

'I wanted to check on visiting hours,' he said.

The nurse smiled up at him. 'We don't have any restrictions, though we only allow two people per patient at any one time.' She leant towards the phone. 'Who is it you want?'

Andrew swallowed. 'Luke Murray.' Barely a whisper.

'Sorry?'

He cleared his throat. 'Luke Murray.'

'Second on the left.' She picked up the phone.

Andrew walked down the corridor, pulling off his gloves and loosening his scarf, his bowels turned to water. He used the gel dispenser at the door to Luke's room.

He held his breath as he went in, released it with a shudder when he saw there was no one else there, just Luke. He stood staring at the figure on the bed, the boy utterly still, his face half covered with an oxygen mask. Machines and pumps and equipment ringed the bed, arrayed around him like so many mechanical vultures.

It was quiet in the room, just the click and shush of some of the equipment and distant sounds from the corridor muffled by the door. He looked, taking in the bandage on the head, the boy's brown arms on the blanket, hands flat at his sides. Steeled himself to focus on the face, the places not hidden by the mask.

A rush of air. 'You can sit down, you know.'

Andrew jumped, nerves flickering like lightning. The nurse smiled. 'It's quite safe.'

'I have to go, I can't stay.' He almost bolted, his pulse racing, but he fought the urge and walked, legs unsteady, back up the ward.

A woman stood aside to let him pass, small and dark-haired, pallid, weary-looking. He nodded his thanks.

Seconds later he heard footsteps swift behind him, turned and saw the same woman, anxious, alert. 'Oi!'

Andrew stopped, puzzled.

'Who are you?' she demanded.

'Sorry?'

Her eyes flashed. 'You will be,' she snapped, 'if you don't tell me who you are.'

'Andrew Barnes,' he said.

She gave a little snort, shook her head, the name not registering. 'What were you doing with Luke?'

'Sorry, I—'

'Tell me.'

'I'm Andrew Barnes.' He blinked. 'Jason Barnes' father.'

She closed her eyes, put her hand to her head. 'Oh God. I'm sorry. I'd no idea who you were, and after what they've done to him already . . .' She shuddered, faltered.

She thought he might have come to cause harm.

'Could you . . .' Her eyes were naked now, bright with pain. 'Would you like a cup of tea?'

61

CHAPTER FIVE

Louise

S he tried to gather her scattered wits by the time they reached the hospital café. Frame yourself, as her grandma would say whenever Louise was slow or reluctant to do something. She framed herself now. Began by apologizing to Andrew Barnes. 'I'm sorry I bit your head off. You must think I'm cracked, but my mind's in bits. And your boy, Jason – I'm so sorry.'

He nodded, then stared down at his coffee.

'He saved Luke's life, doing what hc did.'

Andrew nodded again. Not giving much away. Trying to hold it all in, perhaps fearing that if he started talking it might all come rolling out, like a bag of marbles tipped over, clattering every which way.

'I'm so very sorry,' she said again. She was painfully aware that she still had Luke. Upstairs, resting, getting stronger every hour. She still had such hope that he'd get well and come home, and although things would never be like they were before, there would still be everything to look forward to. The man opposite had none of that.

'Have the police told you anything?' she asked, testing her cup with her fingers, still too hot to drink.

He shrugged. 'Not really.'

He was a wreck, she thought, greying hair dishevelled, unshaven. She guessed he was in his late forties or early fifties, something like that. The skin on his face blotchy, his eyes bloodshot, stubble peppering his jaw.

A pleasant face beneath the stress, but no more than that. His clothes were decent enough, but it didn't appear that anyone was looking after him. Maybe he wouldn't let them. She had clients like that, people who felt that accepting help was a sign of weakness, that it undermined their independence, reduced their self-esteem, or those who were so angry at their failing abilities that they wouldn't countenance assistance, denying there was a problem, bitter and hurt.

She'd showered today, washed her hair, even put a load in the washing machine. Seemed like a big deal at the time, functioning. But her clothes weren't ironed and she knew she looked wiped out too.

'Did he know them? Luke?' he asked.

'I don't know,' she said.

'But the descriptions,' he went on. She saw a glint of anger in the cast of his eyes. 'You read them?'

'Yes, it didn't sound like anyone I could think of.'

'So you think it was random? They picked on him out of the blue?'

'I don't know.'

A man dressed in a Santa suit wandered up to the counter, setting off banter among the staff and customers. Louise wanted to weep.

She wondered why Andrew Barnes expected her to have any answers. What had driven him to come and see Luke? Surely he'd enough going on dealing with his own situation. She felt a flare of irritation with him. Edgy, she moved her drink towards the middle of the table. 'I'm just going out for a smoke, won't be long.'

He dipped his head, picked up his own drink.

She had to go outside and across the road to escape all the no-smoking notices. Other people ignored the exhortations near the entrance and clustered there; she could see two women sucking hungrily on fags and a man in a wheelchair and another youngish lad with a drip. She didn't feel proud of smoking again and she didn't want to flout the rules. The first drag made her cough and her mouth felt dry, her tongue rough; she wished she'd brought her drink out with her.

When she went back to the café, Andrew Barnes had gone.

The man probably didn't know whether he was coming or going. His son had died trying to help Luke; maybe he'd needed to see the cause of his bereavement. She wondered if he had spoken to Luke and what he'd said. She could have asked Andrew about the fight if she'd only taken the chance instead of running off for a fag. It had been at his house after all. How had it started? Thinking about that, about Luke's fear and the violence of what they'd done, made her stomach turn.

She hadn't seen Carl since Saturday, when he'd rung first then come round with takeaway and a couple of bottles of wine. They'd kept in touch by phone, but there had not been any time and she needed to concentrate on Luke and Ruby for now.

She asked him to take the Christmas tree away – see if anyone he knew could make use of it. Ruby stayed close, as if she was frightened to leave Louise. 'You can go round to Becky's,' Louise had told her, 'or she can come over.' Thinking that seeing her best friend might be a break for the girl; but Ruby shook her head.

They'd watched a film on telly, a mindless rom-com. Carl laughed too loudly at the slapstick and she wished he'd leave.

At midnight Ruby went to bed and Carl asked Louise if she'd like him to stay. She shook her head and hugged him, said she'd barely slept but wanted to try and get a good night tonight. Thanked him for the food and the wine.

After he'd gone, she stood in the back garden to have the last fag of the day. There was a full moon rising, bright and luminous, a ring around it, mother-of-pearl. It illuminated the whole of the landscape, bouncing magnesium white off the blanket of snow. The lights in Angie's were off now; Angie would be sleeping in the warm fug of the living room, Sian upstairs.

Louise had wondered about her clients. All the people she'd missed seeing and would miss in the coming week. Some of them – Miriam and Terence and Mrs Coulson (who preferred the formality) – would have got her a Christmas present like last year. Not easy for them to arrange when they were stuck in the house. Miriam's delight at keeping the gift secret from Louise (who had access to her cupboards and drawers in the course of looking after her) had been present enough. Mrs Coulson had flourished a crumpled parcel wrapped in half a mile of Sellotape, and Louise had thanked her, keeping her face straight when she fought her way into it and discovered the packet of assorted mints that Mrs Coulson herself had received for her birthday back in April. As for Terence, he'd arranged for his daughter in Cornwall to buy and post a beautiful pair of sheepskin mittens. They must have cost him a few bob. 'It's perishing out there,' he'd said. 'Don't want you getting chilblains, eh?' They'd be disappointed not to have a chance to give her their presents. She had not bought theirs yet – always last-minute.

Would they know what had happened? Would some replacement carer tell them about Luke, or would they just be told Louise was off sick?

Louise had dropped her cigarette and heard the hiss as it went out, stooped to pick it up and put it in the wheelie bin. The wind blew even harder, buffeting the fence. Across town, just a couple of miles away, Luke lay still. Alone. 'Night, night, darling,' she whispered. And went in.

They stopped the sedation on Tuesday morning. Louise and Ruby had been warned that it was impossible to predict what would happen. 'Some patients open their eyes almost immediately, others can take hours, days. And some remain unresponsive.' Persistent vegetative state. Someone had used the term at some point, but she wasn't going to think about that. He was going to wake up.

There was nothing very dramatic to the withdrawal of sedation, just the unhooking of a drip and a note in his charts. It would take several hours for the sedative to clear from his system. Then they could try rousing him. He was breathing on his own, which they said was really good.

The past three days of bedside vigils had forced Louise to find something to do while she sat there. There was only so much chattering she could manage while Luke lay calm and quiet and so very still. Was he running in his mind? Climbing and ducking and diving? Flying even? Unfettered. She liked to think so, but no one could tell her if he was even able to dream.

So, incapable of reading, her concentration in shreds, and unwilling to sit there like a lemon, she had ransacked the roof space for her rag-bags, pulled out all the cotton pieces and the old card templates and started on a quilt. She'd no clear idea yet whose bed it would go on. There might only be enough for a single, in which case it would be Ruby's. Or maybe she'd hang it on the wall like a picture. The project meant she could sit with Luke, cutting and tacking hexagons. Threads of cotton and scraps got all over the floor but were easily cleared up.

Ruby had loaded an MP3 player with all Luke's favourite tunes and rigged it up to a little speaker so they could play it to him. They had it on for a while. Ruby brought some homework to do – a history project. It was one of the few subjects Louise could help her with if needs be, unlike maths or French. Grandad had been big on history and some of it had stuck.

When it got to mid-afternoon, the nurse looking after Luke came in and checked his vital signs again. There was a whole scoring system used to rank a coma. Based on how easily they opened their eyes, verbal ability, and whether they moved when given pain. Below eight was a coma. Luke had ranked five before the operation.

'Have you tried waking him?' the nurse asked.

Louise shook her head. They had been told they could, but part of her was fearful of trying, thinking what harm in waiting another few minutes, after she'd tacked the next patch, or the next. The nurse seemed to get this. She gave a little nod and said, 'When you're ready, just call his name, touch his shoulder or squeeze his hand. Try it two or three times, and if there's no response, leave it. We don't want to overload him. It's very common not to get a reaction immediately; it doesn't mean it won't happen eventually. Otherwise just chat to him like you have been.'

'We've been playing him music as well,' said Ruby.

'That's great.' The nurse smiled. She changed his IV fluid and checked his catheter bag and left. Her kindness disarmed Louise, made her feel weepy. She closed her eyes and waited for the feeling to recede.

Eventually she put her sewing down. She moved her chair up even closer to Luke and put her hand on his shoulder, his skin smooth and warm. She could feel the bones solid beneath, the muscles. Perfect. She leant her head close to his ear. The bandage concealed all the top of his head. The swelling on his cheek had gone down a bit; a small Steri-Strip crossed his torn eyelid and she could see the scab where it was knitting together. The bruises were yellower now, not as obvious.

He was so peaceful. If she woke him, would he start to feel pain? Would they be able to tell?

'Luke.' She shook his shoulder. Ruby watched intently, her hand over her mouth.

'Luke, it's Mum. You can wake up now, Luke. Come on, Luke, wake up.'

Louise watched for the faintest flicker on his eyelids, any tremor on his face. There was nothing. She picked up his hand and held it in her own. His beautiful hands, long, slim fingers. There were still traces of blood under his fingernails and cuts on his knuckles.

'Luke. It's Mum. You're in hospital. I'm here and Ruby's here and it's time to wake up now.'

Time to wake up now. All the mornings she'd roused him, reminded him, yelled at him, dragged him out of bed and fed him and made sure he got where he was supposed to be going.

He lay unmoving.

Ruby sighed, 'She said it might not happen straight away.'

'Yeah.' Louise's throat hurt. 'I'm going to see about giving him a wash. Do you want to go and get a drink? A burger or something?'

Ruby nodded.

The nurse gave her a bowl and a bottle of special cleanser to use in the water and some cloths. They wouldn't turn him over, but anything she could reach, she could clean.

Louise drew the blanket down. It was some years

68

since she'd seen her son naked, but she felt no embarrassment, though she imagined he would. 'I'm giving you a bath, Luke. You don't like it, you can wake up.'

She swept the cloth over his stomach and down his thighs. Over his shins and round his calves. Counting the old scars: the pale oval on his knee where he'd fallen down the promenade steps at Prestatyn beach, the puckered skin on his arm where he'd burnt himself mucking about with a bonfire. She wiped his feet, amazed that he wasn't writhing around, unable to bear the tickling. She wiped his groin, being careful with the catheter, and then brought fresh water and used a new cloth over his chest and along his arms. She wiped his neck and then his armpits. She could smell his body odour, sharp and musky; she soaped at the tufts of black hair there.

She replenished the bowl again and bathed his hands, lifting each one into the water and letting them soak a few minutes, then running her own fingernail under his to dig out the curls of dried blood. His nails were growing long.

A libation; the word came to her. Something to do with oils and death and purification. The story of Mary Magdalene weeping on Jesus' feet and washing them with her tears, wiping them dry with her hair. 'Opiate of the masses,' Louise muttered, echoing her grandad. She wasn't washing the dead.

She had a hazy memory of her own mum sharing a bath with her. Four or five she must have been, and the bubbles filled the tub. Her mum scooping up handfuls and sculpting a crown on her own head, then Louise's. And singing. The memory never got any clearer. There was no one to ask about it; they were all gone.

She changed the water once again, got a fresh cloth.

Finally, very gently, she cleaned his face, stroking between the bruises, around his mouth, his chin, up along the edges of the bandage. 'You'll do,' she whispered. And kissed him. Oh Luke, she thought, if love could bring you back, you'd be running round the ward, spinning breaks, turning cartwheels. Crowing with joy. And so would I.

Emma

Emma's skin felt sticky, clammy, and her heart kept missing a beat, like it was tripping and losing its rhythm. She'd felt like that when she had the interview for the job, and each time she had her six-monthly review. It wasn't as bad as talking in front of lots of people, but it was still gruelling. And the worst thing was when her brain just seized up so she couldn't even find the right words.

Her throat was sore too, tickly, and she thought she was coming down with something.

The man interviewing her was very nice. He said it must have been traumatic for her to see the incident on the bus and then to learn what had happened. He thanked her for getting in touch and then he asked her to talk him through her journey home that day, starting with leaving work. What time had that been? Did she always get the same bus?

Emma explained, and described where the bus had got to when the three chavs got on. Except she said 'the three of them', not wanting to sound rude. He asked her lots of questions about who said what, were those the actual words? Then it dawned on Emma that they must have the CCTV of it all but without any sound. They could see who did what but not who said what.

The man got even more interested when she told him about the names they'd called Luke, the racist stuff, and again when they'd made threats about the knife. Who did they say had a knife? Was she sure? Did she see any knife?

It was clear in her head, like a film trailer, but as she remembered it all, she also caught the cold, sick feeling inside. Frozen, not wanting to do anything and look stupid, just wanting it to stop.

'It was really, really scary,' she said, needing to explain. 'No one knew what to do. They were so horrible,' she said, 'really aggressive.'

The man nodded as he wrote.

'Then Jason came downstairs.' Saying his name like she knew him, had some connection. But he was just a stranger on a bus. She described the scuffle, felt herself blush, flames in her cheeks as she repeated the swear words. And she described the chase along the pavement. She had to say it in little short bits because she felt like crying. She felt small then, and wrong, and she wanted him to go.

He read back what she'd said and asked her to sign that it was a true record. He told her she might need to give evidence in court. God, no! It was bad enough telling him just sitting in her own place; it would be ten times worse in front of a load of strangers.

The officer got a diagram out, a plan of the bus, explaining it was the exact same layout as the bus Emma had been on. He had some small Post-it notes too. He asked her to write on the notes all the different passengers so he could see where everyone had been. Emma quite liked doing that. It reminded her of the diagrams people had to include for some of their claims, where they had to describe the damage from a leaking dishwasher or what had been broken in a robbery or destroyed by fire: *broken window, all our DVDs melted* or *carpet ruined, and underlay.* Laura once had an old man ring up in a state because burglars had gone to the toilet on his rug (number twos) and he didn't know if he should include it on the form as it wasn't a very nice thing to have to put.

Emma wrote the labels: *Old Couple, Asian Man, Woman 1, Woman 2. Students, 1, 2, 3, 4. Mother and Baby.* She put *Large Man* instead of *Rugby Player.* She set them out neatly. Put herself opposite Luke.

He asked her at what point the verbal insults had turned physical.

'Well, they pushed Luke back into his seat as soon as they got on,' she described. 'Then when he hit him, actually punched him in the head, that was when Jason had come downstairs; I think he saw it and that's when he got involved.' She felt a wash of shame. 'I didn't know it would end up like that,' she said. 'No one was saying anything.' Her cheeks were boiling. 'I didn't know.'

He spread one hand, palm up. 'How could you? These things are so unpredictable.'

I might have got killed, she reminded herself. If I had said anything, they might have come after me with the knife. I might have been dead now. She thought of her parents getting the news, standing by her grave. She had been telling herself that over and over. She was just a girl, a fat girl who wouldn't say boo to a goose. How could she have said anything? But whenever she put herself back there, or heard the name Jason Barnes, saw the bits on the news, or the pictures in the papers, she didn't feel relieved that she'd sat by and done nothing; she just felt ashamed.

Martine wanted to talk to them. She settled Val and Andrew in his parents' living room.

'One of the items we found on Jason was a bus ticket. We traced the bus that it was issued on and recovered CCTV footage.' Martine spoke slowly, with a sing-song tone, as though they were children.

Val nodded, her mouth slightly ajar, tongue tucked into the side of her teeth, a familiar gesture of avid concentration, her eyes eager. She'd never had much patience, Andrew knew. She was quick and competent and swift to pass judgement. Her own strong work ethic, her fierce intelligence, her certainty meant she'd little time for people who floundered. She tucked a strand of hair behind her ear; she was still lovely, he saw, even with the dark circles under her eyes and her hair tangled. She had a Nordic type of beauty, with her white-blonde hair, lightly tanned complexion, eyes a grey-blue like sea ice. He could sense her impatience singing in the air.

'The investigating team have examined the tape, and it now appears that the incident began on the bus.'

'What happened?' Val demanded.

'Three youths, matching the descriptions you have given us, can be seen behaving aggressively towards Luke Murray. This was on the lower deck. Jason, who was travelling upstairs, intervenes when he comes down to get off the bus.'

Val covered her mouth. Andrew swallowed.

'At that point Jason was pushed away and Luke ran off the bus, followed by the three youths, and then Jason.'

'Can you see who they are?' Andrew asked, hope giving him a rush of energy. 'You've got them on film.'

'The images aren't brilliant, but they will be a great help to us. We may be releasing stills along with the e-fits after the holiday.'

'Why wait?'

'People are away, the papers don't come out Christmas Day and Boxing Day's a Sunday. We want to maximize the impact, reach as many members of the public as we can. How are the arrangements coming?'

Andrew saw Val react to the clumsy change of topic, a little roll of her eyes and a blink before she replied. 'Okay, thanks. Thursday the thirtieth at midday.'

Jason's funeral.

They moved back home.

'Stay till after Christmas,' Andrew's mother had begged. 'You don't want to be on your own.'

But Val was adamant. They went on Christmas Eve. Beforehand, Colin had spoken to Andrew, offering to make a visit, check the place out.

'The chair.' Andrew saw Jason tipping forward, the shocking stain glistening on the back of the armchair.

Colin blanched. 'We'll get rid of it. Check the fridge and that. Mum's putting together some groceries.'

'I can shop,' Andrew said.

Colin smiled and shook his head. Big brother. Andrew felt a rush of affection and gratitude. He used to joke with Val about how dull and predictable Colin was, never putting a foot wrong, never veering from his chosen path, but now he relished that dogged, undramatic reliability.

He and Val arrived at lunchtime. Andrew felt self-conscious, exposed and raw, like the fleeting sensation on emerging from a darkened cinema into the bold glare of daylight.

'Oh, look,' said Val. Their fence was a riot of colour, a shrine to Jason. Andrew parked in the drive. There was nothing to see on the lawn; the snow had long since melted, and with it the stain of Luke's blood.

'Come and see,' she said, walking round to the pavement. There were flowers in cellophane wrapping, some already withered, blackened by frost, and cards and trinkets, ribbons and photographs, pools of wax on the ground where candles had melted, a red glass lantern still glowing crimson from the guttering flame inside. The wind was cold, ruffling and crackling the shiny wrappers of the flowers and the scraps of paper. Someone had used a hammer-tacker to staple some of the cards up, though fragments of Sellotape were visible too. Andrew guessed it had been Colin. Thoughtful, organized.

They read all the cards, though many were illegible, the writing blurred by the rain that had fallen. Some of the names were familiar: friends from school, friends who'd known Jason since National Childbirth Trust coffee mornings, since nursery. There were even a few from people Val worked with at the town hall. Somebody had taped a packet of chewing gum to the fence. Val made a little sound as she pointed it out, halfway between a snort and a sob. She had hated Jason chewing gum, both because of the mess when he left it stuck to the side of his bin or she found it trodden into the carpet, and also because of the sight of him chewing. 'It makes you look sloppy and insolent,' she'd said on one occasion. Jason had cracked his gum by way of reply and Andrew had laughed and earned a reproachful look from Val.

'Oh, Andrew.' Val turned to him and buried her face in his neck. He closed his eyes and held her, emptied his mind and drank in the simple physical comfort.

Inside, the house was warm. The wood-burning stove was lit and there was a trace of wood smoke on the air and the scent of oranges and cloves from the pomanders Val had brought back from the Christmas markets in Albert Square.

Without talking, they went into the living room. The chair had gone. The floor was clean. There was nothing to see.

'Do you want a tea?' Her voice was husky.

'Yes please.'

Piles of mail on the kitchen table: cards, letters, bills. They sat together opening and sorting them: Christmas greetings and condolence cards. Val making a note of people who had yet to be told, friends who lived abroad and weren't in any of the loose networks who passed on the news.

'They might want to know about the funeral,' she said about one family who came back to the UK most holidays, getting her phone out.

'It's Christmas Eve,' he said.

She glanced at him, then accepted that it wasn't a good time to ring anyone.

'There'll be time after,' he said.

Now he couldn't settle. He and Val had emptied their holdalls of the assortment of clothes and toiletries that had accumulated at his parents' house, then picked at the casserole that was in the fridge. Val was adding to her lists. He fed another log into the stove.

'His room,' she said, and Andrew's head swam. 'Can we just leave it?'

'Yes, of course.' He imagined it would be messy: the bag Jason had brought home only half unpacked, crusted cereal bowls and dirty coffee cups strewn around the place. 'He might have pots need bringing down.'

She smiled and nodded, faltered, her eyes brimming. 'I can't bear it.' She ran her hands through her hair, pulling at it, her face crumpled.

'I know.' He went to hug her.

'We'll have a look,' she said.

His heart beat hard in his chest as they went upstairs. Jason's door was ajar. Val moved ahead of him to push it open. That's how she copes with it, he thought; she says she can't bear it, but then she meets it head on.

The door swung open. There was the bag, jeans and dirty socks on the floor. The smell of him there, the smell of Jason. Posters on the walls: the Gorillaz *Plastic Beach* album, a Guinness ad, photos of Jason and his mates mucking about in Cornwall, a Peters projection world map.

There were no cups or bowls or plates, no apple cores. No chewing gum wrappers.

'His bin's empty.' Val frowned.

'Colin – he'll have cleared up.'

Val sat down on Jason's bed.

'I'm going to lie down for a bit.' She bent to pull her shoes off.

'Shall I wake you?'

'No.' She swung her legs up on to the bed, pulled at the duvet.

'Okay.' He shut the door.

Desperate for distraction, Andrew plugged in his laptop. The first time he'd checked his emails in days. The inbox filled: 4 ... 11 ... 28 ... 36 ... 41 new messages. His junk box gobbled up most of them. Three were from colleagues or acquaintances expressing sympathy. He skimmed them quickly, not wanting to engage.

There were two messages from the hospital speech therapy unit, referrals for the New Year. He replied acknowledging them, feeling unreal. Impossible to imagine being back there, though what else could he do?

He thought about the Facebook site for Jason. He'd still not looked at it, though Val did. She kept mentioning it and had even added her own thoughts and some pictures. She'd tried to read them to him, but he had left the room, unable to stand with her on this. She had sought him out later, wanting to talk about it, began with, 'It helps me, Andrew, to see how many people care, to read about him.'

He didn't answer.

'It's as if you don't want to remember—'

'It's not that.' He cut her off. 'I can't do it this way.' Wallow, he wanted to say, but it felt so cruel he bit it back. 'Not yet. I'm sorry.'

'I need to be able to talk about him, like we do with your mum and dad – all of us, even the kids.'

Two evenings where in some sort of wake they had sat up late sharing stories. His parents, Val and him, Colin and Izzie and their kids. He had wanted to stop their mouths and cast them out, silence the peals of laughter and murmurs of soft fond recognition. Watching their eyes shine with affection and sparkle with tears, hands moving with gestures to illustrate their tales, he had seethed with rage. Did she not notice that he had said little, contributed nothing, drinking steadily, way more than anyone else, and been the first to leave, escaping with 'a bad head' or 'need to lie down'?

He closed the laptop, took a tea bag out of the jar, found a cup, stared at it, then put it down. He fetched his coat and hat and gloves and set off in the darkening light.

Louise

'Hello.'

It was Andrew Barnes again.

'I hope you don't mind,' he said.

Louise stared at the man. What did he want with them? She hadn't mentioned his earlier visit to either Ruby or Carl. Didn't know how to put it. It seemed private somehow, and puzzling.

'How is he?' He looked anxious, apprehensive, as though he feared she might send him away.

'The same,' she said.

Andrew gestured to his own face, then at Luke. 'He's not got the mask.'

'He's breathing on his own but nothing else.'

'But he still might . . .'

She nodded quickly. 'Yes, it's totally unpredictable. They say that the longer time goes on, the less chance there is that people'll wake up, but it's still quite early on, really.' Seven days. Only three since they stopped sedation, she told herself. No time at all.

'Yes,' he said quietly.

It felt stupid, him standing across the other side of the room. She pointed to Ruby's chair. 'If you want to . . .'

'Thanks.'

He didn't look any better than last time, she thought, and knew she looked worse. She'd caught sight of her reflection in the visitors' toilets, shocked to see grey in her hair. She had always thought that was a myth. And marks like bruises under her eyes. 'They asked for pictures,' she said. 'The police: before and after.' The memory was bitter in her mouth. 'They used them in the appeal.'

He nodded.

She had known immediately which picture of Luke she would give them. Ruby had taken it when they were in Ibiza the summer before last. Luke at the restaurant table, relaxed, smiling. Rush matting and grapevines in the background, a knickerbocker glory with sparklers in front of him – his birthday. They'd teamed up with her mates Fee and Deanne and their kids to go. Deanne had got them a good deal because the apartment was her mum's timeshare. The cheap flights meant travelling at god-awful hours both ways, but it had been a brilliant week for them all. Louise had worried about Luke; it was not long after he'd been in trouble over the graffiti, and before that the fireworks, and he'd been bunking off school. He was the eldest of the kids in the group but he was really good with the others, and then halfway through the week he'd met a girl from London, a holiday romance. Louise hoped they were taking precautions and said so to Luke, who grimaced. 'Leave it out, won't you,' sounding a bit cockney himself. Louise hadn't warmed to the girl, who had a habit of smirking at her whenever they met. She was glad when there was no mention of her after they got home.

'They sent someone in here to take a photo.' She gestured at Luke. She had sat there feeling furious, though not sure why, as the man had adjusted lights and moved drip stands and used a camera with a huge lens on the front then checked to see what he'd got on his screen.

'The fight,' Louise said, a cramp in her guts. 'What happened?' Putting together what the police had told her and what had been reported in the news, it was still so patchy. She knew there were three people involved, thought to be in their late teens, two boys and a girl. All white.

'They think it started on the bus,' Andrew said. 'There's a stop near the house. Jason was coming back from town.'

Had Luke been on the bus? A lurch in her stomach as the possibility struck. Declan said he had gone into town for some Christmas meal with his day-release course. If he had got the number 50 back instead of one of the buses down Wilmslow Road, which he some-times did, then he could have been on the same bus as Jason. Then what? He'd made some smart comment, stared at them the wrong way? Or they'd homed in on him – a mixed-race kid, someone to taunt, to bully.

'They didn't tell you?' Andrew said.

'No.' Why not? She was angry that no one had seen fit to keep her informed.

'They didn't give us many details, but they were bothering Luke first, then they all got off, Jason as well.' He hunched his shoulders over, looked down at his hands. 'I was in the house,' he said. 'By the time I got outside . . .' He shook his head. 'My wife Val, she saw some of it, she called the police. The three of them were . . .' He hesitated, swallowed. 'They were kicking Luke. Jason went for one of them, he managed to pull him off, then as I came out he was pushing the smaller of the boys away. Then they all ran off. We don't know who used the knife.'

She sat for a moment trying to picture it, construct-ing it from what he had told her but at the same time not wanting to. 'Just instinct, isn't it?' she said. 'You see a fight, you want to stop it, especially if it's three on one. Natural reaction.'

'Is it?' He looked peculiar. She couldn't tell whether it was anger or some other emotion; fear maybe. But there was a tremor in his eye, a gleam of something sharp.

She thought of instances: kids brawling outside school, a scrap at a wedding, the pockets of violence on the demos her grandad had taken her on, a set-to once in the off-licence. Always that churning inside and the urge to separate the warring factions, calm them, admonish them. Stop them. 'Yeah, it is. People do it all the time.'

He looked stricken. His son had died doing it. She felt a rush of sympathy, then the grip of guilt. 'I'm so sorry,' she said. 'You must wish he hadn't.'

'My wife thinks he was very brave.' There was a tension to him that made the hairs on Louise's arms stand up.

'And you?'

He frowned hard, the furrows deep on his forehead, the skin along the edges of them bleaching.

If it had been reversed, Louise wondered, if Luke were dead, murdered because he'd intervened for this man's son – what would she feel? Torn open, harrowed beyond sound judgement.

After a moment he took a breath. 'But the stories you hear, people standing back, turning a blind eye, letting it happen . . .'

She remembered fragments of stories: a girl raped on a train, a homeless man set alight. She chose her words carefully, the atmosphere dense between them, his need magnetic. 'Maybe you only hear about them because they're so unusual, out of the ordinary. Or when something goes terribly wrong, like this. All the other times, when someone knocks it on the head and it's over, that's not newsworthy, is it? "Man breaks up fight, trouble nipped in bud, brawl averted."'

There was the faintest hint of a smile on his face.

'The papers were there when we got back on Monday, soon as they'd released his name,' she said. 'All these vans and cars, people with microphones, the phone ringing off the hook. It was like being under siege.' She recalled the sensation of being harried, trapped. They wanted her to come out and speak to them; they wanted to pick apart her feelings for the nation to see. She and Ruby had had to sneak out the back and ring a cab from Angie's to take them to the hospital the next day. 'Have you had them?'

He shook his head. 'We've been staying away; we've only just gone home.'

Of course, she could have kicked herself. 'Home' was where it had happened; how could they have remained there in the aftermath? There was a silence. She looked at Luke. After a while, she spoke again. 'It's not knowing I find hardest,' she said. 'Who they are, why they picked on Luke.'

'Jason walked into the house,' he said. 'He . . .' His voice shook, his grief bloomed between his words and Louise felt her back stiffen. 'He didn't know he'd been stabbed. We didn't know until it was too late.' He paused. 'I keep seeing him.' He stole a glance at her.

Louise didn't speak.

'I don't believe in ghosts,' he said.

'No,' she agreed. She wondered whether he'd told his wife. If she saw Jason too.

He gave a heavy sigh and sat back in the chair, rubbed at his throat. 'Is there anything else they can do?' His eyes, pained, moved to Luke.

'No,' Louise said. 'It's just a waiting game now.'

'Jason was in here – well, next door, St Mary's – when he was born. Premature. He was having fits. For a while it looked like he wouldn't—' He broke off.

Louise tried to think of something to say, keen to divert Andrew from his suffering. 'Luke wanted to go in the army,' she said. 'I made him wait. Didn't want him in danger. You never know, do you?' If she'd said yes, would he have been safer?

'Mum?' Ruby was back from the café. Louise was relieved to see her. Andrew stood up.

'Ruby, this is Andrew, Jason Barnes' dad.'

Ruby swallowed, nodded.

'I'll be on my way,' Andrew said.

'Perhaps we could swap numbers?' Louise said. 'Then if you hear anything else . . .'

'Of course.'

'What did he want?' Ruby asked when he'd left.

I'm not sure, Louise thought. 'To see how Luke was.'

Ruby sat down. 'There's carol singers downstairs collecting for the WRVS. What's that stand for?'

As Louise told her, she thought more about Andrew Barnes, wished there was something she could do to ease his pain, and knew there would never be any way to make amends for the terrible sacrifice Jason had made. The sacrifice that had saved Luke's life.

CHAPTER SIX

Andrew

It was almost dark when he left the hospital. He felt drained, hollow. He kept stumbling. The gusts of wind were spinning litter about, sending carrier bags jinking down the streets. Drifts of food cartons and drinks cans rattled in corners. Squalls of rain spat at him. He was indifferent to the groups of partygoers with their tinsel and antlers, the shoppers laden with bags, the beggar sprawled on the pavement, the pools of water underfoot and the drunk roaring red-faced at the traffic.

Jason went past on his bike. He hadn't any lights on. Andrew went to call out, to warn him, then the chill came over him. He increased his pace, trying to warm up. He couldn't feel his toes. Could do with a drink. There was a pub on the corner, snowflakes sprayed on the windows, coloured lanterns strung round the building. He imagined the scene inside, the yeasty smell of beer, the golden glow in the mirrors at the bar, the giddy bonhomie. Walked past and on until he found a newsagent's and grocer's, grilles over the glass and a notice: ONLY 2 SCHOOLCHILDREN IN SHOP AT ANY TIME. Above that, over the door, the 'Licensed to sell' plate.

He bought a half-bottle of brandy, the brand unfamiliar. The first swig hurt his gullet going down, but soon the numb sensation spread, making his mouth cottony, softening his spine, releasing the rigidity in his shoulders, befuddling his brain. He took another draught of liquor, belched and carried on home.

There were fresh candles outside the house, next to the fence, but the wind had blown the flames out. He wondered who had brought them, who had taken time from their Christmas preparations to remember Jason.

Three faces turned to greet him, conversation suspended. Val and her close friends Sheena and Sue. He felt like an interloper. He'd expected her to still be where he'd left her, curled up in Jason's duvet.

'Oh, Andrew.' Sheena, always more demonstrative than he cared for, came to hug him. There was no way he could avoid reciprocating. He wondered if she could feel the brandy bottle in his pocket, smell his breath. He felt unsteady on his feet, feared he might topple over, pin her beneath him in some ghastly faux-pas.

Sue followed. 'So sorry,' she said. He knew they had been over to see Val while they were at his parents', but this was the first time they'd encountered him since it happened.

'Get a glass,' Val suggested, but he caught the lack of conviction and knew it would be better all round to leave them to it. Good for Val too; she confided in these friends unreservedly. Their friendships went back years, and although at times they all met up as couples at social events, the men, their other halves, never made independent arrangements. He realized there was no one he saw of his own accord any more. He'd be hard pressed to know who to invite out for a pint and a session putting the world to rights if the fancy took him. Everyone had disappeared into marriage and children and he assumed that they, like him, relied for intimacy on their families.

'I won't, thanks.' He was aware of the slur in his

words, his tongue clumsy. 'I'll, er . . .' He was going to say get a shower, but suddenly that sounded callous. He waved one hand upstairs.

He was cold to the core. He hadn't had a bath in years, but now he ran one, deep and hot. His skin prickled as he stepped in, goose bumps breaking out on his arms and legs. He took a drink from the brandy and set it on the side. He sank back, gasping at the heat, until only his face and knees protruded.

Jason aged five, in the bath, screaming in terror as a large moth batted about inside the lampshade. 'It's only a moth,' Andrew kept saying, 'it can't hurt you,' as he rigged up the stepladder.

'I hate moths,' Jason had sobbed. 'Take it away, Daddy.' Hysterical with panic, then screaming, and Val getting him out of the bath into a towel, an edge to her voice. 'That's enough, Jason, stop it now.' Disliking his display of fear. 'Don't be silly,' she'd said.

'He can't help it,' Andrew had protested. The furry moth still smacking into the shade, little puffs of powder exploding as it collided with the glass.

Val glared at him. The wrong response. She believed they must be consistent with Jason, and to be fair, they did see eye to eye on most aspects of parenting, but Andrew recognized in her an impatience, a hardness even, that he didn't share. She talked of toughening Jason up, and resilience and independence, and Andrew would look at the small boy and wonder why love and protection weren't enough for now. The child's neediness, his dependency, seemed to rankle with Val, a burr under her skin. She was a practical, dispassionate nurse whenever anyone was ill; caring for her baby with chickenpox in the same manner as she'd looked after her parents when they each became infirm: her mother with dementia and her father with a series of strokes.

Her whole family had been like that really: practical, unsentimental, sharing a belief in hard work, common decency, moderation and frugality. Val's father had taken over the family ironmonger's in the late fifties and expanded into general hardware. They'd all worked in the shop, Val after school and on Saturdays until she escaped to university. Once their parents were gone, dying within a year of each other when Jason was seven, her brother got out too. Single and in his thirties, he decided to travel. To everyone's astonishment, he had entered a monastery in Thailand. He informed Val by postcard. She never heard from him again. They didn't even know if he was still alive.

They had no way to tell him about Jason.

Andrew had found Val a little intimidating on first acquaintance. Beautiful, with that fine blonde hair and her cool cover-girl looks, but overpowering. It was a union meeting, local authority branch in the upstairs room of a pub. The first he'd attended. He'd have died of boredom but for the antics of this young woman, who repeatedly challenged standing orders and queried points of procedure. He didn't follow all the ins and outs but could see that some sort of power struggle was under way. Val was a shop steward in environmental health. The meeting ended, they adjourned to the bar downstairs and Andrew ended up sitting opposite her. She interrogated him about the proposed cuts in the planning department and invited him to a fund-raising benefit for anti-apartheid.

He thought she was just drumming up business, but she gave him her undivided attention at the event. He offered to walk her home, and she laughed and said she was hoping for more than a walk. She took him back to the room she had in a shared house and they slept together.

The bathwater was cooling. Andrew drained the last of the brandy and got out. As he lay in bed, he could hear the cadence of conversation downstairs. He woke just after three and his head was throbbing, his stomach cramped. He made it to the bathroom just in time, puking over and over again until he was spent and the waves of nausea receded.

He fed the stove, took some ibuprofen and lay down on the sofa. Waiting for morning to come, for the day to pass, for another night to descend.

Louise

More snow had fallen, smothering everything thick and white. Clouds hung feathery in the sky, their edges an oyster sheen. Louise threw scraps out for the birds and watched them come: the robin and the sparrows. A white Christmas. It was cold, too; she could feel the bite of frost in the air, the snap of it as she breathed in.

Much of the country had ground to a halt, airports closed, cars abandoned, trains marooned. It seemed fitting somehow: the muffled unreality of the weather, the suspension of normal life, the eerie hush, the extreme cold and glittering white world an apt backdrop to Luke in his frozen state, in his white sheets in his quiet white room.

Carl had gone home for Christmas. He had offered to stay, said to Louise that he didn't like to leave her when she was in the middle of a crisis.

'You're fine,' she insisted. 'We'll spend most of the time at the hospital anyway. Besides, your mother'd kill me.'

He'd grinned. Carl had told her all about his mother, an old-school matriarch who would clout her kids for the slightest indiscretion and was fierce as a tiger in their defence. Carl was the baby. He tried to get back once a year, at Christmas time. He'd spend almost three days travelling there on coaches and trains.

'We'll take our presents in to Luke,' Louise told Ruby on Christmas Eve. 'Open them there.'

'I thought we weren't doing anything.' Ruby was practising her dance routine; none of their rooms were really big enough, but it was too muddy for her to do it outside. After the holiday she'd be able to use the school dance studio during lunch break.

'Well I've got you both a little thing,' Louise said. 'I'm not taking it back. And you'd better have got me something.' Knowing full well that Ruby had done her Christmas shopping and had made a point of asking Louise on three separate occasions what her favourite colour was.

'Tuck your chin in,' Louise said.

'Since when were you the expert?' Ruby asked, altering her stance and doing a sidestep and slide.

'You look like you're straining, that's all, like a nervous chicken.'

'Mum!'

'Suit yourself.' Louise went into the kitchen. 'Soup or soup?' she called.

'Soup – tomato.'

'Right first time.'

Shrek 3 was on the box. Louise had a shower and sat with Ruby to watch the second half. Ruby was texting every few minutes. Her phone trilling with each reply.

'That Becky?' Louise asked.

'Yeah, she wants me to go over Boxing Day, sleep over.'

'Good idea.'

'I don't know,' Ruby said.

Louise wanted Ruby to have a break, escape the

tension and tedium of hospital visits. She was aware that Ruby was worried about her, was keen to be there and help, but Louise wanted her to have a chance to relax with her friends, the freedom to set it all aside for a few hours. 'Hey.' She waited for Ruby to look at her. 'I'll be fine, it'll do you good.'

Ruby wrinkled her nose.

'Don't you want to?' Louise asked.

'I suppose.'

'Say yes, then.' Louise turned back to the film. The donkey talking a mile a minute. There was something of that donkey in Luke. The irrepressible energy, the impulsiveness.

'What the hell did you do it for?' she'd demanded of him after the fireworks palaver. Luke had bought contraband Chinese fireworks, mortars, and set them off in two wheelie bins. Destroying both bins and setting the nearby fence alight, triggering a car alarm and waking half the neighbourhood.

'To see what'd happen,' he said. And then a glint dancing in his eye at the memory. 'It was awesome – like a bomb.'

'Jesus, Luke. It was dangerous, that's what it was – and stupid. You could have taken your head off.'

'No, they've a long fuse, there was plenty of time,' reassuring her.

The police had cautioned him and warned her. They used all the clichés: *off the rails* and *slippery slope*. One of them did the talking, with the other just chipping in now and again, a cold face on him and a lick of malice in the cast of his eyes, the curl of his lips. She marked him as a bigot. Probably disapproved of her, prejudiced against Luke. Single mother, mixed-race kid.

She'd lost track of the number of times complete strangers had tried to have a cosy little chinwag with her bemoaning immigration and the flood of Pakis/Poles/ blacks into the area stealing jobs/shops/school places, assuming she shared their Little Englander views. A different matter when she had the children with her: sleeping with the enemy then. She saw that there were issues for Luke and Ruby caught between two cultures, two identities. Ruby had come home from school in tears aged nine after being called a coconut (black on the outside, white inside) in the playground. Louise did all she could to inform them of their backgrounds, but that was hard when neither of their fathers were around and they didn't have access to their extended families.

'I've been thinking about my hair,' Ruby announced.

'Never!' Louise said in mock surprise.

Ruby squeezed her knee, just where it really tickled, and Louise yelped.

'I think I will get a wig. Make it a bit Lady Gaga,' naming the flamboyant pop star with her theatrical costumes.

'Fine. There's that place on Oldham Street.'

Louise heard the 'thwock' of the letter box and went to investigate. A manila envelope with her name and address. Inside she found another envelope: Louise Murray c/o Care24, and the agency address. She pulled out a notelet, a painting of violets on the front, and opened it. Crabbed writing, the letters misshapen and crooked, trailing down the page at an alarming angle. She translated.

Dear Louise,
I was so very sorry to hear of your recent misfortune
and wish your son a most speedy recovery.
With very best wishes.
Yours sincerely,
Mrs R.M. Coulson

She shook her head. It would have taken Mrs Coulson most of an afternoon to write the note, her hand shaking uncontrollably, her eyes peering at the jumble of shapes that insisted on moving about on the page. Then she would have had to find a way of getting the card to Louise, asking the carers to help. Louise put the card on the side to take to the hospital.

Mrs Coulson had actually met Luke once, though Louise doubted she would remember. He'd been excluded from school and Louise didn't want to leave him at home unsupervised. She decided he could accompany her on her day's work, see what she did to earn a living for the three of them. Some places, where a new face might have caused confusion or upset, she made him wait in the car, but she took him in to Mrs Coulson's, where she had to prepare and serve lunch and check on any errands or shopping that were needed.

When she introduced them, Mrs Coulson had looked startled. 'Your son?' she'd repeated.

'Yes.'

'I see,' she'd murmured, and kept an eye (not as beady as it had once been) on Luke throughout, as though he might morph into a burglar and make off with the silver. As they were leaving, she'd called Louise back. 'Is he adopted?' she'd hissed.

'No.' Louise tried not to laugh. 'No, he's mine.'

Mrs Coulson made a little 'I see' sort of noise and her eyebrows twitched.

Stick that in your pipe and smoke it, Louise had thought. She wondered if Luke remembered that day. If he had any memories left. Was that where he was now, lost in the labyrinth of past times? Reliving his jaunts with the Woodcraft Folk or play-fighting with Eddie, climbing into his great-grandad's lap for a story or snorkelling by the caves on their holiday in Ibiza. What if he was trapped with bad memories? The sad times after Grandad died, after Eddie's sudden, shocking death; the miserable days eked out in detention or the occasions when Louise had lost her temper, taken him to task for missing school again.

When he woke up, what would he remember? What would be forgotten? Would he still know her? Love her? Her heart swooped with fear. He would surely. Surely he would.

'Hello, Luke.' Louise put the bags down, shucked off her coat. She moved the chair where she could talk to him, leant over and kissed him, stroked his face. 'It's Christmas Day, Luke, Happy Christmas.'

'Happy Christmas,' Ruby echoed, unrolling the scarf from her neck.

'We're going to open our presents here. We've got yours too.' Louise no longer felt self-conscious talking aloud like this, though she did worry sometimes that she might get too babyish in what she said, treating Luke as a helpless child instead of a boy close to adulthood. She did not want to infantilize him, turn him into some travesty of the real Luke.

Personality could change with brain injury. She'd seen it with some of her clients, people who had become quite unlike themselves after a stroke: more fearful and suspicious or alternatively more easy-going and cheerful. But all that really mattered now was that Luke woke up.

'Right.' She sat down and rummaged in one of the carriers. 'This is for Ruby.' She passed her the rectangular parcel and her daughter thanked her, tore the wrapping off. 'Yes!' she breathed. New hair straighteners with various extra tools and attachments.

'And this.' Louise passed her an envelope. She'd saved since summer to give them each some Christmas money, both of them at an age where they liked to choose their own gifts.

'Thanks, Mum.' Ruby came round and hugged her. She smelled of sweet cherry hair conditioner and some new rose and jasmine perfume she'd taken to wearing. But like Louise she was showing signs of the strain, her skin dry and ashy-looking round her eyes.

'And here's yours, Luke.' Louise picked up his hand and folded it round the small parcel. 'It's what you asked for,' she said, 'the new phone in the black.' Would he ever use it? The treacherous thought darted through her mind. The police still had his old one. He might have to change his number. Or would they let him use the old number on the new one, even if they still had it as evidence. No one had said anything to her about whether they had found anything of importance on his phone, anything to help piece together what had happened that night.

She nodded to Ruby.

'This is from me.' Ruby mimicked her mother, placing Luke's other hand on the soft, bulky package. 'It's a T-shirt, TK Maxx, like your old one, but in white.'

'You could say thank you,' Louise teased him, 'instead of just lying there.'

'And this is yours, Mum.' Ruby brought the present to Louise, who made a show of opening it.

'A pashmina. That is so soft. It's lovely.'

'And you like red?'

'I do, my favourite. You asked us enough times.'

Ruby laughed.

Louise draped the scarf round her neck. 'What do you think?'

'Cool. Needs lipstick, though.'

Louise smiled.

'You going to try?' Ruby asked her. Meaning try and wake him.

'Bit later. Sing him your piece.'

'They might not like it; it's pretty full-on.' Ruby nodded to the door to the rest of the ward. Some of the patients were meant to have as much peace and quiet as possible. Overstimulation being a concern with a fragile brain.

'Sing it quietly. Go on, be good practice.'

'Okay.'

Louise settled back, savoured the sound. Ruby never faltered. Her confidence clear, her breathing controlled, pitch-perfect.

An hour later, Louise set aside her sewing, stood up and stretched. She shifted her chair back and took Luke's hand in hers, patted the back of it and spoke clearly in his ear. A command and a prayer: 'Wake up, Luke, open your eyes, come on, wake up now.' She watched. Pinched the flesh between his thumb and forefinger, squeezing hard. He remained limp, made no response.

She felt the disappointment keenly; it didn't get any easier. She fought the impulse to yank him upright, as if she could shake him awake, as if with enough vehemence she could break through the cocoon and free him. She closed her eyes for a moment, regaining her balance.

Ruby gave a rueful shrug and pulled out her phone. Louise imagined teenagers the length and breadth of the land texting over the Christmas turkey, causing ructions.

She got the wash bag from her carriers and pulled out the nail-clippers. His nails were longer than her own, smooth, with a gentle sheen, the half-moons clear, the cuts on his knuckles healed now. She wondered when the bandages would come off his head; if his hair would grow back the same, or if there would be bald patches where they'd opened him up.

Emma

She went home every Christmas. What else could she do? Her mum loved to have her there and did her best to make it cosy. Always made turkey and all the trimmings, even though there were just the three of them.

This year Emma was ill. The cold had broken overnight, her raw throat giving way to a streaming nose and thumping head. The journey was a nightmare. An earlier train had been cancelled, so this one was full of people squabbling about seat reservations and advance bookings and there weren't enough seats. The only place Emma could find to settle herself was in the corridor outside the toilets, surrounded by her bags. It stank. Even with a blocked-up nose she could smell it. There was something wrong with the heating too, like it was set at boiling point, and she was sweaty and thirsty and it just wasn't possible to fight her way through to the on-board buffet.

She was feeling so cranky and weary by the time the train squealed into New Street that she got a taxi rather than wait for a bus and blew sixteen pounds on that.

'Ey up.' Her father took one look at her. 'It's Rudolph! What a conk; you could light your way home with that.' The very first thing he said.

'I've got a cold,' Emma said.

'Never!' he said sarcastically. 'Come on, bring your bags in, don't stand there like a sack of potatoes.'

Her mother usually tried to smooth things over, to cajole him, but he always had the upper hand. One time he'd derided Emma's choice of winter coat.

'Makes you look twice as fat.'

'It's padded, that's the style,' her mum had said. And she had got black, not the white, which was nicer but less practical. Black was meant to be slimming.

But he wouldn't stop. 'Marshmallow Man!' he crowed. 'Like in *Ghostbusters.*'

'Roger, please!' her mum scolded. 'Stop going on at her.'

That made it worse. 'What? I'm not allowed to comment on what my hard-earned wages are spent on?'

'If you can't say anything nice . . .' her mother started, but there was a pleading quality in her voice.

'I'm not going to lie to the girl. I don't know what you were thinking of. She looks a bloody sight.'

He would often laugh as he said these things. Not the sort of laugh that was infectious. A cold, barking laugh so you'd see his teeth, but his eyes looked furious. One time when he told her she couldn't learn piano because it was a waste of money and she'd as much musical talent as a tone-deaf ape and they'd no piano to practise on anyway, Emma had gone to her mother. Rounded on her really, the wildness coming out of her and saying awful things about him: *I hate him, I wish he was dead.*

'No you don't, that's silly talk.' Her mother had calmed her down and Emma stopped crying.

'Why don't you tell him, Mum? Make him stop.'

'Look. He loves me, and he loves you. He never swears, he's never violent. He's never laid a finger on me, never would. He's a bit sharp-tongued now and again, but that's just how he is. Que sera sera. There's a lot worse men, I can tell you. Now, go wash your face and I'll make us a drink. Can you manage an eclair? There's still two left.'

On the rare occasion that Emma did look to her mother for a sense of shared grievance, of solidarity, it was always the same: her mother quick to mollify her. 'It's just his way; he loves you, he doesn't mean anything by it.' Did he love her? Of course he did, she knew he did, and she loved him; she just wished he wasn't always finding fault.

Other times, he pretended he was only joking. He'd accuse Emma and her mum of having no sense of humour, of not being able to take a joke. Usually it was Emma he picked on, but sometimes it was her mum. Her mum would go very quiet and then just disappear upstairs, if she could, and Emma thought she had a cry, but when she came back you couldn't tell. She hadn't got red eyes or a husky voice.

Emma liked it best when he was out and there was just the two of them, like on Sundays when he played cricket and his Tuesday practices, or Wednesdays when he played darts. What was weird was they talked about him even when he wasn't there, passing on things he'd said, sharing his views on this and that, but it was like talking about some rare species. Observing its mannerisms and habits as though they were fixed and a fact of nature.

He should have been a critic, Emma thought. One of those people who write scathing, bitchy columns in magazines about films or celebrities or restaurants. Hatchet jobs. He'd be good at those. Because his disdain wasn't confined to immediate family; he'd carp on about neighbours or workmates or politicians with the same acid tongue. The difference was he did it behind their backs, not to their faces. And he'd entertain his friends at the pub with his put-downs and send-ups. Roger was known as 'a good laugh'. He could have been a stand-up comedian.

* * *

Her mum made a fuss of her and they had her favourite tea: lasagne and apple pie and cream. It would ruin her diet, but there was no point trying to stick to it over Christmas – and not when she was ill as well. She'd start again in the New Year.

Dad complained that there was a new man sharing his office at Clevely and Son and he wanted them to switch to a new type of spreadsheet package. Dad was quite happy with the one they used, he didn't want to have to start fathoming out something else, but Mr Clevely was 'thinking about it'.

'If it ain't broke, don't fix it,' Mum said and doled out the rest of the pie.

Emma told them she'd had to go to the police.

'Causing an obstruction, eh?' Dad quipped, his eyes hard and bright.

'I saw the student who was stabbed and the other boy, the one in the coma.' She told them what had happened, quickly, so he wouldn't make any nasty comments.

Her mum was shocked; she'd seen all about it on the news. She wanted to know if they'd caught anyone. Emma told her no.

'It's awful, that,' her mum said. 'He was from a good family and everything. It was right outside his house. Oh, Emma, I never liked you being in Manchester, and now this.'

Her dad snorted. 'It's everywhere these days, woman. And if you do have a go, half the time it's you'll get arrested. Charged with assault. People screaming human rights, never mind who the bad guy is. What rights did that student have?'

'Disgraceful,' her mother agreed. 'Ted, next door but one, saw some kids knocking over wheelie bins, making

100

a right mess. He rang the police, and do you know what they said? They didn't have the resources to send anyone round, but if Ted wanted to, he could go down to the station and make a complaint. We're thinking of setting up a Home Watch.'

'Improve your house and contents premiums,' Emma, on safer ground, told them.

They watched a documentary about rogue builders; it was shocking, it really was. Emma couldn't stay awake any longer. Mum told her to take some paracetamol and drink some orange juice.

She slept fitfully. Her throat felt like she was gargling ground glass; she was sweating and throwing the duvet off, then she'd get really cold and shivery. She couldn't stop coughing and spluttering, and she felt like someone had stuffed her head with sand.

Christmas Day was just like every year: drinks before lunch, presents after. All done in time for the Queen's speech.

Emma talked to them about her work and told them that her last appraisal had been the best yet but there was a freeze on pay rises at the moment because of the financial situation. That set Dad off on his soapbox about government spending and benefit cheats, until Mum asked him to change the record. But she said it in a nice way, laughing, and he didn't jump down her throat.

On Boxing Day they always went to her aunt and uncle's. They had a bigger house and her nan lived with them now. They'd made the dining room into a bedroom for her and put in a downstairs shower. Nan was much worse. She kept calling Emma Claire. Emma hadn't a clue who Claire was until Mum explained she had been Nan's sister and died in her twenties of complications after an operation. Nan's teeth had mostly gone and she had new hearing aids that made a swooping, whistling noise that set Emma's teeth on edge.

Her auntie wasn't any great shakes as a cook: the beef was leathery and the Christmas pud, which she did in the microwave – 'Do you remember they used to take forever on the stove?' – was so tiny they got like a teaspoon each with lumpy brandy sauce.

Emma's uncle got a bit drunk and wanted to show them a DVD of a cruise they'd taken in the spring. Emma was glad when Nan became agitated and insisted they put the proper telly back on. Thank God they could leave early with Emma being poorly.

Her mum never said a word about Emma's weight. Not once in all the time she was home. Usually she'd tell her she looked well or she was looking trimmer or even ask if she was still dieting. Emma took the silence as confirmation that what she'd suspected all year was true. She was still gaining. She just kept getting bigger, and nothing worked.

The two Kims were like straws, could eat anything and never put on weight. Laura was bigger but still only size 14. She would exercise more, Emma promised herself. She couldn't afford a gym, but she would get into the habit of taking the train both ways to work and walking through town. She wasn't going to just give up. And she'd have to be a lot bigger to qualify for gastric-band surgery. Meanwhile it was impossible not to eat over the holiday; the fridge was stuffed with food, so she just got on with it. Tucked in with the rest of them.

CHAPTER SEVEN

Andrew

Boxing Day and he found Val at the kitchen table, her chin on her hand, elbow propped, staring out to the back garden. Papers strewn about, Post-it notes and pens. It looked like she was preparing a report for work. She often brought work home, responsible for training across all the departments at the town hall. But he knew this current project was personal: the burial of their son.

'Do you need a hand with that?'

She turned, took a breath like someone coming round from a sleep. Dragged herself into the present. The here and now. 'No, it's okay. Just think,' she said, 'they're out there today, opening their presents, stuffing their faces, swigging—' She broke off. 'Do they think they can get away with it!' Her face was mobile with emotion, her eyes burning. 'How can they sleep? How can they function? The families must know.'

He thought of the figures in the garden, the lad rearing up and away from Jason. He rubbed at his face. 'They'll find them,' he said. He went and stood behind her, put his hands on her shoulders, kissed the top of her head.

'You okay if I go for a walk?'

'Sure.' She put her hand up to squeeze his.

His shoes were still soaked. He thought of the journey home on Christmas Eve, swigging the brandy, stepping in puddles.

Outside, the wind cut into his face, icy blasts that drove heavy, brass-tinted clouds across the sky. Frost glimmered on the fences and shrubs. Black ice gleamed malevolent on the tarmac.

He had no sense of where he was going, no route planned out. He just walked and walked until his body warmed and the aching in his limbs made him feel halfway alive.

The house was quiet on his return. On the table, Val's lists. The bewildering range of things to do for Thursday. Val's neat print marched in serried ranks down the page.

NURSERY – BUY TREE
TAKE WATERING CAN/SPADES
FELIX – FLUTE
REHEARSE BEARERS (COLIN, NICK,
HARRY, MARLON)
FEES FOR CELEBRANT
B&B DETAILS
BAR
DECOR FOR CC

She always made lists. Andrew remembered the long period of limbo waiting for Jason to come home from hospital. The first few weeks not knowing if he would or not. Val constantly refining the lists of clothing and equipment. Not daring to buy anything for long enough. Colin and Izzie had offered them plenty of baby gear, but they decided not to have it in the house until they knew for certain that Jason would pull through.

In the incubator they used special materials; ordinary fabric would have been intolerably harsh against his raw, fragile skin.

They watched him grow from a scrap of skin and bones and a flickering heart, the whole of him smaller than Andrew's hand, to a young man with his dragon tattoo and muddy-blond tresses and lazy smile.

'He's so laid back, he's horizontal,' Val had complained one summer when she'd come in from work to find Jason, then fifteen, still in his pyjamas, scoffing cereal and playing on the games console. 'Why won't he get a job?'

'He doesn't need the money,' Andrew suggested.

'It's not about the money,' she said, 'but the experience.'

'What – working in a fast-food joint for crap wages?' Andrew said. He was with Jason on this one.

'He'd learn something. Customer service, how to operate a till. You worked when you were his age, didn't you, at the golf club.'

'Collecting glasses. Everyone worked back then. There were more jobs, less pocket money.'

'That's where we've gone wrong,' she said darkly.

'Hey.' He put his arms around her waist, drew her close. 'We've not gone wrong; he's a lovely boy. Lazy as sin, but lovely with it.'

'Well if he's here all day, he can do more at home.' And she'd followed through, leaving lists of chores, instructions for the washing machine, the hoovering, reminders about the dishwasher and tidying his room.

When Val surfaced, he expected her to ask him where he'd been, why he'd taken so long, but she just said, 'Hi. There's some minestrone if you want. Colin and Izzie called. And your mum rang. They've got someone for the bar at the cricket club.' They were hiring the cricket club for the celebration after the funeral.

'Good,' he said.

'Your suit. It'll need cleaning.'

'Right. I can take it,' he said. She was doing it all. He knew keeping busy, tackling the practical tasks, helped her cope, but he could at least do some of the running around. 'I can get the tree too. A rowan.' He steeled himself. 'Drop his clothes off.' Just the thought of it, that they were picking out burial garments for his eighteen-year-old son, lit the anger inside. The anger was good, though, hot and clean and fierce. Far better than the fog of grey desolation, the marsh of despair that threatened to suck him under.

'Okay,' Val said. 'They're on his bed.'

He went upstairs and stood outside Jason's door. He felt the rage burn, pushing his heart harder, searing his guts, curling his hands into fists. Then came the pictures in his head. Those fists slamming into the feral lad, smashing his face, beating him again and again until there was nothing left. Hands throttling the girl, choking the life from her. A knife for the bug-eyed one, plunging it into him again and again, watching the shock and then the pain and fear fill those eyes. Hurting them, hurting them so they knew what it felt like. Killing them, over and over and over again.

Louise

Louise stared at the television, shock radiating through her like lightning. Police had released CCTV images of the three young people wanted for questioning on suspicion of Jason Barnes' murder. They showed them getting on a bus. Two lads and a girl. The boys wore hoodies, and the girl's face was obscured too, by the fur-trimmed hood on her jacket. Then on to the screen flashed a sequence of three e-fit portraits, and the voice-over was describing them. The broadcast moved on to the next story.

Louise was trembling. She grabbed her cigarettes and went outside. Seeing them on the camera like that pushed her close to imagining what had come after, when they had chased Luke down Kingsway, pictures in her head that she censored. Redacted they called it nowadays, didn't they? Big black lines through intelligence and military reports. Big black clots in Luke's brain. Redacted.

She smoked her cigarette down to the filter and tasted the bitter scorch on her tongue. She resisted the temptation to light up another, and went to the corner shop to see if the pictures were in the lunchtime edition. She needn't have wondered: it was on the sandwich board outside. EXCLUSIVE: GOOD SAMARITAN MURDER – SUSPECTS PICS.

'All right, Louise,' said Omar at the counter. 'How is he?'

'Same, thanks.' She picked up the paper.

'Scum,' Omar said, nodding at the front page, 'that's what they are, scum.'

It didn't really help.

The e-fit drawings were clearer than anything you could make out on the CCTV that had been shown. The CCTV could have been anyone, but the sketches were distinctive. The big lad had popping-out eyes, it said he had red hair, and the other one had a mean mouth, he looked a bit wizened. The girl was nice-looking, a heart-shaped face.

Sian was coming into the shop as Louise was leaving. She blushed as she said hello.

'How's your mum?' Louise asked, force of habit.

'Not bad, but her legs are up again,' Sian stammered. 'If there's anything I can get you—'

Louise cut her off. 'We're fine, love, ta. Thanks all the same.'

Back home, Louise made a coffee and read the article through carefully. Luke was only mentioned twice. *Luke Murray (16) was being kicked by the assailants when Jason Barnes (18) came to his aid.* And, *Murray remains seriously ill but stable in hospital. He has not regained consciousness since the brutal attack.*

She wondered whether to text Ruby, but decided to leave it. Ruby had stayed a second night at Becky's, coming back in between to change and to visit the hospital.

Her phone went. Declan. 'How's Luke?' he asked.

Louise told him there had been no change.

Declan had been into hospital once and it had been painful to see. He'd blushed deep red on arrival and hadn't the wherewithal to chat along to an unresponsive body on a bed. He'd barely exchanged a word with Louise. When he left, she told him that as soon as they had any news she'd let him know and he could come visit again. Letting him off the hook.

Time was the two lads had been inseparable, egging each other on, both drawn to mischief, hot-headed, impulsive. Both prone to giving cheek. But in the last couple of years Declan had started messing with pills, and nowadays he was out of his skull half the time, spending his life in front of the Xbox cocooned in a haze of chemicals.

'Are you at home? Can I knock on?'

Louise felt a spike of unease. Why on earth would Declan want to visit her? 'Yeah,' she said. 'See you in a bit.'

When he arrived, she offered him coffee but he just wanted milk. His eyes were watery and red-rimmed, his lips chapped, his hair straggly and unkempt. Louise felt a wave of sadness for him. He'd lost his way. His life a narrow rut growing deeper, his health precarious. He'd be old by thirty at this rate. And what alternatives were there? There was no one to guide him, to champion him. His mum as lost as he was. He'd never work, not legally; he hadn't the discipline or the self-belief, let alone any marketable skills. It was such an awful waste.

He nodded at the paper. 'You seen the pictures?'

'Yes, have you?'

'Only on telly.' He leaned closer. 'This one,' he pointed to the bigger lad, 'I think it's Gazza.'

Louise felt her blood chill, cold spackle her skin. 'Who?'

'Gazza; his real name's Tom Garrington. Don't know him really, like, but Luke had a run-in with him a while back.'

'When? What?' Her rapid-fire questions disconcerted Declan and she bit her tongue as she watched him struggle to focus.

'A while back.'

'How long? When?'

'Erm . . .'

'Summer?'

'No. Halloween.'

'What happened?'

Declan puffed out his cheeks, released a slow breath. He looked hounded, head hanging low between his shoulders, eyes averted.

'Declan, whatever it is, it's fine. This could be really important.'

'There was a party – this empty house off Braithwaite.' One of the roads on the estate. 'Everyone went. They was all, like, off their heads, man.' He slid a frightened glance her way. 'There was a lot of gear.'

'Gear?'

'Stuff.'

'Drugs?'

'Pills and coke and that meow stuff.'

Oh God. 'Go on.'

'That Gazza, it was his birthday, he was with this girl. Well, dunno if he was with her but he was next to her, slagging her off, she was crying. She was off her face, man.'

'This girl?' Louise touched the picture in the paper.

'Nah. Anyway, he's saying a lot of shit, how he's going to cut her up and stuff, and Luke just tells him to pack it in. Then he's yelling at Luke, like well stressed, man, abuse and that. Luke's ready to thump him. Gazza goes for him but Luke trips him up and he falls in all this crap, like where people have left pizza boxes and dead drinks and fag ends and that. Well rank. Everyone laughs, man.' Declan tugged at a strand of greasy hair, looking guilty. 'Then Luke gets his phone out, "say cheese", takes a video, like. We had to leave then. Luke sent the file round. Put it online.'

For this. For this they had kicked him half to death. Pity and grief and dismay crept through her.

'Why didn't you say anything before?'

Declan flushed. 'It were ages ago. I'd forgotten.'

'Was this other guy there?' She tapped the paper.

'Dunno.'

'You need to tell the police.'

He sighed, slumped, stared at her, mouth hanging open.

She fought the anger heating her flesh and resisted the impulse to grab hold of him and shake him and tell him to frame his bloody self. 'Yes, everything you've told me.'

'I've not much credit left.'

110

She bit her tongue. 'Wait.' She dialled the number the police had given her, her pulse racing, her stomach knotted and a great weight crushing her heart.

You'd have thought the police would have been falling over themselves to hear what Declan had to say, but they kept them hanging around the reception bit at the police station long enough. Louise gave the gist of why they were there to three separate people one after the other, like it was a memory test.

Finally DC Illingworth, a woman about Louise's age, glowing with a violent tan and dressed in a purple pinstripe shirt and black slacks, took them into a small room and sat them down. It was just a little box, table and four practical chairs, steel frames and padded seats.

DC Illingworth apologized for the cold and turned on the convector heater. Once she'd established who they were – Luke's mother, Luke's friend – and taken their dates of birth and addresses, she asked Declan if he would like Louise to stay or whether he'd prefer to talk to her on his own.

'She can stay,' he said ungraciously. Louise could see he was slightly embarrassed at being given the choice. She was relieved. Declan needed a steady hand to keep him on track at the best of times. His mind wandered, making him prone to telling rambling stories that never quite reached their destination. She wondered how stoned he was today and thought about asking for a coffee to sharpen him up, but held back.

'You recognized one of the e-fits in the paper?' The detective drew out a copy of the newspaper from the file at her elbow.

'That one.' Declan pointed to one of the faces. 'Tom Garrington.'

'How do you know him?'

Louise waited while Declan told his story, listening for any deviation from what he'd said earlier. DC Illingworth interrupted a couple of times to ask questions, and each time Declan had to gear himself up to find his thread again. Louise stiffened with impatience. Her legs ached and she realized that she had them twisted and was pressing the top of one foot against the other calf, cutting off her blood supply.

To her credit, the police officer was very patient with the lad and didn't try rushing him. When Declan got to the end – their swift departure from the party in the empty house and Luke sending the clip round – she turned to Louise. 'This is what Declan told you?'

'Yes,' Louise turned to Declan, 'but you missed out the drugs.'

Spots reddened on his cheeks and he gave a little twist of his head, sliding his eyes sideways like she was a fool for bringing it up.

'We need you to be completely honest, Declan, completely open; don't leave anything out,' the officer said.

''Kay.' He nodded, bit at a fingernail.

'So tell me about the drugs.'

'Just there was a lot there, all sorts. Everyone was high, you know.'

DC Illingworth sat forward. 'Do you still have a copy of the video Luke took?'

Declan nodded. Louise felt sick. She didn't want to watch it. She folded her arms and looked down as Declan found the file and passed his phone to the detective.

As DC Illingworth played the clip, Louise could hear the mess of chatter and music, then Luke's voice clear and close, bubbling with laughter, 'Say cheese.'

Oh you bloody idiot, Luke. You sweet, stupid idiot. When would he wake up? When would she hear him talk again? Would he be able to talk? Were those to be his last ever recorded words, 'Say cheese'?

'I need to make a copy of this,' the woman told Declan, 'but it is very helpful to have it.'

Louise understood that it would back up Declan's story. Declan wasn't exactly a straight-up guy who you'd buy a used car from, but this was proof.

'You'll arrest him?' She gestured to the phone still in Illingworth's hand.

'If our enquiries . . .' The detective was hedging her bets.

'But that's proof!' Louise objected.

'It's proof of this specific incident.'

'But that's why!' Louise heard her own voice high and tight. Too loud in the small space. 'That's why they attacked him.'

'You're probably right, but we have to follow procedures. We have to be methodical, meticulous—'

Louise snorted and shook her head, wired with exasperation.

'If we don't stick to the procedures, gather sound evidence and build a watertight case, then no one gets justice. And that's what we're all here for.' Illingworth held Louise's stare.

'How long?'

The detective shook her head. 'It's an impossible question.'

It's an impossible bloody situation, Louise thought. 'I need a break.' She stood up so abruptly that she had to reach out and catch the chair to stop it falling. 'Is there anywhere I can smoke?'

'I'll take you outside. You can stay here, Declan.' The boy was halfway to his feet. Probably gagging himself. Well he can wait, Louise thought, and then hated the meanness in her.

The detective left her in a small courtyard where a shelter covered a metal bench. Her hand was shaking as she lit her cigarette. Rage. At the delays, at the plod-plod way of dealing with it all. At the whole bloody world. She closed her eyes and smoked.

You'll give yourself a heart attack. Her grandma's words to her grandad when the miners' strike was on and he'd be yelling at the television: 'I was there; it wasn't like that, pack of lies!' The news covered running battles between the police and the pickets who travelled to support the strikers. 'They were beating us up!' He'd throw his arms up, his face deep red. 'A load of southerners working for the Tories, no idea about mining, about what this means, about those communities.'

'Sit down before you fall down,' Grandma had said. 'Why are you so surprised? We all know whose side the press are on, most of them.'

He had fallen down eventually. Louise had found him on the kitchen floor, coffee spilt. Only five weeks after he was made redundant. There'd been a terrible split in the union ranks in the run-up to the firm's closure. Militants, 'bloody Trots' as he called them, dividing the membership, running dirty-tricks campaigns and smears, accusing some of the moderates of being moles or spies, in bed with management,

'Divide and rule,' he sighed one night when Louise was helping him fit new vinyl flooring in the bathroom. 'Oldest trick in the book, and now we're doing it to ourselves.'

His anger had turned sour and dirty in those last few months, and after he was out of a job he became bitter. Like the fight had gone and all he could do was brood.

Now Louise realized he was probably depressed. Even with all his learning and reading, all his political analysis, the job had defined him. He was a docker, his comrades were dockers, and when that was taken from him, he was a hollow man. His wife and Louise and Luke weren't enough to complete him.

Her cigarette finished, Louise took a moment gazing upwards, where the shreds of white and pink cloud trapped the sunset against the deep blue of the sky. There was a gap in the rumble of traffic and no other sound broke the silence. No drill or dog or music or voice. As if the city held its breath. Then the drone recommenced, and bone-weary, she went back to join Declan.

She was calmer by the time they were through. Her anger had settled to a slow, smouldering burn deep in her belly rather than the roar and crackle of flames in her head. She asked to speak to DC Illingworth on her own.

'I need to know what's going on,' she said, keeping her voice level. 'No one's telling me anything. I didn't know those pictures would be in the paper. No one said Luke had been on the bus. I should be told these things, not have to read about it in the papers.'

She sensed a reserve creep into the police officer's manner, a shutter coming down. 'You have a family liaison officer?'

'You tell me,' said Louise. 'I was given a name and number but I've never been able to reach them. They've not phoned me back.'

'Has anybody been to the house?'

'No. Look, I don't need babysitting, but I shouldn't be the last to know.'

'I agree.' The detective gave a thin smile. 'Let me check this out. You don't mind waiting?'

'No.' Waiting was her new way of life. Maybe she should have brought her patchwork with her.

She texted Ruby to tell her she was running late and to call at Angie's if she needed anything.

After ten minutes, Illingworth bustled back in, all

efficiency. 'Right. I think there's been some crossed wires at our end, probably the result of the holidays: officers on leave and so on. So, I've had a word with DI Brigg, the senior investigating officer, and he's happy for me to be your designated point of contact. It makes sense, as we've met already. Any developments that we are able to make public, I'll let you know. You understand there will be times when we are made aware of new evidence or information but need to keep it confidential.'

'Okay.' She could hardly argue otherwise.

'Here's my card, that's my direct number.'

'Thank you.'

'And thanks for coming in today with Declan.'

'Only way to get him here,' Louise told her.

'It really has been invaluable. Thank you, Louise.' She smiled. Bright and friendly. Laying it on a bit thick, Louise thought. Anxious to smooth over the cock-up, get Louise onside. Stop her complaining. The police had a grubby history of failures in dealing with ethnic-minority victims, a past they were eager to see dead and buried. Someone like Louise raising a fuss about her experience, given that Luke was a mixed-race victim, would be terrible PR for them. The possibility that she might need to do that, if things didn't improve, if Illingworth didn't keep her word, was there. A strategy. She'd go to the papers if she had to. They were all desperate to talk to her as it was. Them and the TV news crews clustered round the house. *How does it feel, Mrs Murray? Louise, has Luke opened his eyes yet? What would you like to say to our viewers?* Pushing their business cards through the letter box. Shouting about exclusives, and *Hear the victim's point of view.* Yes, she'd do whatever she had to do to make sure Luke got the justice he deserved.

CHAPTER EIGHT

Emma

Leaving to come back to Manchester, she felt deflated. That after-the-party feeling even though the party had been crap. Arriving home, the flat was cold and she turned the heating on full. The fish were fine; she fed them and checked the temperature. She'd lost two in September to a fungal disease, and she still worried that the others might get sick. She'd nothing much in and she was starving again, so went to get a Chinese. It was good for takeaways where she was, but the Chinese was her favourite. She ate every last scrap, then she had some of the Christmas cake Mum had given her.

Mum texted her: Dad had got her cold. Good, thought Emma, and then felt horrible. She was a horrible person, that was the trouble, and sooner or later her new friends would find out and she'd be on her own again. Like she was meant to be.

She finished the cake and some mince pies, and a Yorkie bar. But it still wasn't enough. She'd only ever told one person about it: the locum GP who she saw in the middle of A levels when she got an ear infection and needed antibiotics. Emma was exhausted by the endless revision for the exams, and by the other thing. She hadn't planned to say anything; she'd expected to see Dr Henry, who treated all her family, but he'd been called away due to a bereavement and a young woman was covering his appointments: Dr Sulayman. The doctor was quite pretty but she had funny eyes, like a squint, and one eyelid lower than the other. Like she'd got stuck mid-wink. She spoke quietly, like Emma herself, and after she'd examined Emma's ear and done the prescription, she turned back to her and asked, 'And how are things with you generally?'

It was like snapping open a jack-in-the-box. Emma's mind flooded with her miseries, and to her horror she began to cry, right there in the consulting room. Dr Sulayman was so nice. She gave her tissues and a cup of water and told her to take her time and tell her what was making her so unhappy.

Emma didn't know how to answer her. 'Everything' was too vague. She shook her head.

'Are there any problems at home?'

'No,' said Emma quickly. She couldn't bear being disloyal. 'But sometimes I can't stop eating, even when I'm full.' There, she had said it, and the doctor would hate her now. *Greedy pig.* Emma chewed her lip.

But Dr Sulayman said it was a very common problem and there were ways to deal with it, like following a healthy eating plan and trying to minimize stress. Counselling could help as well, especially in dealing with any underlying issues.

Emma could hear him jeer, his voice rattling away like a machine gun, 'Oh, she's psychotic now, is she? Just our luck, we really picked a winner there, eh? There was none of this in my day, people just got on with it.'

'How long have you been binge-eating?' The doctor said it normally, like it was a cold or flu. Something ordinary.

Emma considered. Since Year 10; she'd loved sugary things before that, and pies and chips. 'A sweet tooth,' her mum would say. 'A fat pig, if she doesn't watch it,' her dad would add.

'About three years,' she said.

'And would you say it's getting worse?'

Emma nodded.

'Do you ever make yourself sick?'

Emma almost denied it, but it was like the doctor already knew. She dipped her head. 'But just this year.'

'When you look in the mirror, you think you look overweight?'

'I am.'

'You're doing A levels now?'

'Yes.'

'And that must be putting a lot of extra pressure on you. Have you applied to university?'

Emma shook her head.

'Had enough of school?'

'Yes.' And he said she'd never get a place, not with the competition, and university was all well and good but half the graduates couldn't get jobs, and why waste the time and money, even if you had the brains, which she was seriously lacking.

'And my dad thinks it's a bad idea.' It felt like a rip, a tear in the picture of how things were supposed to be, and Emma wanted to take it back.

'Why's that?'

'I'm not clever enough.' Her stomach flipped. 'You won't tell anyone, will you, about the eating?'

'No, complete confidentiality. And what does your mum think?'

'Whatever he tells her to.' Emma's face was on fire. She shouldn't be thinking this, talking like this. She felt terrible, but Dr Sulayman was so kind and not shocked or anything.

'They don't know about your eating disorder?'

'No.'

'You have any brothers or sisters?'

Emma shook her head.

'Friends you could talk to?'

'No.' There were a couple of girls she hung round with at school, mainly because they were the leftovers, like she was, the losers, and you had to sit next to someone at school. None of their conversations ever got too personal.

'Your parents think university is not for you. What do you think?'

Emma shrugged.

'Is there something else you'd like to do? Do you have a career in mind?'

Emma shrugged again. She didn't know what she wanted to do. The trouble was, there was no one thing she was really good at.

'It sounds like everything's very uncertain for you at the moment, exams, not sure which direction to go in. But it also sounds like you've been unhappy far too long.'

Emma bit the inside of her cheek.

The doctor paused, then brought her hands together in a silent clap, fingers pointing at Emma. She had lovely nails. Emma hid her own.

'Here's what I suggest: I will put you on the waiting list for counselling, and before then,' she swivelled in her chair and opened one of the desk drawers, pulled out a leaflet, 'here we are.' She held it out to Emma. 'You read this.'

Eating Disorders – an introduction and guide to treatment. Emma wanted to give it back, tear it up. This had been a bad idea. She only caught fragments of the rest.

'Resources listed . . . linked to low self-confidence . . . feel better about ourselves.'

How? Emma thought helplessly. Beginning to wish she hadn't told Dr Sulayman any of it.

'Do you see a dentist regularly?'

'I don't like the dentist,' Emma said.

'One of the side effects of bringing back food . . .' – and she didn't mean from the shops – 'is the acid corroding the enamel. You've lovely teeth . . .'

Emma blushed. Lovely teeth!

'. . . but this could cause irreparable damage both to them and to the lining of the oesophagus as well.' She said it so gently, not like a lecture. 'The dentist might be able to help you protect your teeth.'

Emma did that anyway. She always brushed her teeth straight after, and she drank loads of milk and ate cheese. She imagined losing her teeth, being gummy as well as fat. The urge to leave was massive. She stood up.

'Lots of girls have this problem.' The doctor got to her feet. She was tiny next to Emma. 'And people overcome it. Support from family and friends can be a big help.'

Emma shook her head. Forget it, then.

'Sometimes people need to create a bit of space, some independence, especially if the situation in the family reinforces poor self-esteem.'

'I need to go,' Emma said quickly.

Dr Sulayman handed her the prescription and smiled. 'Take care, Emma, and good luck with your exams.'

Emma hadn't kept the appointment with the coun-sellor when it finally came through. But she had eventually read the pamphlet and she had looked up some of the websites it mentioned. She didn't like it; it made her feel grimy and guilty, and anyway she could manage, she just ate a bit too much sometimes.

She got a C and two Ds in her exams and put her name down for the new Tesco that was opening down the road.

* * *

Andrew

The depth of winter, Andrew thought. Winter had depth, summer had height. Barely seven and a half hours of daylight at this time of year. Now, close to midday, the sun had reached its zenith, a brassy ball in a cerulean sky. Light glancing off all the shiny surfaces: the metalled road, the cars, the glass in the buildings and stretches of river glimpsed from the bridge.

Andrew turned in at the garden centre. The car park was surprisingly busy. A sign at the entrance offered Christmas Trimmings and Lights at HALF PRICE!!! The thought that people were here stocking up for next December was depressing.

The trees were at the far end of the complex, corralled in pens, some with horticultural fleece round the pots. Stocks were low. Autumn or spring was the time to plant, not midwinter. He scanned the labels. Compared the pictures on them to the spindly plants on offer. There was only one rowan tree. *Red berries and white flowers, ideal small tree, attractive to wildlife*, he read. *Grows to a height of 10 metres.* It would grow, its roots in the soil drawing nourishment from Jason. Macabre. Of course, death was macabre, that was the point, and all the rituals, like scattering ashes in rose gardens or planting bulbs by graves, were variations on the theme: life in death, the circle of creation, the wheel of life. But it should have been his father or his mother he was here choosing a tree for, not his eighteen-year-old son.

Jason. They'd picked the name because they liked the sound of it, though people teased them at the time that it was after the *Neighbours* soap star, Jason Donovan.

Following the first miscarriage, they had learnt to be circumspect in hope. Not to tempt fate. Jason was the fourth pregnancy. Only when Val reached twenty-six weeks did she suggest they get some baby name books. Andrew favoured short, unfussy names: Jack, Tom, Joel; Anna or Rose for a girl. Val wanted something more unusual: Lewis or Jeremy, Suzanne, Bethany. Occasionally she got carried away.

'You can't call a child Ferdinand,' he'd objected, laughing. 'He'd never live it down.' He drew the line at Lorelei, too. 'It needs to be something people can pronounce – and spell. Jason had been the only name they'd agreed on for a boy.

'Can I help?' The assistant, a chubby-cheeked girl with blue hair, set down her wheelbarrow.

'The rowan.' He cleared his throat. 'It's the only one you've got?'

'Yes. Doesn't look up to much now, they never do, just sticks really, but it'll surprise you.'

'They're good for birds?'

'Yes. Or there's the silver birch, they're popular, we've a few of them, or the aspen, you know, the ones that shiver.' She fluttered her hands. 'The leylandii are good too.' She gestured to a stand of them behind him. 'A lot of birds nest in them, but they are quick-growing.'

He didn't like the shivering idea. And he was pretty sure the leylandii weren't on the list from the woodland cemetery. He knew they were the ones that grew like weeds and caused more neighbour disputes than anything else. It seemed fitting now that the rowan was one on its own, an only one, just like Jason had been the only one.

'I'll take the rowan.'

'And keep the receipt; any problems and we offer a full refund.'

A preposterous image of digging up the tree from its woodland site and hauling it here for his money back snuck into his head.

He manoeuvred the tree into the car with the top sticking out of the open passenger window.

He still had to call at the funeral home. He should have gone there first. Jason's clothes were in the back, in a carrier bag. Jeans and a long-sleeved T-shirt, underwear, his shoes. The shoes they had to bring home from the hospital. Big as coal barges. A fragment of the song came into his head: *Herring boxes, without topses, sandals were for Clementine . . . Thou art lost and gone for ever, dreadful sorry, Clementine.* Singing it with Jason in cod-Yankee accents. Jason picking out the tune in between on a harmonica.

This wasn't happening. It didn't make sense. It was as if he was playing a role, grieving father, but he wasn't really committed to it. It was all pretence. Any moment the curtain would fall or the camera stop rolling and the chimera would disappear. Everything would go back to how it should be.

He had tried to talk to Val about it, the unreality, but she'd reduced it to a formula: denial – it's a part of the process. Before he had a chance to take it any further, to ask her if she too felt this bizarre disconnect, she was moving on to something else. Her energy, close to mania, exhausted him.

He sat until the light began to fade, his buttocks growing numb in the seat. The sky changed, the ink of night stealing across from the east. East, the Orient, from *orior*, to rise. Many early maps didn't include the compass points; they had their own orientation based on the purpose of the map, the culture of the particular cartographer, their understanding of space and representation. Only later did the demands of trade and travel force a cohesive format on to mapmakers: the use of scale, the four points of the compass, the lines of latitude.

He and Val were like those early mappers. Each charting their own course, not even agreeing which way was up or down.

He stretched, then turned the engine on, reversed the car and set out for the funeral parlour. Glad to be sheltered in the encroaching dark.

The coffin had arrived. Val had put it in their conservatory. 'This time of year,' she said, 'and they still do same-day delivery.'

We never sleep, he thought. No two-week Christmas breaks for those in the funeral business. There'd been a strike once, he remembered, of gravediggers, headlines about the dead lying unburied, corpses rotting, families distraught.

'I've told the boys to come round tomorrow teatime.' Jason's closest friends, the lads he'd been at the pub with that last night, heartsick and passionate with all the righteous intensity of youth, wanted to be involved in celebrating Jason's life. Val, with her customary zeal and focus, had been researching options for humanist ceremonies, eco-friendly coffins and woodland burials. She swiftly involved them in the details and asked if they would like to decorate Jason's cardboard coffin. Now it was here, plain, dun-coloured, grotesque. Andrew went out and got the rowan tree, carried it in and stood it beside the coffin.

The phone rang. He moved to get it, but she said, 'Don't answer it. It's the newspapers. They've been ringing every ten minutes. Over and over. I spoke to Martine, she said to ignore them, not to say a word. They'll give up eventually.'

'What if Mum or Dad wants us?' The phone rang on and on.

'I've told them to use our mobiles for now.'

They paused and listened. The phone sang out for another five rings, then stopped. 'I'll take it off the hook,' he said.

'I've tried that – it does that horrible siren noise after a bit.'

He looked at her, then went into the hall. He unplugged the base station and the telephone jack. 'Sorted,' he called out. 'I've disconnected it.'

She didn't answer. His neck prickled. He walked back through to the conservatory. She was sitting down on one of the rattan chairs, head in her hands, her shoulders moving as she wept.

'Oh, Val.' Tears started at the back of his eyes. He moved to her, moved to hold her, her crying raw and guttural and accompanied by a rocking motion. He held her and tried to soothe her, whispering in her hair. 'Oh, I'm so sorry, love. Oh, darling, I'm so sorry.' Knowing that he couldn't make it right, couldn't kiss it better. That all he could do was be there and walk beside her. Even if they were making the journey in different ways, disagreeing about the direction, they must walk on because there was no other choice.

They clung to each other like that until she quietened and his feet had gone numb and his shoulder and top were damp with her tears.

He didn't know what to say, how to move them back to the business of living, of dealing with the dead. In the end, he resorted to the basest practicalities. 'Tea, something to eat?'

She shivered, looked at him. Grey eyes lucid and naked, red-rimmed. 'There's a shepherd's pie, it'll microwave.'

He squeezed her shoulders and clambered upright, the burn and bite of pins and needles sizzling in his legs.

She'd rallied by the time he'd got the food on the

table, though he noticed she ate little as she updated him on the progress she'd made for the other arrangements. How she'd asked Jason's friends to choose some music, but told them it would be nice to include the Bobby McFerrin song 'Don't Worry, Be Happy'. 'Remember?'

'Lovely,' he said, but there was a lance in his heart.

That holiday. Driving down to Cornwall with a compilation tape that Andrew had made playing loud. All of them singing that song, rewinding it time and again for Jason, who was seven. In the wake of Val's parents' deaths, a horrible year, the mantra seemed tailor-made for them all. Jason had made a video on the camcorder to go with the music. Stop-motion Plasticine cat and mouse, meant to be dancing, swaying their heads to the laid-back beat, but getting the movements right had proved too difficult. The end result was hilarious, had Jason breathless and Andrew and Val in stitches.

Jason had got car-sick on the drive home. Andrew thought that navigating with the road atlas would entertain him, but before they'd reached the M5, Jason was pasty-faced and they had to stop. Val had blamed Andrew. 'Everyone knows reading causes car sickness; what were you thinking?' Then Jason had been sick in the car, once they were on the motorway. The reek of it was horrible and Jason was crying, and they had to wait to get to the services to try and clean him up a bit.

'Andrew?'

'Sorry?' Had she said something? What had she said? He saw a flicker of displeasure.

'The stuff for Colin's there. I've emailed the text, but he wants the actual picture to scan for the cover.'

'Right.' Colin was doing the programme for the service. He ran a print and design company and had everything to hand. 'I'll take it over now.'

* * *

With nightfall and clear skies, the frost had come. Andrew scraped the ice off the car windscreen, shaving delicate white curls on to the ground.

His neighbour Robert came out of his house and paused when he saw Andrew; he half raised an arm in greeting, a muddled look on his face, then let his arm fall, nodded and strode off. Not knowing how to deal with me, Andrew realized. Embarrassed, uncomfortable.

He was almost at Colin's when he heard his phone. He checked it once he'd parked. *Missed call from LOUISE.* He felt a tilt of surprise. She'd left voicemail. He pressed to retrieve the message, wondering if something had happened to Luke.

'Hi, Andrew, it's Louise Murray here. There was something I wanted to tell you. Ring me when you can. Bye.'

Andrew hesitated. He could ring now, but then he'd still have to go in and give Colin the file. If it was more bad news, then it might be better to call afterwards.

Colin insisted he sit and have a coffee with him and Izzie. Their kids came through and each hugged Andrew, a simple act of fondness that threatened to unseat him.

'How's Val?' Izzie asked.

Andrew shrugged and gave a rueful smile. 'Keeping busy. I suppose after the funeral, that's when it will really hit home.'

'And the photofits?' asked Colin. 'Have they any leads?'

'We've not heard. But someone must know who they are. The simple fact that there's three of them going round together. People must know.' But he was aware that there were cases where no one came forward.

128

Where the wrongdoers were sheltered, protected, helped to get away with it. Could he have done that? If Jason had done something wrong, would Andrew have covered for him, told lies and hidden the truth? He couldn't imagine it, not for something serious. Would he have seen Jason locked away?

He changed the subject, told Colin and Izzie which of the wider family were coming on the day.

Colin cleared his throat, messed with his coffee mug.

Now what? Andrew thought.

'Mum and Dad, they'd like to do more,' he said.

Andrew frowned.

'They feel helpless. They're devastated.'

'Join the club,' Andrew said.

Izzie blinked, taken aback.

'Sorry,' Andrew said. 'It's just . . . there isn't . . . I can't . . .' Inarticulate, he rubbed at his head.

'They were glad to have you there, they were worried about you leaving so soon. Mum feels like Val takes everything on herself. Perhaps too much,' Colin said.

'It's just her way,' he answered. 'She needs to do this.'

'But if there's anything Mum—' Colin persisted.

'We'll say, we'll ask!' He got up, indignant but trying not to let it show. Astonished that they were chiding Val and, by extension, him. Tired of family etiquette in the midst of their tragedy. 'I really need to get back.'

Colin stood up too, and followed him out. Patted him on the back and made reassuring sounds. Big brother. Andrew's annoyance melted. For a moment he wanted to be small again, to stay with Colin and be teased and bossed about and allowed a go on the Scalextric. Free of all that awaited him.

Colin watched from the doorway, so Andrew drove away and parked up a couple of hundred yards down the road to make the call. The wheelie bins were ranged along the pavement, ready for collection. The general refuse ones and the blue paper recycling bins. Cardboard boxes were piled high beside them outside the nearest house. Packaging from Christmas presents: Hot Wheels Garage and Table Top Football.

Andrew rang Louise Murray.

'Have you heard from the police today?' she asked him. She had a warm voice, slightly husky – that would be with the smoking. A strong local accent.

'No.'

'We've got a name – the oldest lad.'

'What!' He felt a shiver run through him, and his heart leap against his ribs.

'Luke's friend recognized him.'

He needed to see her, to hear it properly, find out more. 'Where are you? Are you at the hospital?'

'Just leaving to go home.'

'Where's that?'

She didn't reply immediately, and he thought he'd freaked her out. 'Sorry, if we could meet . . .'

'There's a student pub, just south of the junction of Mosley Road and Wilbraham.'

'Yes, I'll see you there. Won't take me long.'

The pub had several rooms off a central bar. The floor was sticky underfoot, and garish banners for high-strength drinks caught the eye. The decor was a mix of Soviet retro-chic and Victorian gin palace.

Louise was in the second room he tried. On her own, apart from a foursome at another table. There was a coal-effect gas fire in the hearth, pub mirrors advertising drinks around the walls. She had a full glass in front of her, but he still offered to buy her a drink. She declined. He ordered a pint at the bar. Tried to remember when he last had a pint in a pub. With Jason, up in Durham,

130

a pie and a pint when they'd moved his stuff into halls. He took a mouthful of the foam as soon as it arrived so that it would be easier to carry without spilling.

He set his drink down on a beer mat, took off his coat and sat opposite Louise. He didn't bother with pre-ambles. 'This friend recognized the picture?'

'Yes. Declan, Luke's friend.' She gathered her dark-brown hair in one hand, pulled it back as if to make a ponytail. Then let it loose. 'Declan and Luke met the lad at a party. Luke and he had a barney and the boy went for him. Luke tripped him up.' She sighed. 'Then he filmed it.'

'Luke did?' Andrew leaned forward, his hand tight around his glass.

'Yeah, on his phone, a video.' She gave a little shake of her head, her eyes clouded. 'And he sent it to everyone he knew.'

Andrew had heard the terms: *happy slapping, cyber bullying*. He tried to sort out what this meant. 'He knew them, then?'

'Not well, but he'd met that one. He's called Tom Garrington.'

Tom Garrington. Andrew waited, expecting the name to signify something, to explain or illuminate or resonate. But nothing changed. Tom Garrington. Four syllables. 'You've told the police?'

'Yes, that's why I rang. See if you'd heard.'

He looked away. Gazed at the fire. Befuddled. His cheeks warm, skin clammy. He drank some beer. 'When did you tell them?'

'This afternoon.'

This was important, Andrew thought, this was the start of all the answers. Who and why.

'I asked if they were going to arrest him, but she said that it might not happen straight away; they have to follow procedures.'

'But if they know who it is . . .' He stared at her.

'I know!' She nodded her head, emphatic in agreement.

She talked some more about how they had a copy of the video, then she excused herself. She wanted a smoke. She pulled her bag over her shoulder. 'You won't disappear on me again?' she teased him. He saw she had dimples, and her almond-shaped eyes narrowed and almost closed as she smiled.

He drank the beer, the taste hoppy and fruity. He stared at the nearest decorative mirror, *Bell's Whisky*, elaborate letters, ribbons and bells. He thought about what she had told him, and began to feel ill at ease. Disturbed. Soiled, somehow. Because of the pathos? The tawdry background to the attack. A squabble, a lad on the floor, humiliated, and teenagers sniggering over the short film, showing it to their mates. The lead-up to Jason's unthinking action had been petty and trivial. *Call an ambulance. I think they've killed him.*

It all seemed to get in the way of what mattered, the arrangements for Thursday, for saying goodbye to Jason and honouring his life, celebrating him. All this was like smearing dirt over everything.

When Louise came back in, he could smell the smoke on her and feel the cold air around her. He had finished his drink.

'Do you want another?' she asked him.

'I'll get them. What are you having?'

'No, it's fine.'

'I'll get them,' he repeated. He assumed he was better off than she was. He knew she was a lone parent, and somewhere in all the column inches, he had read that she was a care worker. Low-paid, on the bottom rung.

'Thanks,' she said, 'just a Coke.'

'Nothing in it?'

132

She wrinkled her nose, thought about it. 'Oh, go on then – rum. Thanks.'

The pub had been a good choice, he thought. A roomy, anonymous sort of a place. Not somewhere he might run into anyone he knew.

She was on the phone, texting, when he went back. She thanked him for her drink and finished the message. 'My daughter, Ruby,' she explained.

'I remember.' A fleeting impression, a lovely-looking girl. Willowy, beautiful eyes. 'How old?'

'Fourteen.'

'When you got in touch, I thought it might be Luke.'

'No, still under.'

He hadn't meant that he thought Luke might have woken, but that he might have deteriorated. Why had he thought like that? Because he'd seen the state of the boy, perhaps, and couldn't imagine him recovering? Or because his own situation was so dark it made him pessimistic?

'It was out of character, for Jason,' he said slowly. 'I don't think he'd ever been in a fight in his life. Not a proper fight. He just wasn't that sort of kid, you know?'

She nodded, did that thing with her hair again. 'Well he wasn't fighting,' she said. 'He was trying to stop it.'

'Yes.'

'Luke . . .' She blew out a sigh, stretched her back, 'he's a handful. He's had his moments, got into the odd scrap at school, but he'd never start anything. Self-defence half the time. That and being too cocky for his own good.' The words were harsh, but he heard the love behind them.

'This trouble with Garrington . . .' The name felt odd to say. 'What was that about?'

'Declan said that Garrington – they call him Gazza, actually . . .'

133

'Oh, please,' he moaned. The image of a pudgy footballer known for weeping and later for his chaotic personal life mushroomed in his mind, and then the thought that these nicknames, Gazza, Baz, Mozzer, were typical for young thugs.

She shrugged. 'Well, he was having a go at some lass. Nasty – threats and that. Luke told him to pack it in.'

Andrew was surprised; he'd expected something more loutish, laddish. Not the chivalry she described. She seemed to read his thoughts, and there was an edge to her tone when she said, 'He wasn't looking for trouble; he was doing the right thing.'

But trouble had found him, trouble had caught up with him, dragging Jason in its wake.

The second pint was nearly gone, slipping down faster than the first. Andrew was aware of the softening in the set of his shoulders, the tension in his gut uncoiling some.

'I keep thinking,' she said. 'If he hadn't filmed it, would it have been okay? Would they have let it go? He always has to have the last word. Drives me mad.' Her face fell suddenly, lines puckered her brow. 'God, I'm sorry. Going on like this when you—'

'It's fine,' Andrew said. 'No one knows how to be, you know, how to talk to us. I laughed at something on the radio the other day. Laughed. I was mortified. How could I laugh? Even we don't know how to be.'

'I don't think there are any rules,' she said softly.

'Maybe not.'

They talked a little longer, about their sons, the similarities and differences. Then he said he'd better leave. 'Thanks for ringing.'

'Something's bound to happen soon,' she said. 'Now they know who he is.'

'Yeah.' He buttoned his coat and they walked out together.

He felt awkward again as they parted; the intimacies they had shared suddenly lost currency as they stood like strangers on the pavement. But once he was in the car on his own, he found himself replaying bits of the conversation, and recognized that for much of the time he had been comfortable in her company. That there had even been moments of pleasure in among all the chatter. Flashes where they were just two human beings communicating, and doing it reasonably well.

Jason's shrine, the mementos and cards, glimmered with frost. Val had gone to bed when he got in. Andrew didn't want to sleep yet. He took the whisky into the conservatory and sat there, opposite the cardboard coffin and the rowan tree, and drank himself numb.

CHAPTER NINE

Emma

Emma reapplied the dressing. It was happening more and more. It was the murder, she knew it was. She couldn't stop thinking about it, even dreaming about it. It seemed like every time she turned on the television or saw a paper, there was something there about Jason Barnes and Luke Murray. She knew what she did was sick, but she couldn't stop. She'd never forget the first time: her eighteenth birthday.

They'd bought her a mobile phone, one with a camera on. It was lovely. She put her home number in, and her aunt and uncle's, and the hairdresser's. Then she took the money her nan had given her and went into Birmingham and trudged around New Street and up Corporation Street looking for a dress to wear for their meal out that evening. She tried on dozens, her arms aching and the hangers biting into her fingers as she browsed the rails. There were so many different styles: minidresses with bold prints, floaty romantic styles, metallic sheaths. She finally settled on a sleeveless maxi dress with an empire line and a full skirt; it was giant paisley in greens and browns. It hid her legs, which was good. The neck was scooped and quite low, but she had a green necklace at home that might look okay with it. She wasn't sure about how it made her arms look, but by then she was too tired to try anything else, and she couldn't go home empty-handed.

She got ready in her room, curling her hair and

putting on green eyeshadow to reflect the colours in the dress. Her mum called to her when they were ready, and she went down and waited in the lounge doorway. Her mother smiled and nodded. Her father turned and did a mock double-take. 'Gordon Bennett – what is it wearing?'

'Roger!' her mum protested.

'That's bound to frighten the horses. Whoever flogged you that was having a laugh.'

'I like it.' Her voice shook.

'Well, you've never had a clue.'

'Roger, don't.'

'What's wrong with it?' Emma demanded. She wouldn't cry, she wouldn't. Her mother shot her a warning glance, but it was too late.

'Where shall I start?'

'If we don't go now, we'll be late,' her mother said.

'You look like you're wearing a tent – Jolly Green Giant, that's it. We could all go camping.'

'Don't!' Her mother moved towards Emma, frowning.

'I'm only being honest. Do you want her to be a laughing stock?'

Her mum sounded really cross. 'It's a perfectly nice dress and you're not being honest, you're being mean.'

There was a silence, heavy, dangerous. Emma filled it, stammering over the words. 'Well I like it and it's my birthday, it's my money. Shall we go?'

She braced herself for more from him, but he just gave a dry little laugh and scooped up the car keys.

At the restaurant, Emma chose the most expensive dishes: tiger prawns, fillet steak. She swallowed mouthful after mouthful. Her father made a fuss about the wine being undrinkable. and the waiter had to bring a different bottle.

She went to the toilet before dessert; the place was empty and she stuck her fingers down her throat and made herself sick. She felt raw with emotion, a bleak pain that threatened to drown her. She washed her hands and rubbed water on her teeth. She looked in the mirror, loathing her reflection: her upper arms like pasty white balloons, her podgy face, the colours in the dress sickly under the fierce lighting, her dangly earrings tawdry. The idea just came. She took one of the earrings out. Returned to the stall and locked the door. She drew up the dress and opened out the wire hook of the earring. Pushed it against her inner thigh, increasing the pressure until it pierced the skin and she felt it sting. She pulled the wire out and watched the bead of blood swell. A berry. She did it again. And once more. She closed her eyes and savoured the new feelings, the throbbing pain and the tide of relief that moved through her.

Then she wiped the blood away, replaced the earring and went to eat her Double Chocolate Hot Fudge Sundae.

The next day she surfed the internet and found a temporary job vacancy at an insurance company in Manchester. She applied online, having to retype much of the form because her fingers were shaking. She had an interview first thing the following week. She was sure she'd made a complete idiot of herself, stammering and blushing and getting muddled up, but they asked to start immediately. One of the managers gave her a number to ring for a vacant flat in the same block as his brother. He could give her a reference.

'You silly little idiot,' her father ranted. 'What happens when the contract ends and you're out of a job with rent to find? You'll come running back then, no doubt, expecting us to bail you out. You can't just up sticks and move to Manchester for three months' work.'

Emma had let him talk, tried to ignore his comments, thought only of being somewhere else, somewhere better. Of being someone else, someone new. And now here she was, independent, in her own flat, sitting on the toilet lid, cleaning a razor blade.

Andrew

The morning of the funeral, and Martine turned up. She apologized for the intrusion, but she had news.

'As a result of the publication of the e-fits, a number of names have come up, one of them repeatedly, and the inquiry team will be regarding these as persons of interest,' she said.

'Meaning what?' Val asked, her face set with tension and interest.

'The team will be keeping them under surveillance and gathering additional evidence.'

'Who are they?' Val said.

'I can't tell you that at present.'

Val stood up. 'Why not?'

'We need to be sure, we need to establish that we have found the right people, and if we have enough evidence to make any arrests, you'll be informed.'

Martine had no idea that Andrew already knew it was Tom Garrington she was talking about, and that Luke had made a bitter enemy of Tom at the party. He was tempted to challenge her with these facts, but he hadn't spoken to Val about meeting Louise, about the name she had given him, there hadn't been a chance, and it would be dreadful to tell her now in front of the police officer.

* * *

Val's friends Sheena and Sue arrived and they went out to greet them. The weather was calm, grey, cold and foggy. A sweaty scent clung in the air; Andrew couldn't put a name to it. Then Colin and Izzie and their two arrived, and Jason's friends. Warm greetings were exchanged, murmurs of mutual sympathy, questions about the schedule for the day. They waited for the hearse.

Ideally they'd have used a horse-drawn carriage and walked behind it, respecting Jason's views on carbon footprints, but the woodland burial site was miles away, and it simply wasn't practical. Andrew thought of the old rural maps he'd seen in Ireland, where mass paths were rights of way to enable the devout to reach their parish church to celebrate mass. He recalled images from a film, though its name was lost to him now, of villagers carrying a coffin across a hillside for burial.

He moved among the visitors crowding the house and felt that distanced sensation again. The notion that he was going through the motions, living someone else's nightmare. He remembered being in a similar state at their wedding, even though that was a happy occasion. The focus on the right sequence of trivia, the whole thing more of a rehearsed ordeal than a joyous celebration. The distortion of ritual.

He faltered when he saw his parents, their wobbly faces, the ravaged expressions in their eyes. Hard to conceal their pain. He hugged his father, thinking, why Jason and not you, but with no hint of malice as he felt the old man's belly bulging out, and noted the rounding slope of his shoulders.

Andrew hadn't expected the press. They were set up at the ready as the cortège entered the cemetery site.

Family and friends emerged from the cars to the snick and whir of the lenses. He watched as Jason's good friends, along with Colin, took instructions from the director and carried the coffin into the chapel.

Two nights before, the boys had turned up to decorate the coffin, armed with memorabilia, computer printouts and photographs, PVA glue, felt pens, paint and scissors. Andrew had cleared space in the conservatory and found a wallpaper table to put the coffin on. The event took on a party atmosphere, helped along by the pizzas and six-packs of beer that the boys had brought.

The collage grew: riotous, lively, spreading over the sides of the coffin. One of the girls, an art student, used paint to connect the different images together, spirals and tendrils and leaf shapes.

A map, thought Andrew. There should be a map. He went to find his ordnance survey maps of the Peak District. He selected the one that included the little campsite where they had gone for weekends when Jason was small, and the hills where they'd hiked in later years until Jason rebelled and started sleeping all morning whenever he was off school.

Andrew had cut a large shape from the centre of the map and pasted it on to the lid as one of the boys told a story about getting lost with Jason on the school outdoor pursuit camp when they were in Year 6. How they had followed a stream downhill, sure that once they reached the valley they could trek back along the road to the base. But the stream had led down to a farm. Fields full of llamas and ostriches like somewhere in South America, and it turned out to be the wrong valley, and the farmer had to ring the outdoor pursuits centre and get someone to come and pick them up.

Andrew laughed and glanced round for Jason,

141

wanting to catch his eye and share the joke. His heart shrank.

He hadn't wanted the decorating session to end, but it did, and the young people left, and with them went their energy and brilliance and noise, and aspects of Jason.

In the chapel they gave testimonials and played music. Felix played a piece on the flute. Andrew gritted his teeth and hardened his heart as 'Don't Worry, Be Happy' filled the space. There were other tunes, other brave speeches, and then they left the chapel and paraded through the grounds to the woodland: the coffin, the mourners, someone carrying the rowan tree, the watering can, the spade. A motley crew, Andrew thought as they gathered around the grave. Trestle tables had been set up to take the coffin while they prepared the straps that they would use to lower it into the hole.

The mist was still rising in the woods as the weak winter sun met the dew. People wept and laughed and exchanged teary smiles and blinks of recognition. Without too much trouble the coffin was lowered into place, and the humanist minister gave a brief address and read a poem that Val had chosen. Felix played the flute again while Andrew and Val manoeuvred the tree into place just near the head of the grave in a second, much smaller, hole and covered the roots and watered them. Jason's friends filled the grave with soil, and that was when Andrew felt close to breaking down. He held it in, a giant hand throttling his neck, pressing on his chest. Val trembled beside him. He put an arm around her. She was wearing a veil. 'I'm going to cry my eyes out,' she had said to him earlier. 'It's either that or sunglasses, and in sunglasses I'll end up looking like some B-movie Mafia matriarch.' They had told people to wear whatever they liked. Some had gone along with it, sporting vibrant colours, but most clung to the safety of sombre shades.

The reception was wonderful. People relaxed and mixed. His father had insisted on paying for a free bar, and it wasn't only youngsters that took advantage of the fact. His nephew had sorted out a laptop loaded with music, and people could pick tracks to play. There was a wall of photos of Jason and the people who loved him. The food kept coming.

Close to eleven o'clock, Val caught up with him. 'There's a taxi coming.' They'd agreed to leave the car and collect it the next morning.

They slipped away. The temperature had plummeted, and Andrew's teeth were chattering by the time they got into the cab.

The driver was a young Asian lad. He struck up conversation as he pulled away. 'Good do?' he said blithely.

Andrew squeezed Val's hand, felt his eyes prickle. 'Great, thanks,' he said, and gave their address.

Louise

Louise started back at work. She couldn't afford to miss any more shifts. She might be able to get a hardship payment from the union, but she hadn't had time to look into it.

Most days she worked eight till four so she could have some time with Ruby and visit Luke in the evenings.

Deanne came to the hospital. She was only just back from Christmas with her husband's family in Wales.

143

Louise had texted her, and they'd spoken on the phone several times. 'Oh Louise, oh God,' she'd said when she set eyes on Luke, and her eyes had glittered.

Louise hugged her friend and closed her own eyes against the grief.

'Can he hear you?' Deanne pulled away and looked at Louise, who shrugged. 'No idea. No one has. We talk to him anyway. Ruby made a tape.'

'How's she been?'

Louise gave a breath out. 'Brilliant really. But something like this . . .' The enormity of it hit her again. She frowned and shook her head, determined not to cry. What did it mean for Ruby? Her brother so hurt, the uncertainty, the new routine of snatched meals and hospital visiting. 'She's got her audition soon. She needs to practise.'

'She'll get in,' Deane said. 'They'd be mad not to take her.'

'I think she's worried about going, if she does get a place. She'll be boarding during the week.' Her throat ached, the pressure building inside, the urge to let go and weep, which she had fought so hard.

'Home at weekends?'

'Oh yeah. The fees are means-tested and there are grants and stuff. The woman said we'd be fine on that score. She's bought this wig.' Louise smiled, still sniffing, pedalling back from the brink. 'Dark crimson. She looks amazing.'

'She *is* amazing. Do you want me to have a word with her? Buck her up a bit?'

'No, ta. I need to do it. I'm not going to let this spoil things for her. It's all she ever wanted, Deanne.'

'I know.' Deanne took her coat off, went and sat down. She stared at Luke. 'It's a crying shame,' she said.

That was all it took and Louise was gulping and

sobbing and the stupid, bloody tears were spilling through her fingers.

'Louise! Aw, babe.'

Louise was up, half blind, seeking the door, the sorrow hot and fierce inside her. Deanne followed her out, hugged her close.

'I didn't want to bloody cry,' she said when the worst of it was over, when she could no longer breathe through her nose and her lips were all swollen.

'Course you need to cry,' Deanne said. 'You're not a saint, Louise. You're flesh and blood. With all this . . . Jesus.' She rubbed Louise's back.

'I didn't want Luke to hear me crying. He's going to wake up, Deanne. He's going to get better. If he can hear, what's he going to think? Crying doesn't help anyone.'

Deanne sighed. One of the nurses came along the corridor, smiled as she passed them by. Once she was out of earshot, Louise said, 'Declan knows who did it – the main one. You remember Declan?'

'Dopey Declan?'

'Yeah. Apparently Luke had a set-to with this lad Gazza. Pulled him up for threatening a girl at a party. Gazza went for him and Luke tripped him up, took a photo and sent it round. Declan's told the police; needed a kick up the bum from me first.'

'Oh God,' Deanne said. 'I need a smoke.'

'I'll come with you.'

Deanne looked, her face fell. 'You haven't?'

'Something's gotta give.'

It was dark outside, the sky a sickly blend of sulphur yellow from the city lights and leaden grey. The air was cold, still, trapping the smell from a brewery and the high, acrid exhaust fumes.

They smoked, and Deanne talked about Christmas at the in-laws, the tensions, the food, the boredom. Louise caught a shadow in her friend's gaze, a current of something sour in between the words.

'Did the kids like it?'

'Yeah, they were fine, a bit bored but okay.'

'And?'

Deanne cast her a glance, took a long drag on her cigarette, blew the smoke up into the beam of light from the street lamp.

'Me and Tony.' Deanne wrinkled her nose. 'We're breaking up.'

'Oh no.' After what? Twelve years, thirteen? Three kids.

'Bastard's seeing someone else.'

'And that's it? There's no . . .'

'Yes. And no. I've told him I want him out by the end of the month. You can imagine the atmosphere.'

'Who is she? Someone you know?'

'No. Some little tart he met on his travels.' Tony was a rep selling soft toys to outlets round the north. 'Lives in Preston.'

'Oh Dee, I am sorry. Do the kids know?'

'Not yet.' Deanne ground her cigarette out. 'We need a night out.'

Louise felt weary at the prospect. 'I don't know . . .'

'No arguments. Me and you and Fee. Nothing too demanding. Cocktails.'

'But Ruby . . .'

'She can stay at mine – I'll pay her to babysit. Or rather Tony will.' Deanne looked at Louise. 'It's not like we've got much to celebrate for New Year. You with Luke, me not with Tony. Jesus, Fee better have some good news for us.'

* * *

It ended up being just the two of them – New Year's Day evening, when the rest of the world was too hung-over to get out. Fee had begged off: food poisoning from dodgy prawns.

Louise made the effort. Ruby helped her put her hair up in an elaborate twist, and she dug out a dress and heels and a glittery shawl. It was as much for Deanne as for herself, but also a way of sticking two fingers up at the situation. Life goes on.

Tony wasn't there when Louise and Ruby got to Deanne's. Deanne looked formidable in a leopard-print sheath and half a ton of gold jewellery. Ruby had sat before for the boys, and they'd go to bed when she said. It wouldn't be a late night anyway; both Louise and Deanne had work the next day.

They went to Roxies, a cocktail bar near the canals in town, where Deanne had once been manager. The guy serving remembered her and gave them two-for-one. After her first Margarita, Louise felt like going to sleep; after the next, she got her second wind and started to enjoy herself. Deanne told her all about the finer details of finding out that Tony was a cheating bastard. The discovery of his affair and the ensuing fallout had all taken place at his parents', leading to ridiculous scenes where they had whispered arguments and tried to hide what was going on from the rest of the family.

'I ended up bloody texting him,' said Deanne. 'Can you imagine, rowing by text! Slagging him off and him sending "sorry, sorry" back. It all blew up big style the day after Boxing Day. I caught him on the phone to her. So much for "sorry, sorry". I got his phone. Stuck it in the dishwasher.'

'Deanne!'

'Prat.'

'You wouldn't go see someone?'

'Counselling? Nah.' She shifted the umbrella in her drink, took a sip. 'Maybe if I thought there was any hope of a future in it, but . . . I don't think he loves me any more.'

Louise saw the brief twitch as Deanne's lips tightened, saw the hurt.

'I'm spitting mad at him, but when I think of the kids, I want to cut his dick off. How can he do it to them? Those boys adore him, Louise. And trying to imagine the place without him.' She shuddered. 'Do you still miss Eddie?'

Louise smiled. 'Yeah, specially at a time like this.'

'Carl not stepped up?'

'Oh, he would, given half a chance. Carl's all right, but he's not the love of my life, you know?'

'Fuck buddies,' Deanne supplied.

'Oh, charming,' Louise scolded her. 'Ey up, incoming at four o'clock. We're being given the once-over.' Three men had arrived and were waiting to be served. They looked as if they had come from work: suits and ties. Louise wondered what sort of work they did, given it was a bank holiday. One of the men, looking her way, leaned into his friends and made a comment. Something funny; they all laughed.

Deanne swivelled in her seat. 'Three into two won't go.'

'Are you mad?' Louise asked her.

'The one with the striped shirt is mine.'

'In your dreams.' Louise took a drink.

'Is that a dare?'

'Whoa! No,' Louise said. 'You're not going to blame this on me. You know what you'd be doing?'

'Rebound sex.'

'Revenge sex – even worse. I am going home after the next drink. And you are coming with me.'

'Am I?'

'You'll have to. I'm taking your babysitter home with me.'

'Bugger,' Deanne said. 'Smoke?'

They took their drinks out on to the roof terrace, where patio heaters belted out warmth on to the tables and benches. Fog hung over the city, diffusing the lights.

'I can't imagine going with someone else,' Deanne said. 'There's only been Tony for so long.'

'No rush, is there,' Louise said. 'Not like you'll forget how to do it.'

'Like riding a bike,' Deanne shot back. Cracked them up.

'It's a bit weird at first,' Louise said once she'd stopped cackling. 'The dates. Someone unfamiliar. You get the jitters and that, like when we were kids.'

'Where did it go, Lou?' Deanne was suddenly sombre. 'All those years.'

'Hey, we grew up. You've got three lovely boys.'

'I know.' She flicked repeatedly at the end of her cigarette with her thumbnail. 'I never saw it coming. Thought we were in it for life. Saw other people's marriages fold, affairs, divorces, never thought it'd be me.'

'No.' Louise smoked, heard a burst of laughter from inside the club rising above the jazz funk that was playing. She shivered, stamped her feet.

'What will you do if Luke doesn't wake up?' Deanne said.

Louise froze; she felt her skin chill and a frisson of fear bubble through her veins. And then a hot needle of anger at the question. 'He's going to wake up,' she said sharply. And ground out her cigarette underfoot.

CHAPTER TEN

Andrew

Garrington. It was like a small seed stuck in his teeth, grit in his shoe. He ignored it for long enough.

They made love, the first time since it had happened. The familiarity, the physicality, the release were a reassurance. Val slept afterwards. He lay and watched her. So busy in her waking life, so active and energetic, when she slept she was still. Would lie in one position all night long. He saw she had lost weight, her face thinner, almost gaunt. He felt a crush of fear that she might get ill, that he might lose her too, and promised himself that he would help her.

In the becalmed weekend after the funeral, waiting for life to resume, he and Val found tasks to occupy their time. A blitz on the garden: clearing up the last of the leaves now the snow had melted and bagging them for compost; tidying the borders, the straggly spikes of lavender and the desiccated remains of Michaelmas daisies and asters.

He sorted out the polytunnel, repaired a small tear near the back, checked over the cabbages and leeks and dug up some of the potatoes. There were a couple of squally showers on the Sunday, and as the rain drummed on the plastic, he closed his eyes and took himself back to camping holidays: the three of them, and later just him and Jason. The smell of earth and wet wool and wood smoke. The murmured conversations that they held, rolled side by side in sleeping bags, the delicious hooting of an owl in the night, and dawn waking them as light seeped through the canvas. Showering in whitewashed sheds, littered with moths, and Jason reluctant even to use the toilets.

The past was solace, but the future stretched ahead barren, hopeless, hostile. A place of thorns and bones and sinking sands. Andrew decided the trick was not to think about it, not to look ahead, beyond. Not to imagine.

They had lost a date palm. The brutal frost left it scorched and black.

'We should get rid of it,' Val said. 'It looks awful.'

Andrew tested it with the saw. The dead wood was fibrous but not too tough. He began to cut it into sections, and Val put the perished leaves in the recycling bin and hauled the pieces of trunk over to the drive – they'd go to the tip.

Garrington. Still there as he drove the saw to and fro, the pungent smell of sap in the air and a burning in his shoulder, still a little tender from falling when he'd chased after them.

Val brought out tea and he took a break. Sat beside her and gulped hot mouthfuls, his fingers smearing the mug with dirt.

'Nearly done.' She nodded at the stump.

'The roots'll be the worst bit, spade and fork job.' He thought of their ragtag procession for Jason. The coffin and the tree, the spade and the watering can.

'I'm going back in on Tuesday,' Val said.

He nodded. He'd already decided for himself that he'd start back then, but Val had spare holiday left that she could have taken.

The phone went. He'd reconnected it eventually, and they hadn't been pestered by the press since. He groaned as he got up, his muscles stiffening already.

'I'll get it,' Val offered.

'No,' he said, moving towards the house. 'It'll be my mother, or Colin.' They rang every day. 'They said they'd do a meal tomorrow.'

'Hello?'

'Hi. Is Jason there, please?'

Andrew went dizzy; he felt as though he'd been kicked in the skull.

'Hello?' A woman's voice, young, an unfamiliar accent.

'I'm sorry, there's been . . .' His words were thin and dry. 'I've, erm . . .' He faltered.

'I can't get him on his mobile.'

'I've some very bad news,' Andrew said. 'Jason died on the seventeenth of December.'

'Died?'

'Yes.'

'But . . . Oh God!'

'He was attacked when he tried to stop a fight; he was . . .' Andrew didn't want to say killed. 'There was a knife.'

'Oh God.' She sounded shell-shocked.

'I'm sorry, we told everyone we could.'

'I've been home – Denmark.'

A foreign student? 'You knew him from university?'

'Yes. I'm so sorry.'

'No, no, that's fine.' And of course it wasn't.

'The funeral was last Thursday.'

'Yes. Yes, I see.'

He heard her breathing change and understood as she quickly ended the call. He replaced the phone. Allowed his mind to swoop around those unforgettable images: the crimson snow, Jason's blanched face as he sat in their lounge, his body in the hospital anteroom. Then he forced himself back outside to dig up the roots

152

of the palm. He continued even when the drizzle came and made the spade slippery to handle. Even as the crumbs of soil sneaked into his gloves and rubbed against the skin. He tugged out the last of the roots and discarded them. Broke up the clods of soil and forked it over. It was dusk by the time he'd finished.

He showered while Val prepared a meal. He complimented the food, hoping to entice her to eat more.

'What time are we round at your folks tomorrow?' she asked him. He hadn't told her that the call had been from one of Jason's new friends.

'Six,' he invented. He would call and fix that up with his mother after tea. If it didn't suit them, then he could easily tell Val the plans had altered.

Garrington. Like a splinter under his nail. The more he tried to disregard it, the more it nagged at him.

He lasted until late in the evening. Val had gone up, and he was having a nightcap, ostensibly watching a rerun of *Coast*, the documentary series about the British coastline.

He moved abruptly, went through to the study and wrestled the phone book from the stack of directories.

Frost . . . Gane . . . Gardner . . . Garrington. One entry: *V*, 22 Waterford Place, M20. He felt a shiver of excitement, a sort of sickly triumph. He tore the page out and folded it up. Put it in his pocket. The thrill of discovery beating inside him like a new heart.

Louise

Carl had brought vodka. Cherry vodka. From the distillery near his village, he said. The Poles were big on vodka, Louise had learnt, usually flavoured with fruit or herbs or honey. He'd brought duty-free cigarettes too. It was good of him, but within half an hour of Carl being there, Louise found her mind wandering. It was hard to concentrate on his stories from home; she felt irritated at the way he shook his head when he chuckled.

Driven to distraction, she thought, that's what it feels like: everything's popping up and zipping about and none of it is important any more. Too much clutter in her head, and all that mattered was Luke and Ruby.

She looked at Carl, the broad cheekbones, the honey colour of his skin, blond hair, his eyes, cat-like, wonderful eyes, and sighed. 'I think we should give it a break – us, I mean.'

He looked dazed. 'Really?'

'It's not you, Carl, it's me, Luke, everything.'

'But I want to help.'

'There is no help.' She turned her glass to and fro on the table. 'It's all I can do to give Ruby the time she needs, with work and hospital.'

'You make it sound as if I am work for you,' he complained. She saw petulance in the set of his jaw.

'I don't mean to.' She didn't want to get into it. Her mind was made up and nothing he could say would shift it. She didn't want to pick over it, analyse it. Or hurt him any more. 'You've been really good. I'm sorry.' She frowned, pinched at the bridge of her nose. *Now please, go.*

'You want us just to be friends?'

Did she even want that? 'Yeah,' she answered. Though she couldn't really imagine it.

That tightness in his jaw again, then he cleared his throat. 'Very well,' he said, stiffly, formality his way of coping.

'Please take these.' She pushed the bottle and the cigarettes his way.

154

'No, they are yours,' he objected, getting up.

She stood too, awkward now, not knowing whether to approach him, to thank him. A farewell hug. He made no move, and she took her cue from him.

She was relieved when he had gone. She'd always known that she and Carl were a time-limited affair. Had realized that it would not lead to them moving in together or, God forbid, babies. She thought he had too, but perhaps he'd harboured hopes for more.

There had never been that wild, desperate attraction she'd felt for Roland, and later for Eddie. She'd been misguided with Roland, but she'd have married him in the blink of an eye if he'd asked. And with Eddie it was pure joy, as the dizzy, chaotic sensations of being in love settled into a deep love and respect, a delight at being together. She wondered if Roland had married his African fiancée, and if he'd stayed true. Perhaps he had taken other wives, as was legal in his part of the world.

Would it have made any difference to how Luke had turned out if he had known his father? Would letters or a clutch of meetings have been enough to temper his alienation from school, his waywardness? Occasionally Louise had Googled Roland's name, but she never found any reference to him. She had asked Luke directly when he was twelve or so, 'Would you like to try and find your dad, make contact?'

'No,' he'd replied, his lip twisting with derision. 'What for?'

Her attempt to prolong the discussion had led to him walking out of the house.

Had Roland ever given a second thought to the child he'd left in Manchester? He knew she'd been pregnant, but had already left when Luke was born. He never knew whether he had a son or a daughter, or even twins. She found it hard to conceive of that level of indifference. And given how he had treated her, at the end of the day perhaps it wasn't unreasonable to assume that Roland in Luke's life might have made things worse, not better.

She picked up one of the packets of cigarettes. It was only half nine; Angie would still be up.

'I'm just popping next door,' she called up to Ruby. ''Kay.'

Louise looked at the vodka, then changed her mind. She'd regret it tomorrow if she started on that. Another time, she promised herself.

Andrew

The first day back was the worst. It was like an obstacle course, with each encounter a negotiation of sympathy and reassurance, a battery of questions or an exchange of platitudes. Andrew spent much of the time clamping down on his emotions, on his empathy: setting his teeth against colleagues with teary eyes or faces stark with embarrassment; tensing his muscles against pats and strokes and even hugs.

The clients, most of whom didn't know him from Adam, and hadn't made the connection between him and the city's latest tragic murder, came as a blessed relief. With them he could immerse himself in the business of work. The woman who had had a stroke, the post-op cancer patient and the car-crash survivor: he was there to help while *they* were the victims of misfortune, lives suddenly altered beyond recognition, changing course, tacking out into the unknown. With him they could regain the use of muscles, tongue and teeth, remaster breathing and vocalization, practise the mechanics of talking, learn to speak again. With each patient he would assess where function had been lost or compromised and create individual treatment plans including exercises to be done at home, or in hospital, between his sessions. He liaised with medical and physio staff too around issues of diet (those whose condition left them at risk of choking), emotional and psychological barriers to compliance and the impact of medication on recovery.

At lunch he steered clear of the canteen, avoiding the risk of running into more well-wishers; bought a sandwich and a drink from the machines instead and ate it in his car. He rang Val to see how she was faring, and they compared notes.

'I've decamped to one of the meetings rooms,' she said.

'And I'm hiding in the car.'

'I might be late,' she said.

'That's not like you,' he teased her.

'Someone's cocked up the environmental health training report. I need to rescue it before it gets sent out.'

'Can't get the staff.'

She gave a little laugh. 'See you later.'

'Yeah, bye.'

He sipped his coffee and watched the parade of cars prowling around hunting for a parking space. It cost him an arm and a leg to leave the car, and though he might be able to cycle the five miles to work, the prospect of cycling back at the end of the day kicked that idea into touch. One car paused to the back and side of his, its owner making motions with his hands, translating as: *You coming out?*

Andrew shook his head, mouthed: *Sorry.* Sat there until his break was over.

* * *

His final patient that afternoon was a young man, early twenties, whose long-term abuse of solvents had left him with damage to the throat and vocal cords. Andrew read his notes carefully and made his own examination: feeling the patient's throat and neck and jaw, looking inside his mouth, where he saw the scar tissue on the lining of the mouth and throat, and also the badly decayed teeth, the enamel now translucent, grey, the dentine destroyed.

'You getting any rehab?' he asked.

The man shook his head. The skin around his mouth was crusted with a virulent rash.

'Are you on the waiting list?' Andrew asked him.

He nodded.

'Because any more abuse like this and your cords'll pack up for good, yeah?'

The patient shrugged, and Andrew felt a flash of anger. This lad destroying his health, mistreating his own body, no idea how precious life was. He turned away, pretending to study his notes, waiting for the fierce emotion to ebb away and rational thought to return. As in – maybe he doesn't see his life as precious: low self-esteem, shitty background, his life a burden half the time, something he only wants to escape from.

'Put your lips together,' Andrew said. 'Good. Now open them, not too wide, right. Sit up straight. Now, do that again, but first take a breath down here,' he indicated on himself, below the diaphragm, 'and as you open your mouth, push the air out, like so: "Pah! Pah!"' The man copied him, then grinned sheepishly. 'What we'll do,' Andrew said, 'is build up a way of speaking that minimizes the strain on your vocal cords. A lot of it is about relaxation.'

At the end of their fifteen minutes, he sent the man away with a copy of exercises he had to do, with no idea whether he'd be back at the same time the following week or if that was the last he'd see of him.

He caught up with his emails, and the online newsletters he subscribed to for work. There was a piece inviting papers on selective mutism. People, usually children, who stopped speaking, or never started, not because of any physical impediment but due to psychological factors, in particular acute social anxiety or phobia. Most children eventually developed coping mechanisms and so learned to communicate in public. Because Andrew dealt with adults, he'd never worked with a patient like that, though in his training he had shadowed a therapist treating a four-year-old girl who had become mute once she started school. The name for the disorder had changed in recent years, from elective mutism to selective. Reflecting the understanding that people suffering from the condition did not choose to stay silent but were physiologically unable to speak in certain situations.

He thought of the people on the bus, the people who had sat dumbly while Jason spoke up. If only one or two of them had found their voices and backed him up, echoed his sentiments, then it all might have been so different. Luke safe, Jason alive.

He waited until it was dead on 5.30, then went to the office, where the clerical worker, Harriet, had her coat on. 'Can you check a record for me?'

'Don's waiting.' Harriet got picked up at 5.35 on the dot by her husband Don, which saved the couple car-parking fees. Harriet believed she was overworked and underpaid and behaved as though she was the only person in the NHS with that cross to bear. Everyone else was living the life of Riley and exploiting her.

'I need it now, really,' Andrew complained. 'Just had a referral from surgery.'

She looked like she might spit at him.

'Just log me on,' he said. 'I'll find it.' He tried to sound exasperated at her lack of co-operation, and prayed she wouldn't smell a rat.

'I'm not supposed to,' she said.

'You do it then,' he challenged her.

She tutted loudly, inserted herself between him and the computer terminal, booted up, sighing pointedly every three seconds, and then typed in a password. 'Make sure you log off and close down,' she said, and stalked out, her heels clipping the lino.

Once in the system, he began to type: *Garrington, Thomas.*

Emma

It was a training day. Something to do with improving customer service and team communication. Emma hated anything like that. You never knew what was going to happen. They'd had one just after she was made permanent and they'd had to play games in a group. Variations on stupid kids' games like musical chairs and blind man's buff. She'd read there were places in Japan where the workers had to sing together at the start of every day. She shrivelled at the thought of it.

This training involved the junior staff and another ten people from the Liverpool office. For Emma it started badly and got worse.

They sat on chairs in a big circle and the trainer, a man called Vernon, with one of those funny little goatee beards, asked them each to introduce themselves. But instead of just saying their name, they had to talk for thirty seconds and tell as much of their life story as possible. *Not me not me not me.* Emma prayed fast and hard, but he asked her to go first. Her face burned and she felt sweat prickle under her arms. Now she'd stink all day too.

'I'm Emma and . . . erm . . .' Some spit caught in her throat and she coughed. Someone laughed and Emma felt her mind blur, the sense and the shape of the words dissolve. They were all looking at her.

'Keep going,' said Vernon cheerily. He had a timer that was counting down the seconds.

'I'm twenty-one.' She looked at her hands. She could feel everyone's eyes poking holes in her neck and her belly and her forehead. 'I'm from Birmingham,' she said.

'That's great, Emma. Speak up a bit,' called Vernon. It wasn't great, it was pathetic. She could feel the embarrassment hanging like a pall in the room, saw her own knee tremor, her foot dance on the carpet. 'I'm from Birmingham,' she repeated, glue in her mouth, trying to find her thread. 'I live in Manchester now, in East Didsbury.' She didn't dare raise her face, wouldn't look to see what Laura and the Kims were making of her feeble efforts. What was she talking about, supposed to talk about? Her mind was blank, full of grey wool. She felt the sweat run down into her bra. The bra was pinching her; the underwire felt like it was trapping her left breast. She bit her thumb hard, trying to find some sensation, something to jolt her back on track. Should she tell them about her tropical fish? Or that she'd seen the people who killed Jason Barnes? Been close enough to touch them. She glanced at Vernon. 'Sorry,' she mumbled.

'And time's up! Always tough going first,' he said, pretending she hadn't just made a complete dick of herself.

'And next, Damon, go!'

Emma sat still as the exercise proceeded, hoping to be forgotten. Wishing she could disappear. When they divided into groups of four, she found herself with three friends from Liverpool and could barely follow the banter that they shared in their Scouse accents. She smiled when they did, hoping that would suffice, nodding puppet-style through the discussion about which qualities had highest priority when dealing with customers.

After feedback came coffee. Emma hid in the toilets for most of the break, nipped back and ate three biscuits and drank half a cup of tepid coffee and took her seat again without exchanging a word with anyone.

Then came role play. She wondered if she could fake a heart attack, or whether she'd have one anyway. Vernon paired her with Little Kim. They watched several couples act out scenarios outlined on index cards that Vernon passed round to the 'claimants'. The person playing the claims officer never knew what they were going to be faced with. Some of the people were very funny, ad-libbing. They could have gone on the stage.

The card Vernon gave Emma said: *Irate customer complains about her accidental damage claim being refused.*

They sat on chairs in the middle of the circle. They each had an old phone with a wire trailing from it, as a prop. That was stupid anyway, thought Emma; the people who dealt with calls wore headsets now.

'Okay,' said Vernon, 'off you go, Kim.'

'Good morning, my name's Kim, how can I help you today?'

'I'm going to kill you,' Emma blurted out. The room erupted with laughter.

'You're obviously upset,' Kim managed when she'd stopped giggling, 'but I can't help you without your details. Could I have your policy number?'

'No,' said Emma and put the phone down.

Kim scowled and looked at Vernon. Emma saw a flash of irritation cross his face before he recovered and smiled. 'There's always one,' he said. 'Thank you, Kim and Emma. Remember to tell the abusive caller that calls are being monitored and recorded and that it's company policy to end abusive calls. Next.'

At lunch, Emma left. Better for them all that way. She wondered if Vernon would tell. She got a text from Laura mid-afternoon. Heard her phone go as she was fixing the dressing on her leg. *U ok? x*

Felt sick x Emma replied. Laura cared; even though she'd made a fool of herself and upset Kim, Laura was still talking to her.

Don't blame u l8r x

Emma felt so much better then. She got the tub of ice cream out; she deserved a treat.

'Gavin wants to see you,' Laura told her the next morning as she hung up her coat.

'Right.' Was abandoning a training course a sackable offence? A written warning?'

'Tell him you had cramps,' Laura said. 'He'll hate that.'

Emma cleared her throat. 'Is Kim okay?' She could still see Kim scowling, sense her irritation that Emma had ruined the exercise, not given her a chance to shine.

'Course. It's not like you can help it, being shy.'

Emma wanted to collapse with relief. All night she'd imagined a conspiracy, the three of them sending her to Coventry, a wall of silence, or sniggers. An earlier memory scoured through her: a special assembly at school. She was six. Her class had to walk up on stage and chant a poem, something about forests and tigers. Emma was one of the smallest and was made to stand at the front. She wet herself.

'Thanks,' she said to Laura. 'I'd better see Gavin.'

'Remember – really bad period pains.'

Oh, she did like Laura. She was smart and funny, and she was kind too, like now.

Gavin was okay about it. As soon as Emma mumbled that she'd felt ill, he didn't ask for any more details. He said her attendance record was excellent and gave her a handout from the afternoon and recommended she read through it – especially the bullet points at the end about good practice. Then he let her go.

Emma had brought in shortbread and handed it round at break.

'Not stuck poison in it, have you?' Little Kim teased her. 'Your face! I thought you were going to kill me.'

'You should have broken the phone,' Blonde Kim said to Emma. 'Vernon would have gone mental.'

'That beard,' said Little Kim. 'Looked a right prat.'

'Look what I've got,' said Laura. She rummaged in a carrier and pulled out a wodge of holiday brochures. Handed one to each of them. *Greek Island Escapes*, read Emma's. Her heart raced. She saw aquamarine sea and white sand, like in the film musical *Mamma Mia*. Little coves with restaurants by the water's edge, olives and donkeys. Laura and Emma and the Kims all sun-bronzed, drinking chilled wine beneath palm-thatched umbrellas. In their room, getting ready to hit the disco. She knew the three of them had been to Tenerife last year. But now Laura had given *her* one of the brochures.

'Be cheaper to book online,' said Blonde Kim.

'I know,' Laura said. 'This is research. We each come back with two resorts that sound good, decent nightlife and not too far from the airport, and then we choose a shortlist and see what cheap deals we can find on the net. But we need to work out dates. Avoid the school holidays.'

'I can't do June,' said Little Kim. 'Our Maryanne's wedding.'

Emma ate another biscuit. She felt the anticipation frothing inside her. They could have barbecues on the beach and go on boat trips. The four of them bessie mates.

'September's too long to wait,' said Blonde Kim.

'May, then,' said Laura. 'Be warm then.'

'Where are we looking?' Little Kim tried to see Emma's brochure.

'Spain and the Canaries.' Blonde Kim waved her booklet.

'Greek islands,' said Emma.

'Croatia, Montenegro and Corsica,' said Laura.

'And I've got Turkey,' said Little Kim.

'Will they let us have time off together?' Emma asked. What if Gavin said no, only three of them could take holiday then?

'Yeah, if we book it before anyone else, we'll be okay. So that's your homework tonight, girls.' Laura grinned.

Emma looked at the pictures, buildings like sugar cubes, harbour lights at night. She couldn't wear a bikini, not even a one-piece swimsuit. She could say she hadn't learnt to swim. But then what about sunbathing? Long shorts would cover the marks, but it would be horrible to get all that way and be by the sea and not be able to go in. She imagined a Victorian bathing suit, long stripy pantaloons and a flouncy skirt. Oh God. If she tried not to do it any more between now and May, then maybe she could explain it, like she had some sort of eczema, or she'd had an accident. Something that left puckered lines and puncture marks criss-crossing her skin on the inside of her thighs.

Who was she kidding? She couldn't possibly go. But how would she tell Laura? They'd hate her if she turned down the holiday. But they'd hate her even more if they knew how sick she was. She didn't know what she was going to do.

CHAPTER ELEVEN

Louise

Terence had had a fall. Louise found him in the hall when she went to get him washed and dressed and breakfasted. She couldn't see any obvious signs of injury, but he was very pale and confused. She rang for an ambulance, let the office know, and waited with him till they took him in. She cleared out the perishable food and turned off the heating.

He'd been born in the house and she knew he hoped to die there too, but she didn't know if he'd come back this time. She'd miss their sparring: he was a dyed-in-the wool royalist who'd voted Tory all his life and liked a good argument. Sometimes it reminded her of the banter when her dad had still been around, arguing with her grandad. When Terence had discovered Louise held her own opposing views, he made a point of engaging her in debate: picking a topic from the *Telegraph* or the television news and throwing it before her like a gauntlet. 'Look at that,' he'd announce. 'Nanny state gone mad. Kids banned from playing conkers because of health and safety.'

And she'd happily pitch in. 'It's not true, another of those urban myths. Very fond of them, the *Telegraph*.'

'Never needed health and safety in the old days,' he'd bluster.

'That when people were losing limbs at work, chopping their fingers off?'

'But you can't deny . . .' he'd say, and launch into

why immigration was out of control, or they needed to bring back grammar schools or National Service, or how tax by stealth was crippling the nation.

'Nothing to do with greedy bankers or the world economy taking a dive or the rich robbing us blind, then?' was Louise's answer to his economic position. The debate was good-humoured and lively and neither of them ever budged an inch. And when she drew it to a close each time, as she completed his notes so that the next carer could see what was what, he'd slap his hands, large liver-spotted paws, on to his knees and proclaim: 'We'll have to agree to disagree.' She would miss him.

Her next call was a new client, a woman with Parkinson's who'd had a spell in hospital after a knee replacement and had just been discharged by the rehab team. Louise tried to get to know her a bit while she made and served her lunch and emptied her commode, but the woman was monosyllabic.

Louise did Mrs Coulson's lunch too, an hour later, and her shopping. Mrs Coulson complained that it was after two o'clock, and Louise reminded her that because there were a limited number of them trying to get round everyone at the same times of day, there was always someone had to be last.

It was a perennial complaint, that and not spending enough time with people. The client often didn't realize that the office allocated their time slots, and that while Louise might be paid for a half-hour or an hour with a particular client, she wasn't paid for the travelling time in between house calls.

With the care market carved up and divvied out to the cheapest private contractors, running costs were pared to the bone, wages pegged as low as possible. Looking after the frail and vulnerable was just another business, with people out to make profits.

Louise had a fag after Mrs Coulson. One of Carl's duty-frees. She leant against her car, collar done up tight. There was a group of little kids on scooters and bikes playing together, Asian most of them, and a couple of white kids. They shouted to each other, excited voices and Mancunian accents ringing in the air. One of them, a little boy with glossy black hair wearing a loose tunic and trousers and an open anorak, suddenly threw down his scooter and started singing and dancing, his arms flashing like semaphore and then his hands on his waist, thrusting his hips like Michael Jackson. A little star. His mates cheered and crowed and Louise laughed.

She remembered Luke's break-dance phase in the last years of primary school, spinning on his head and flipping back and forth like a contortionist. It was the move to high school when things had really started to sour. It was a tough school, a big comprehensive, and Luke loathed it. It was in his second year that he first got into serious trouble, for hitting another student. When Luke explained, his eyes burning, unable to sit still, that he'd exploded after weeks of low-level bullying – taunts and tricks and having his things ruined – Louise tried to get the school to drop the exclusion. They refused; it was a zero-tolerance offence, though they did give the other kids involved a week's detention. Luke lost his faith then. Bitter at his treatment and bored senseless by many of the lessons.

One of the little kids yelled, 'Last one to the corner's a dumbo,' and they all swarmed off, pedalling and scooting furiously.

It was Ruby's audition soon; Louise must make time to watch her practise. Like Deanne said, they'd be mad not to take her, but then who knew how tough the competition was. And if there was any problem with the bursary, she simply wouldn't be able to go. Louise wondered if she should raise the prospect of disappointment, to prepare Ruby just in case, or if that would undermine her confidence.

In the car, she reached to get the mints, catching sight of herself in the rear-view mirror: washed out, dark hollows beneath her eyes. Ten years older. More.

At the hospital, the nurse on reception recognized her and said that Dr Liu would like to see her before she left. A spurt of hope leapt in Louise's chest. Her pulse began to race. 'Has there been any change?' Ready to run to see Luke, to talk to him, revel in his response, gaze into his eyes, see sense there, emotion, life.

'No,' the nurse said. 'We'd always get in touch straight away if that was the case.'

'Of course.' The hope sputtered, guttered out, leaving an ache inside. 'Is she free now?' Louise asked.

'On her break, but I can tell her you're with Luke when she gets back.'

Louise greeted him as she always did: 'Hello, Luke, it's Mum.' And kissed him, then held her palms against his cheeks. 'Ruby's not coming tonight, she's making tea, well, sticking some pasties in the oven. I don't know about you, love, but I'm knackered.'

She got herself settled in the chair by the bed but didn't bother getting her patchwork out. Her eyes felt scratchy and dry and she preferred to take his hand, and close her eyes as she stroked his arm and talked. 'I saw Angie last night,' she said. 'She's doing all right. And Declan sends his love. And I know you're probably lying there thinking, "What do I care and why's she wittering on like this?" but if you don't like it, you'll have to wake up and tell me.' She talked on, dipping into memories too, hoping that they might reach the parts the trivial gossip didn't.

She was back in the present, passing on Deanne's news, when she heard the shush of the door and Dr Liu came in.

'Hello, Luke,' said the doctor. She always made a point of speaking to him, and Louise liked that. 'Shall we talk next door?' she asked Louise.

In the little side room they sat down. Dr Liu had Luke's notes, a huge folder of charts and reports and records that had accumulated in the three weeks since he'd been admitted.

'How are you?' Dr Liu asked.

'Okay,' said Louise.

'I wanted to have a little chat with you. I've been reviewing Luke's condition and assessing his treatment plan.'

Louise tensed; she could sense something coming, something bad.

'We've talked before about the Glasgow Coma Scale and Luke's score.'

Louise nodded; knew that it rated his responses or lack of them to a range of stimuli. Knew Luke's score was low.

Unbidden, she remembered his baby book, how the midwives, then the health visitors, had marked his weight and height on the charts, ensuring that he was thriving. Recalled her anxiety, as a young mother, that they might find fault, that he'd fall below the desired percentile line.

'We've repeated the tests today,' the doctor said, 'and got the same results. I must stress that every patient is different and that we still know very, very little about the working of the brain and its capacity for healing.'

But . . . Louise could hear the word looming large.

'But,' said Dr Liu, 'we've not seen any alteration in Luke's condition. And although there are no hard and fast rules, the likelihood that there will be any recovery reduces sharply after the first few days. It's been three weeks now.'

Louise hardened herself, stony, impermeable, unwilling to absorb any of this. She sat still and stiff, neither nodding or smiling.

'Luke is therefore facing the prospect of continuing in the same state for the foreseeable future.' The doctor paused.

Louise remained unbending.

'You understand?'

Louise gave the smallest of nods; she could feel the pulse in her temple, the beat and swish of blood in her head. An acidic taste in her mouth.

'In the longer term, because he is unable to make decisions about his treatment, that will fall to you. I'm talking about very difficult decisions about his quality of life, about whether to maintain life support in the form of food and drink.'

Louise ground her teeth together. She could not think about that. How dare the woman sit here and say those things? She stared down at her hands, at the skin around her nails, red and angry, her nails dull and scratched.

'But those are decisions for the future. In the shorter term, we need to consider where Luke can best be cared for. Given that there is no medical imperative to keep him in the hospital—'

'You're giving up on him.' Her head was swimming. Everything crooked.

'Not at all. But everything we are doing for Luke here can be done equally well in a residential care facility.'

Louise thought of some of the homes she'd worked in, those residents able to leave their rooms plonked in chairs in front of the television, the wanderers drugged up and befuddled, the smell of urine.

The doctor went on, 'What we are proposing to do is to refer Luke on, with a view to moving him in the next couple of months.'

Louise stared at her.

'I want to assure you that if there was anything else I could suggest in terms of other treatment options for Luke I'd explore it, but we may have to accept that the trauma was so severe that recovery, even on the most basic level, is not a realistic prognosis. I am sorry. Is there anything you'd like to ask, anything you don't understand?'

Why Luke? Why? Shrieking inside her mind. A lament. Louise shook her head once, biting her cheek. She did not speak. She went back to sit with her son.

Andrew

They drove to Durham on the Saturday to collect Jason's things. Term hadn't started. Andrew borrowed Colin's estate car, which had more space in the back than theirs.

The drive up took longer than they'd expected. Heavy rain had caused flooding on some sections of the M1, then they got caught up in a tailback where a lorry had shed its load of pallets. He suggested they leave the motorway at the next exit, but Val argued it would take even longer using the back roads.

He loved the look of Durham as they approached, the Norman cathedral and the castle dominating the skyline, the whole place compact and dripping with history. At street level there was a malevolent one-way system and an acute shortage of parking places in the narrow lanes. The place had been built for people and horses, not vehicles.

They found their way to the halls of residence and parked there. Val shivered as they got out of the car, and he suggested they go get a bite of something to eat and a cuppa before making a start. It was partly consideration for her, but also a desire to delay the chore that faced them.

The café they found was a traditional place, steamed-up windows and the scent of frying bacon and wet clothes. Andrew had an all-day breakfast, suddenly ravenous, and Val chose egg on toast but didn't clear her plate. He should talk to her about it, he thought; he would talk to her about it, but not now, not yet. He didn't want to put any more pressure on her.

He still hadn't told her about Garrington, about knowing the identity of one of the thugs, and the more time passed, the less he wanted to confide in her. It would mean explaining about Louise Murray and how he had visited Luke, and that would feel disloyal. And if he felt it was disloyal, then it surely would read like that to Val. Keeping it from her thus far would be seen as something worse than it was, as a betrayal at a time when she was vulnerable.

They had Jason's key and made themselves known to the manager of the halls, who they'd spoken to on the phone. She greeted them warmly. Andrew liked the lilt of her accent. 'We're just up here,' she said. He was glad of the guidance; although he had been here before, helping Jason move in, he would never have remembered the way.

'If there's anything you need, just give us a call.' She left them outside the room.

Andrew opened the door. The space was small and cluttered and shouted Jason from every angle: his guitar, his rugby shirt, his photos. Andrew took a sharp breath and moved towards the desk at the back wall where books and CDs and files were strewn about. Val took a step after him and stopped in the middle of the room between the bed and the chest of drawers.

Andrew scanned the desk. What had Jason been reading, working on, listening to? Hungry for more knowledge about his son. When he turned back to Val, she moved to him. They embraced. All the nevers, thought Andrew. He will never come in that door, play that song, read another word. He eased himself away from her.

'I'll fetch the boxes,' he said. 'I'll do the books, if you can empty the drawers.'

She nodded, and they set to work.

Louise

'Oh, Louise.' Omar looked crestfallen, shaking his head at her when she went in the shop for milk. 'It shouldn't be allowed.' He waved his hand at the bundles of newspapers he was undoing for the shelves.

Her eyes flew from one headline to the next. COMA BOY'S REIGN OF TERROR – DEATH IN VAIN? STUDENT GAVE LIFE FOR TEENAGE THUG. COMA VICTIM'S LIFE OF CRIME. Luke's face and Jason's staring out at her in black and white.

Louise felt her heart clench, gasped at the savagery of the words.

'Don't read them,' Omar said.

She was dizzy, frightened. 'How can I not read them?'

'It's all lies,' he said.

'I need to know what they're saying.' She got out her purse.

'Keep your money,' he said. 'If I could, I'd burn the lot.'

She forgot the milk. Ran home and spread the papers out. Ten minutes until she had to wake Ruby.

It was lies, most of it. The facts twisted beyond all recognition. Supposition and exaggeration and righteous indignation stuffed between barbed comments. Luke had been out of control, uncontrollable, feckless, reckless, known to the police, excluded from school, a thug, prone to antisocial behaviour, a budding criminal, an arsonist, a vandal, a drug-user, disturbed. He'd been raised in a broken home, by a single parent who had children by two different men. Neither of the children saw their fathers. There was no mention of Eddie's sudden death. Luke had caused explosions in an arson attack, defaced public property. Neighbours reported living in fear. A source close to the family did not want to be named.

He was the devil incarnate, her spawn.

Something broke inside her. This was her boy, her lovely boy, lying sick in a coma, his skull broken, and they could write all this about him. The cruelty of it sang through her, circulated like acid in her blood. And a great swell of doubt came crashing after it. Was it her fault? Could she have done more? Done better? Was this a broken home? She had filled it with love and encouraged laughter, tried to keep it warm, kept the fridge stocked, their clothes clean. Revelled in them, even when she was ragged with fatigue. She'd have done anything to prevent Eddie's death; she had not chosen to be left on her own raising a family. And in her heart she did not equate lone parents with broken homes. Weren't they simply victims of unsuccessful relationships? While a broken home was a dysfunctional one, surely, one without love or care or comfort.

She recalled the visits to school, her attempts to broker some sort of peace between Luke and his teachers, Luke and the attendance officer. She had done her level best to listen, to try and find out how she could help him, why he was so unhappy and restless.

The possibility that she had fallen short, that there were mistakes, inadequacies in what she had done, made her sick with guilt. Shame clawed through her.

But when she returned to the papers and read them anew, the anger returned. This was not Luke, this was not fair.

Shivering with rage, she rang DC Illingworth, never mind how early it was. 'Have you seen the papers?' she demanded, a tremor in her voice.

'No,' the woman replied. 'What is it?'

'It's bloody character assassination,' she said, close to tears, 'that's what it is. My boy's a victim here and they're making him out to be a right villain.'

'Louise—'

'Please,' she blurted out, 'read them!' She ended the call.

'Mum?' Ruby was there in her school uniform. 'What's going on?'

Louise only hesitated for a moment – there was no way she could keep it from Ruby; she was bound to hear about it. 'The papers, they're saying things about Luke, things that aren't true.'

'What sort of things?'

'That he was a criminal, that he was terrorizing the place.'

'Oh, Mum.' Ruby's eyes filled.

'I know it's not true and you know it's not true, but it's there in black and white and some people will take it as gospel.'

'Can't we sue them, then?'

Oh, Ruby. 'I doubt it.' She tried to focus, to

concentrate on what was important. 'Listen, you might get some bother at school. Do you want me to talk to Miss Morley?'

'No, it'll be all right.'

'But you would let me know if . . .' A spike of panic in her guts; was she neglecting Ruby too? Should she keep her off, cocoon her here?

'Course.' Ruby poured cereal, drained the last of the milk, pulled one of the papers closer.

'How do they know all this?' Louise wondered aloud. 'The stuff with the police, the cautions, that's not public knowledge. He was only fifteen, it's meant to be confidential. So either the police have leaked stuff, or someone who knows Luke told them. But why? Why would anyone do that?'

'It makes him sound horrible,' Ruby exclaimed. 'There's our house.' She pointed at an inside page. The picture made the place look smaller, meaner than it really was. Barren. Taken so that the great tree, with Luke's lights in, was not in view.

The only reference to Luke's attackers was right at the end of the piece, which repeated that the police had issued e-fit pictures of two men and a young woman wanted for questioning in the assault that led to the death of Good Samaritan Jason Barnes.

'Why would they write all this?' asked Ruby.

'Because it sells papers. They can stir it up, get people talking. You know what spin is; this is spin. Your great-grandad called them the gutter press, this lot. Best used for wiping yer arse on.'

'Mum!'

'His words, not mine.' She drew a breath; her chest ached. 'Just remember, if anyone says anything at school, you know Luke, and what sort of person he is. And this isn't him.'

178

DC Illingworth rang back before they left. 'I'm so sorry, Louise.'

'Can't you do anything? Make them take it back? What if it affects how people see things when we get to court? Isn't that illegal if there might be a trial?'

'They've been very careful; there are no details about the incident itself in what they've written.'

'Aren't your press office meant to stop them printing stuff like this?'

'We do our best, but we have a free press. Publishing material like this doesn't help anybody, but as I say, there's nothing there that might materially affect our ability to press charges or mount a prosecution. You could try for a right of reply or an apology, but we really wouldn't advise it. It could make things even worse.'

Louise felt boxed in, nowhere to turn. 'How did they find all this out, the stuff about the cautions? I was told at the time that none of it would be disclosed.'

'That's right, it's common practice with young offenders.'

'But someone's disclosed it.'

'This hasn't come from us, Louise, if that's what you're implying, I can assure you of that.' There was a tart edge to her tone.

'So I just let it go, do I? See him slandered like this?' Tears of frustration started in her eyes.

'I know, it's hard. But it's like feeding the machine: anything you give them can come back and bite you. You speak to them and they'll want more. Our press officer is already in touch, so there shouldn't be anything else. And even if we make arrests and charge people, the trial wouldn't be for several months.'

Louise glanced at the clock, signalled to Ruby that she should set off. 'Why hasn't anything happened yet?'

she asked. 'You've got the name. What are you waiting for?'

'Let me check with the team and get back to you.'

'So you don't actually know?' Louise felt she was being fobbed off.

'I want to make sure I'm completely up to date. I'll speak to you later today,' the detective said neutrally.

Hadn't she done her best? Should she have been harder on Luke? Tough love? She had lived all her life in the belief that people were basically good, that with children you set boundaries and you loved them, you praised them, and they would come good. So where had it gone so wrong? She felt wretched. She had not been able to protect him when it came to it. They had ridden him down and savaged him. And now she could not even protect his reputation. She could not defend him and set the record straight. Tell the world that the reckless arson was just a firework in a wheelie bin; that he was cheeky, never malicious. That he had never been violent, never a thug, terrorized no one.

All day she wrestled with it, a net of worry, of impotent rage. A web of doubts and questions. Deanne called her mid-morning, then Fee and even Carl. All of them outraged, spitting tacks at the injustice of it. She was grateful to them; it helped to know she had them rooting for Luke. But the dribble of unease, the seasick lurches of guilt, wouldn't go away. Louise felt dirty, tarnished, the smears undermining her self-belief. Yet she had to squash this, bury it deep, in order to be a rock for Luke, for Ruby.

Mrs Coulson regularly took one of the tabloids. It always sat on the tray table at the side of her chair, but today when Louise visited it was absent. Louise didn't say anything and neither did the old woman. The kindness disarmed Louise and she felt a lump in her throat as she said goodbye.

She'd just put the key away in the key safe by the back door and was walking to her car when Andrew Barnes rang her. There was a bitter wind, a north-easterly, thrashing the trees, making her eyes water and pinching her cheeks. Clouds dense and low swung overhead, making her giddy. She turned her back to the wind, hunched over the phone. Litter skirled down the street, bags and a plastic bottle, fast-food cartons, smacking against walls and skittering around parked cars.

'I've seen the papers,' he said. No commiserations or anything.

Guilt leapt inside her. *DEATH IN VAIN*. She stiffened. 'Right.'

'It can't all be . . . well, it's not all true, is it? What they said.'

The fact that he had to ask the question saddened her. How little trust he had, in her, in Luke. She had shared something of Luke with him – had he not heard her? Did he now not believe her? He'd come looking for her at the hospital, came there twice, and then they'd met in the pub, and each time she couldn't quite figure him out. It was like he thought they had some common cause, but it didn't really feel that way to her. He must hate her, surely. His son was dead, hers still alive. His only child gone, while she had a second child to comfort her. *DEATH IN VAIN*. There they were, the perfect middle-class family, Jason the golden hero, whilst Luke, Luke was now the undeserving cause of Jason's death and Louise the inadequate, feckless single parent.

'Louise?'

Wordless, confused, she was unable to deal with him on top of everything else. She hung up.

181

Andrew

Andrew was cooking, making spicy chicken and basmati rice, rinsing the rice under cold running water prior to boiling it when Val got back.

She came straight through, her arms full of newspapers. 'Have you actually read them?' Her eyes blazing, her face flushed. She slapped them down one after the other.

'Yes,' he said. He'd passed the hospital shop on the way to his department and they were there, startling, making his heart stop. The ground shifted underfoot. He'd even bought them himself. Scoured them feeling like a voyeur, his pulse too quick and heat in his face. His first reaction was a dreadful sense that there was some truth in the damning reports and that Jason's honest response had been a terrible mistake. That prospect plunged him into an icy lake of despair, of senseless, meaningless loss. It couldn't be true. It mustn't be true. Then he had torn at them, cursing, shredded them and stuffed them in his bin, ink smeared on his hands. Val had rung him at work and he'd cut her short, 'Yes, it's outrageous. Completely. But look, I've a patient due, we'll talk later.'

And in the middle of the afternoon, unable to quell the unease, he had rung Louise, anxious to settle the questions he had, hoping to reassure himself that Luke wasn't the villain he'd been painted. She'd been too upset to talk.

Now he said, 'You can't trust what they—'

'This is what Jason died for?' Val shouted. 'A thug, a yob who should have been locked up already.'

'Val, you don't know—'

'He'd been in trouble with the police. He was too disruptive to stay in school, he was setting fire to things, terrifying people.'

'It's exaggerated, the tabloids, for Chrissakes, you know how it works.' Why couldn't he just agree with her? He'd shared the same sense of dismay, harboured the same doubts.

'You're defending him!'

He shook his head.

'I wish he'd died,' she said. 'I wish Jason had done nothing and that Luke Murray had died instead.'

Silence split the air. She stared at him, jaw up, defiant.

'Oh, Val.'

'It's true.' Her mouth trembled. She shook her head quickly.

'I know.' He thought of Luke lying silent in his hospital bed. Of Louise, in the pub, talking about her son. 'It's easy to hate him. To blame him. Reading all that crap. To wish Jason had been a million miles away. It's so easy. A scapegoat. But it's wrong, Val. Half of it'll be exaggerated, sensationalized. That's not the answer.'

'Why not?' she demanded. 'This is our child we're talking about, not some abstract, hypothetical case. This is ours, ours!' She hit the table. 'He died for nothing.'

'No.' He wouldn't have it.

'So you think this scum deserved saving?'

'Val, please calm down.'

'No, I won't calm down. I'm so angry. I have every right to be angry. You should be angry,' she yelled.

'I am!' he said. 'What is this? A competition? Who's angriest, most heartbroken? Who's most traumatized? Who misses him most?'

She flinched.

'I am angry, but I'm angry with the ones that hit him. Luke Murray wasn't holding the knife. And I will not accept that what Jason did was worthless. I'm proud of him.'

'Proud!' She groaned, tugged at her hair. 'He was stupid.'

'No! He had the guts, he had the humanity to help someone in trouble.' Andrew's voice trembled; he tried not to shout. 'He didn't stop and judge them first: ask if they'd got a drug habit or messed up at school. He just went to help. I love him for that.' He swallowed. 'I love him so much for that. He didn't look away or sit silent like the rest of them. Imagine if everyone did what Jason did, what a world we'd have.'

Tears stood in her eyes. 'You are so wrong,' she said. 'And he was wrong,' she went on. 'He misjudged—'

'Don't!' He tried to silence her. She was tearing it down. Making his death meaningless, pointless, pathetic. 'You were the one said he was brave, remember? Would you rather he had been a coward?'

'He'd still be here,' she said.

He felt the space between them, a chasm, steep-sided, too wide to bridge. Jagged rocks like knives far below.

'But he wouldn't be our Jason,' he said.

She gathered together the newspapers; she was still wearing her coat. 'I'm going to Sheena's.'

'I've made some food.'

'I'm not hungry.'

She couldn't go like this. Leaving everything so tangled. 'Val, can we talk?'

'There's nothing to say.' Resignation blunt in her voice.

'Please?' He wanted to tell her he loved her, but the words wouldn't come. He watched her walk away and heard the front door close quietly behind her.

He moved to turn the gas ring off and caught a glimpse of Jason out in the garden, sitting on the bench, bent over his guitar, then glancing up, hair falling away from his face and smiling at Andrew.

CHAPTER TWELVE

Louise

When Louise got back from work, she made some pasta and tuna for their tea, then booted up the laptop. The pieces were there on the internet, and after them threads of messages readers had posted. Outraged and virulent, most of them. Luke was Borstal material; he'd obviously grown up without moral guidance or discipline, etc., etc. These people believed what they'd read, swallowed it hook, line and sinker. About Luke, about her. The impotence, the inability to shout the truth from the rooftops was tempered by the miserable shame Louise felt, the sense of failure.

Ruby said school had been weird but okay. Some of the kids thought it was cool that Luke had been in the papers again and didn't really care what it said about him.

'The cult of celebrity,' Louise muttered.

Intent on maintaining a brave face, after tea she persuaded Ruby to run through her pieces and watched her.

'Excellent!' she said.

'The wig moved a bit.'

'I never noticed,' she said.

Their visit to Luke was brief that evening. Louise read some of the papers out to him. Some deluded part of her hoping that he'd be so annoyed at what had been said that he'd wake up fighting. He never moved. Not a flicker.

* * *

Louise went round to see Angie later that evening. The last snowfal had all but gone now, rain most of the day, so just a drift left along the fence where it was shaded and sheltered, though more was forecast. Gusts of wind rattled the branches in the sycamore and made the lights swing. She'd keep them on, she decided, a bit of Luke shining in the dark. A beacon. She could hear the clatter of a gate somewhere close by, and a dog whining and yapping.

She was disconcerted when Sian opened the door in tears.

'What's wrong?' Was Angie bad? Had she collapsed again? Louise went to put her arm round Sian, but the girl moved away into the living room and Louise went after her.

'The stuff in the papers,' Sian said. Angie looked miserable too.

'Oh love, ignore it,' Louise told the girl. 'It's a pack of lies. They'd write anything to sell a few more copies. We know it's not true.' Sounding stronger than she felt. 'You know Luke. He's no angel, but he's not a devil either. He's not got a mean bone in his body.'

They were both looking peculiar. Uncertainty stole through her. 'What is it?'

Angie bit her lip, put her hand to her head.

'I didn't say any of that,' Sian said in a rush. 'Not what they put. They changed it, they made it sound really bad.'

'Sian?' Louise said, perplexed.

'I'm so sorry, Louise.' The girl started crying. 'I didn't . . .'

Louise felt everything collide: the girl weeping, the headlines, Andrew Barnes on the phone. 'You talked to the papers?' she said, quaking. A bad taste in her throat.

186

'They kept ringing. They just wanted to get an idea of what Luke was like. Human interest for people. I never said those things, Louise. I never.'

Louise covered her eyes and pressed her lips tight together, felt the rapid thud in her chest and the busy swarm humming in her head. It was all such an awful mess.

'I'm sorry.'

'Oh God.' Louise sat down heavily on the sofa.

'I'm so sorry,' Sian sobbed.

'It's okay,' Louise said, still smarting with shock and aggravation but knowing that the girl needed her forgiveness. 'It'll be okay.' The words shallow in the overheated room.

Andrew

He stood watching the house; the night was cold and foggy, the pavements and fences shone with a dull gleam under the street lights. The thick air tasted of tar and seemed to cling to his clothes, making them damp.

The house was a bog-standard three-bedroom semi. One of thousands built by the local authority in the post-war period. Council houses. Many of them sold since in right-to-buy schemes, but this one didn't bear any of the marks of owner occupation. No big extension, fake stone cladding or laughable mullioned windows, no garage crammed into the space at the side of the house. Just red-brick, a door in the middle, a window either side of it and two on the storey above them. And a satellite dish. In front of the house, a concrete driveway, an old Vauxhall parked there. There was a yellow glow of light through the glass in the door and electric blue from one of the upstairs rooms. Someone watching telly? Him?

Two weeks since Louise had given him the name, and still nothing had happened. Bland reports from Martine claiming they were making progress but never any specifics. And after two weeks he was still free. Going about his business. Laughing in their faces.

Thomas Garrington.

Andrew hadn't been able to find him on the hospital system. He had to guess at dates of birth around Halloween. Louise had told him Garrington was celebrating his birthday when he and Luke clashed at the party. He had to guess which year, try days either side. He must have entered thirty different combinations, and nothing. Perhaps Garrington had never been to Wythenshawe Hospital. Perhaps he'd been born at MRI, or the family had moved to Manchester in recent times and managed to get rehoused.

While he had been hunched over Harriet's terminal, stabbing at keys and crossing off combinations, he hadn't thought about what he might do with any information he found. The acquisition of it was all that mattered. Knowledge is power.

In the same way, he was unaware what he might do if Thomas Garrington appeared now. But the very prospect of it made him clench his fists, sent his breathing up a gear. Seared in his memory was the glimpse he'd had: Garrington and the girl by the front gate, yelling as Jason and the other boy struggled over Luke. The look on Garrington's face: exhilaration. Wild and high and excited.

Andrew heard footsteps in the fog and stepped back into the alleyway. The steps grew closer, were drowned out by the noise of a passing car, then he saw a man and his dog across the other side of the road. When they had gone, swallowed up by the fog again, he resumed his vigil.

The anger came in waves. He didn't resist but let it carry him out to the depths. Allowed the pictures to bloom in his head: saw himself knocking the boy down and beating him senseless with a baseball bat, spurred on by the meaty sound of wood on flesh and bone; driving into him with the car and reversing back over his body, the satisfying jolt as the wheels went over him; felt the heft of a butcher's knife in his hand and the ease with which it slid into the boy's chest and throat and belly, watching his expression alter from belligerent to wary to fearful then anguished. Peeling back the layers of pretence. You hurt too. You bleed.

Or fire! Push a Molotov cocktail through the letter box and watch the colours at the windows change. Him trapped behind the glass, fists banging on the double glazing, face contorted.

The images were lurid, heightened and of no comfort whatsoever. They simply fed the anger, tinder to the flames.

There had been other times in his life when there had been a hint of this rage, like when his boss mounted her bullying campaign: micromanaging him, belittling his work and his demeanour, alternately carping and mock-concerned. Until the sight of her, the scent of her perfume, made him seethe. But never anything as raw, as profound as this. He wanted to howl at the moon, bay for blood.

The door opposite opened and the whole of Andrew's skin prickled. Framed in the light, one hand on the door jamb, the other scratching at his belly, was the boy. Looking down towards his feet where something moved. A cat. Andrew saw the lad nudge the animal gently with his foot. His bare foot. The cat leapt over the threshold and was lost in the dark. The boy closed the door.

He was still there, living, breathing, scratching. Letting the fucking cat out.

Andrew's phone rang, loud in the muffled night. He dug it from his pocket. It was Louise.

'I don't want you to contact me again,' she said.

He was surprised. 'Why? What's wrong?'

She gave a little laugh, no humour in it. 'You really don't know?' She sighed. 'Luke's alive, Jason isn't. It's not fair, is it? Every time you see me or Luke, you must wish it had been different. It's only natural.' She spoke brusquely, sounded brittle.

He wasn't sure what to say.

'And now with the garbage in the papers – I'm sorry about what happened to Jason, but he saved Luke and I can never be sorry for that. I just think it's better if we—'

'Garrington, Gazza, he's here. He's still here, at his house. They've not done anything.' His words were spilling like skittles. 'Why haven't they arrested him, they know it was him, they've had the name two weeks, what the hell do—'

'Where are you?' she demanded.

'Outside his house. Ten minutes' walk. I've just seen him, Louise, large as life—'

'Where? What's the address?'

He told her.

'Don't move.'

She was there in no time at all. Pulling up and waiting while he opened the door and got in. Then driving away, crunching through the gears in a way that told him she was livid even before she spoke.

She stopped the car alongside the park; the street smothered in fog looked empty. She snapped off her seat belt. 'What the hell were you playing at?'

'The police have done nothing.'

190

'Oh, and you were going to, were you? What? Thump the guy? Put a brick through his window?' She was quivering, her eyes bright and intense.

'He killed my son,' he said tightly. 'And he's not even been picked up.'

'And he put my lad in a coma.' She rounded on him. 'What happens when he is arrested and it comes out you've been stalking him?'

'I wasn't stalking.'

'Intimidating a suspect, interfering with an inquiry. You could mess it all up.'

'But—'

'I want them sent down, I want them punished. I want justice, not some middle-class prat like you ruining everything. Playing at terminator. What makes you think you know better than the police?' She was trembling with fury, spittle at the side of her mouth, which she swiped away. She hit at the steering wheel. 'What if he'd seen you, legged it?'

'He didn't see me,' Andrew said, his mouth dry and palms clammy. 'And I wouldn't have done anything.'

'Just being there was doing something.'

'Why is it taking so long?' he burst out.

'I don't know!' she yelled back. She closed her eyes. Silence stretched between them. He looked out at the huge poplars, bare branches shrouded in fog. He heard the slam of a car door, the cough of an engine.

She spoke. 'Swear to me that you won't go near that house again, you won't try anything else.'

He took a breath. 'I promise.'

'I never should have told you, I thought you could be trusted. You acted like we were on the same side.'

'We are.' He was desperate to reassure her, redeem himself. 'I'm sorry.'

'You wanted to hurt him?'

'Of course, but only in my head.'

'We're better than them,' she said quietly. 'Jason was better than them, my Luke . . .' In the quiet he heard her swallow, heard the ticking of the car as the metal cooled.

Andrew pinched the bridge of his nose, screwed his eyes shut tight.

'I'll take you home,' she said.

'I can walk from here.' He opened the door. 'Thanks.'

She looked at him but didn't speak. She looked so tired; worn out but not defeated.

He watched her drive off until the red rear lights had gone. Then he turned for home.

The phone went at seven, waking him. His thoughts flew to Jason, something wrong . . . then he slammed into the truth, a brick wall of pain – Jason's gone. Amended his fears: his father, perhaps? He hurried on to the landing, snatched up the handset.

It was Martine. She didn't waste time on small talk. 'Andrew, we arrested three people this morning.'

His knees went weak. 'Who?'

'I can't give you names at the moment.'

He heard Val. 'What is it?'

Martine went on, 'They match the descriptions. I'll get back to you as soon as I know more. Would you like me to come round?'

Val was there, eyes puffy from sleep, her hair tangled.

'No thanks. We'll be fine.' He put the phone back. 'They've arrested them,' he said.

'Oh God.' She swayed, put a hand to the wall to steady herself.

'Three of them – that's all she could say.'

'Oh God,' she repeated, covering her mouth. 'So have they been charged?'

'I don't think so. She'll ring later.'

Val nodded slowly. She seemed to reach some sort of decision. 'Good. It's good.'

'Of course, yes.' But it was unnerving, too. 'Shall we stay home? I don't know how long . . . don't know if I could concentrate.'

'And the press might be back.'

'Yes. We'll stay here.' He shuddered, goose flesh on his arms. Outside it was lashing rain; he could hear it slapping the windows, hear the wind buffeting the house. He moved to hold her. His arms went round her and he felt her tense, withholding the full embrace he longed for. He stepped away. 'You okay?' Though that wasn't the question he wanted to ask.

'Fine,' she said. The lie between them like a line in the sand. A border between alien territories. 'I'll get a shower.'

Above him, around the roof, the wind howled.

Louise

Louise spent the day on pins, checking her phone every ten minutes. Losing track at work so she almost gave Miriam two lots of her lunchtime tablets. Smoking too much even when her mouth tasted foul and she was behind on her schedule.

It poured down all day, sullen clouds dumping bucketfuls of rain over and over, the wind hurling it sideways, so she had to try and smoke in doorways, even in a bus shelter at one point, to avoid getting soaked through. She wouldn't break her rule and smoke in the car, but boy was she tempted.

She'd not slept the night before, too wound up about Andrew's vigilante stunt and what it might have led to, and about the papers. Not only what they'd written about Luke, but also the way they'd conned Sian, who wasn't the brightest button in the box. They'd preyed on her goodwill, her friendship with Luke's family, to get hold of the information, then warped it as much as they could. Louise had got out of bed in the end, wrapped herself in layers and a blanket against the cold in the house and done some sewing until her fingers went numb.

When the phone went during breakfast she had expected the agency with a change to her visits, but it was the police. The news made her physically sick, the shock of it.

Now she was waiting for more. She had called at the hospital straight from work. Aware with each visit that she was avoiding Dr Liu, not ready to face any more discussion about moving Luke or the impossible decisions she might be forced to make after that. She bathed Luke and brushed his teeth. The dressing on his head had been removed and his hair was growing back, dark fuzz, the texture of hair on a kiwi fruit. The scar looked livid, pink and lumpy where they had operated. Fee had given her some aromatherapy oil, a mix of basil, bergamot and peppermint. She massaged him with it, his torso, arms and legs, gently round his neck, his feet. The scents, peppery and fresh, filled the room.

'Do you like the smell, then?' she said. 'Meant to help your memory this, stimulate the brain.' When she'd finished, she drew the sheet over him and sat and held his hand. 'They've arrested them, Luke. The three that hurt you. They picked them up this morning.' She watched for the slightest twitch, saw only the steady pulse in the side of his neck, the slow rise and fall of his chest as he breathed.

She reached and tapped the side of his face. 'Luke,

wake up now. It's Mum. You can wake up now.' She pressed a fingernail into the sole of his foot, her eyes fixed on his face. Altered her tone: quick, instructive, 'Luke, wake up!'

There was nothing.

'Ring them, Mum,' Ruby said again.

'I've told you, they'll ring me.'

'What if they've forgotten? Or think it's too late?'

'Then I'll kick up a stink,' she said.

'What if they let them go?'

'Then they'll tell us.'

Ruby looked so worried.

'Why would they let them go? Look, you're getting me all stressed now. Haven't you any homework to do?'

'Done it.'

The phone rang. Louise snatched it up. Ruby stared, shoulders hunched, her eyes huge.

'Yes?'

'It's me, Louise: DC Illingworth.'

'Yes.' Her mouth was dry; she strained for a clue in the way the woman spoke. Good news, bad? She nodded to Ruby, reached out a hand. Ruby took it.

'The three people we arrested this morning have now been charged with the murder of Jason Barnes and the attempted murder of Luke.'

Louise gasped, felt dizzy, as though she'd topple over.

'One of the three has made an admission of guilt, a confession, and that's enabled us to bring charges more quickly than we'd anticipated.

'Oh God.' A confession!

'What?' Ruby was mouthing, slicing her free hand with impatience.

'The people involved are Thomas Garrington aged eighteen, a seventeen-year-old woman who cannot be named for legal reasons and Conrad Quinn, aged eighteen.'

She unscrambled the words, struggled to take it all in: the numbers, the unfamiliar name. 'What legal reasons?'

'Under eighteen.'

'What happens now?' Louise asked.

'They'll appear in the magistrates' court in the morning, and then next week there will be a plea and case management hearing in the Crown Court. That will set a date for the trial.'

'Thank you,' said Louise, her voice breaking.

'I think I can speak for the whole team when I say how pleased I am that the individuals have been apprehended and charged. I'll be in touch soon. You are entitled to attend any of the court hearings if you wish.'

Did she want to? The thought of seeing them made her stomach turn.

'I'll call tomorrow,' the detective said.

'They've got them,' Louise told Ruby. 'They've charged them all.' And she started to cry.

Emma

She showed the letter to Laura at work. Laura scanned it. 'You're going to be a witness?' She glanced at Emma.

Emma nodded, miserable. 'I wish I didn't have to.'

'It might fall through,' Laura said. 'It's months away. I know someone who had to go, about their neighbours: the bloke had attacked his wife. Anyway, when my friend got there, all hyped up, they said it was off. The bloke changed his plea.'

Emma considered this, but knowing her luck, the thing would go ahead and she'd have to appear.

She'd had to go in to the police station, once they'd arrested the suspects. The police had called at work and she'd had to go and ask Gavin for the time off. He had no problem with it but she half hoped he might have some reason to refuse.

The people weren't lined up like on telly. She just had to look at videos of different people and pick them out. It was easy, really. The Gazza guy with his red hair and staring blue eyes, the other one with that tattoo and his pokey face and the girl prettier than all the other girls in the clips shown to her.

Now, with it all being reported in the papers, Emma knew their names: Thomas Garrington and Conrad Quinn. The girl was just called Girl A because she was under eighteen. Conrad Quinn had confessed, he'd pleaded guilty so he'd be a witness like Emma.

'Might be exciting,' Laura said.

She doesn't understand, thought Emma. Emma wanted to do the right thing – she still felt a sting of shame when she thought back to her silence on the bus – but she was bound to freeze up or get tongue-tied and make a fool of herself.

That weekend she went home to celebrate her mother's birthday. They were having a meal on the Saturday evening. Emma had bought Mum a necklace, lovely rose-coloured beads interspersed with pearls, which would go with some of her clothes.

The restaurant overlooked the river and they had a table in the conservatory right next to the water. Emma waited until they had finished the meal, and she'd had three large glasses of white wine, before telling them about the witness summons. Her dad was on it like a hound on an injured fox.

'You a witness! God help the prosecution. Tell them to give you a megaphone or no one will catch a word you say.'

'Roger,' her mum chimed in, on cue.

'Well,' he leaned back, belched softly, 'you know what she's like. Whispering Winnie.' He made stupid sibilant sounds, angling his head to and fro, some ghastly impersonation, malice flickering in his gaze.

Emma dug her nails into her palms, felt the hate for him black in her heart. 'Why do you always put me down, Dad?' The directness of her question startled Emma as much as it did her parents. Her mum shifted and laughed awkwardly and her father stopped still.

'Any more coffee?' her mum said.

'I asked you a question.' Emma forced herself to keep looking his way, even though her face was aflame with heat.

He leant forward and lowered his voice. His eyes glinting. 'You will not ruin your mother's special night out with this silly attention-seeking claptrap.'

'Roger . . . Emma . . .' Her mum was flustered.

Emma pushed back her chair.

'Where d'you think you're going?' he snapped.

'Toilets,' Emma said. 'Something's made me feel sick.' As she turned, she caught her foot on the chair and stumbled.

'Hah hah!' he cackled, delighted. 'See that! Hah! Nellie the Elephant.'

'Oh, Roger,' her mum said sadly, 'that's not fair.'

Emma didn't cry; she wouldn't cry. Nellie the Elephant, Whispering Winnie. Hateful. And what hurt worst of all was that he was right.

Louise

They had to set off early to allow for the traffic. Ruby was wound up with anxiety, chewing at her nails. 'Stop it,' Louise told her. 'If you have to chew something, chew some gum.'

'I haven't got any,' Ruby retorted.

'In the glove compartment.' Louise's stomach was fluttering too – like a bird had got trapped in there – but she tried to act calm for Ruby's sake.

Ruby fiddled with the radio, tuned it into Radio 1 Xtra. She sang along to the tunes she liked.

Louise concentrated on the road, negotiating the slew of commuter cars and heavy goods wagons. It was sleeting and the wipers were going at full tilt to clear the windscreen.

She hadn't told Ruby about Dr Liu's plans to move Luke from the hospital; hadn't told anyone. Nothing would happen yet anyway. 'In the next couple of months,' she'd said. That could be March. They could get Ruby settled into a new routine by then. Travelling to Liverpool early on a Monday, back Friday night. They should be able to get help with her travel expenses.

'Mum!' Ruby yelped as a 4 × 4 swerved in front of them from the inside lane. Louise braked, cursed, sounded the horn. The vehicle flashed its lights in reply. A sarky thank-you. Louise flung a V-sign his way, shaken up.

'I'd like to get there in one piece,' Ruby grumbled.

'Tell him, not me,' Louise said.

They were just in time. The drama school was in its own grounds, a grand old Victorian villa with pillars at the entrance door and big bay windows. Trees thrashed their branches in the wind and icy rain as Ruby grabbed her holdall from the boot. Another heavy squall bounced off the car roof and the gravel.

One of the students took Ruby's name, showed her where to leave her bag in the changing rooms and gave them a tour of the buildings. The house was warm and bright, with the former bedrooms now classrooms and downstairs rooms used as rehearsal spaces and offices.

Outside, behind the villa, a converted garage functioned as the dance studio, next to a purpose-built music centre. Ruby's eyes roved hungrily over everything. There were plenty of students about, both boys and girls. Louise noticed the way they checked Ruby out as they passed and Ruby doing the same.

'We've had loads more people applying,' their guide told them. 'The *Glee* factor.' She mentioned the American TV series about a school choir and their ambitious musical routines. It had been compulsory viewing for Ruby when it started.

The student halls were a modern block. Canteen, lounge, showers and cubicle-style bedrooms. They were able to see inside one – it was smaller than Ruby's bedroom at home, little more than a cell. But if all went well and she made friends, she'd only be in there to sleep.

Back in the main house, they were served coffee and biscuits and Ruby got changed and waited to be called. The auditions were in one of the rehearsal rooms. In the quarter of an hour until her slot, Ruby couldn't sit still. Louise let her prowl about, working off some of her energy. She looked amazing: the glowing red wig framing her sculptured face, her eyes big and luminous with long lashes, her mouth generous. It was a face Louise never tired of looking at. The same with Luke. Ruby wore a red leotard and red and black striped tights, black boots. Her body was long and slim and fine. She stopped pacing and turned to Louise, panicking. 'I can't remember it! The poem. Oh Mum.'

'Hey, you'll be fine. It's just nerves. Run on the spot.'

Then the student called her and Ruby went.

Louise fiddled with her phone. She had a voice message on there from Luke: 'Hey, I'm staying at

Declan's, yeah. See you tomorrow.' His voice was warmer than she had remembered, in spite of the bland, businesslike content of the message. She had played it to him recently; she'd try anything to reach him. She listened again now. 'Hey . . .' What she'd give to hear him say that now. One word. *Hey*.

'Mrs Murray?'

Louise felt a prick of shock, as if she'd been caught doing something she shouldn't. She slid her phone shut, smiled and went through to meet the principal, Vicky Plessey. They'd spoken on the phone before, and Louise had seen her picture on the website: a vivacious, Liverpudlian with long blonde hair. She couldn't be much older than Louise. Her office was a hymn to art deco – mirrors and statues, velvet curtains, framed posters. She began by telling Louise that Ruby was an impressive applicant, obviously committed to performance. How would she find living away from home?

'I think she'll be fine. She'll make friends, I'm sure, and she'll be home at weekends.'

'Is there anything we need to be aware of, anything that's altered since you sent in the application from?'

Louise didn't know whether to say anything about Luke. If she went into details, if she identified him as the boy who had been savaged in the press, it might alter Vicky's view of Ruby. Turn her from a gifted teenager to the sister of a young criminal. But if she said nothing, there might be problems further down the line for Ruby, because no one would know Luke was in hospital.

'Ruby's brother is in hospital,' Louise said. 'A brain injury.'

Vicky frowned in concern. 'Oh, I am sorry.'

Louise rushed to speak, keen to deflect any questions. 'So she may need to visit, depending on how he does.'

'Of course. The welfare of the students is our first priority.'

Before Vicky could ask anything, Louise said, 'When will we hear if she's got a place?'

'By the end of the week,' Vicky said.

'And the bursaries – does that depend on who gets in?' Louise realized it might be a bit crass homing straight in on the money side of things, but it was crucial Vicky understood their situation.

'Yes. We only offer two bursaries each intake and demand is increasing year on year. Though we do have a separate expenses fund.'

'Like I explained on the phone,' Louise said, 'Ruby wouldn't be able to come here if we had to find the fees.'

'I understand.'

Did she? Louise wondered. Had Vicky Plessey grown up in a home where school trips were out of the question and buying new shoes might mean keeping the heating off for a month. Could she imagine that? Every purchase being weighed, the permanent worry about managing money gnawing inside.

Back in the changing room, Ruby was ready to leave.

'How did it go?' Louise asked.

'Good,' she grinned, 'good. I slipped on the last turn but I changed it into a slide and I don't think they could tell.'

'How many people were there?'

'Three!' she said. 'And they laughed at the poem.'

'Hey, well done you. We'll hear by the end of the week.'

The call came on Thursday. Louise texted Ruby straight away, even though her phone would be off till school ended at three p.m. At 3.03 Ruby rang home, whooping and hollering with joy.

That evening they celebrated and Ruby flung a hundred questions at her mum, none of which Louise could answer. 'What about my washing? Do I keep the same doctor? If I go on the train will I have to pay full fare? Will there be a public show this term? Do they have teacher training days?' At bedtime, Ruby lingered in the doorway perched on one leg, practising her balance. She put her foot down. 'Will you be all right, Mum?'

'Me? Course I will.'

'But you'll be all on your own.'

Louise bit her cheek. Breathed in hard. 'Hey, I'll be fine. You're amazing, you know. I'm so proud of you.' She hugged her. 'Now. Bed.'

Ruby went. And Louise kept on breathing steadily, eyes shut tight. Till she was fit again, danger past. Her delicate grasp on life, on self-control, regained.

CHAPTER THIRTEEN

Andrew

The time until the trial, set for October, stretched out like a barren plain, a place of thin air and stunted grass and dust storms.

Andrew felt as if he and Val were shrivelling up, desiccated, living through a drought. As the time crept on, there were hazards to overcome, earthquakes splitting the ground beneath them, cracking the surface and threatening to suck them into the dark anew. Andrew's birthday, Mother's Day, Jason's birthday in May. Taurus.

'I'm a bull, Dad, what are you?' Crunching his toast, jam on his cheek.

'A fish.'

'And Mum?'

'A ram.'

'Hah! I'm the strongest. I don't think they should have bullfighting. It's mean.'

'It is.'

'Why are they called star signs?'

'Because the whole idea is based on the stars. In the ancient world people thought the stars affected everything that happened on the earth. I've a map somewhere, a chart.'

'Get it!' Jason eyes alight as he puts the last bit of crust in his mouth and clacks his sticky fingers together.

'Wash your hands, then.'

* * *

Val was on sick leave. She'd made it through until the end of February, then had in effect been sent home from work. She couldn't function properly, she couldn't concentrate, she was depressed. She started taking antidepressants. He tried to help, to pamper her, to keep her company, but often as not she gave him that blank look that chilled him to the core.

Jason's birthday loomed, growing closer, denser, darker, a storm on the horizon. Nineteen, Andrew thought. But he wasn't, wouldn't ever be. Andrew asked Val what she wanted to do, how they should mark it.

She closed her eyes, shook her head. He couldn't do this on his own; he felt drained. He expected they would spend time at the grave, but what else? She kept the shrine going. Simplified now, as the original candles had melted, the flowers and cards ruined by the weather. He wondered if this was healthy, but was happy to go along with it.

One bleak, stifling Sunday, he tackled her, head on. 'Val, we need to talk to someone, get some help.'

'No.'

'Why not? We can't go on like this. You're so unhappy, not communicating. We never talk, we never make love, we barely exist.'

She covered her eyes. He reined in his temper, lowered his voice. 'I don't know how to reach you any more. I don't know what you want from me.' He felt cold and tense inside.

She said nothing. He looked up to the ceiling, to the lampshade they had chosen, the paper they'd hung together. 'I need you,' he said. 'I love you, Val, I don't want to lose you too. But I don't know how to make things right.'

'You can't. You can't make it right.'

'I can't bring Jason back.' His voice shook, he cleared his throat. 'But you and me, our marriage, we need to work things out.'

She shook her head.

'You're depressed, I know that, but talking to someone, someone who's experienced, the bereavement service, we could do it together. Or separately if you want.'

She sat there, dull, uninterested. 'No.'

'You won't even try?' He felt the ground rumble and shift. The future ripple and disintegrate. He heard the release of her breath. 'Do you even want to be with me?' he asked her.

'I'm not sure,' she said.

And his heart broke.

Emma

Emma knew she had to say something to Laura soon. She had intended to pull out of the holiday before they even booked it. Had sat there, her guts in turmoil, as they voted on which destination to try for. Meekly giving her passport details to Laura, who was going to scour the internet for deals that very evening. She promised herself she would ring Laura after work and explain. But then she hadn't been able to. She stalled each time she picked up the phone, shame stealing over her skin. It was impossible to do it, to tell Laura, to say the words, because she'd have to explain why, and how could she tell anyone such disgusting things?

And the next morning Laura was so excited: she had found a brilliant full-board deal in Corfu, mid-May, with daytime flights. Less than three hundred pounds each. Emma had paid her deposit.

The balance was due six weeks before leaving and the date crept closer. At night, Emma lay awake and wondered about ways round it. But any excuses she came up with, she always found a way that it might unravel on her and end up costing her the friendship. If she said her passport had expired, Laura would insist she go get one Priority Service. Or if she said there was a family wedding or her mum was having surgery, so many other lies would have to be told.

Then they had a night out. Little Kim's boyfriend was playing drums in a band and they were on at The Academy. Emma liked the music, it was a mix of folk and pop with lots of fast tunes that some of the crowd jigged about to. There were no seats, everyone had to stand. The venue looked a bit run-down really, a big barn of a place. Blonde Kim and Laura had both smuggled bottles of vodka in and shared them out, so they just bought soft drinks at the bar to mix.

Emma felt giddy and a bit sick by the time the band had finished, and agreed to go on to a bar in town with everyone. The band came, and friends of theirs, and Emma enjoyed being in the middle of the group and no one bothering about her but just accepting she was one of them.

The man who did the sound desk for the band, Simon, ended up sitting next to Emma. He chatted away to her about the band and then about cycling; he was in a cycling club and did races and things. He asked her if she'd ever been to the velodrome, and if she had a bike, but she said no. She thought he'd stop talking to her then but he didn't. He had nice brown eyes. He bought her a drink, carried on chatting. He had a gap in his top teeth. A nice gap.

When Emma went to the loo Laura was there, redoing her eyeliner.

'You're in there, Emma,' said Laura. 'You fancy him?'

'Jesus!' Emma coughed, giggled. 'Dunno.' He didn't fancy her, did he? No one ever did. Why would they?

'Take him back to yours and try 'im out.'

'Laura!'

'Well give him a kiss, drop your handkerchief or something. I'm on my tod out there, but you're in with a chance.' Laura was single, had been since the previous summer.

'Do you like him?' Emma said. 'We can swap places.'

'Don't be daft,' Laura said. 'It's you he's interested in.'

'How do you know?'

Laura sighed. 'Because it's you he's talking to, you muppet. Go on, before he forgets what you look like.'

I can't, thought Emma. Even if I like him, I could never . . . If I let him kiss me, let him take me out, I could never let him touch me, not properly. Because then he'd know . . .

'I can't go on holiday, Laura,' Emma blurted out, 'I just can't.'

'What?' Laura looked puzzled. 'Why not?'

'I just can't.'

'Why? We've paid the deposit now and everything.'

'I'm sorry, I can't.' Emma made to leave, her heart tripping, but Laura caught at her wrist, swung her back. 'Hang on, don't go all weird on me. Is it the money?'

'No.'

'What, then?'

Emma tried not to cry, but she felt the tears sliding down her face.

'You're not going till you've told me,' Laura said. She wasn't nasty but she was determined to have an explanation.

'I can't.'

'Emma! I'm not doing bleeding twenty questions.'

The truth clogged in her throat. Laura kept watching her. 'I cut myself,' Emma said quietly, 'on purpose.'

'Okay,' Laura said slowly.

Emma stared at her, stunned. 'With a razor blade,' she said, in case Laura hadn't actually grasped what she was saying.

'What's that got to do with the holiday?'

Emma clutched at her head. 'The scars on my legs.' She waved a hand towards her thighs. 'I can't wear a swimsuit.'

Laura smiled, gave a little snort. 'That's why?'

Emma nodded.

'Come here,' Laura said. She hugged Emma. 'You dozy cow.' She stood back. 'Just get a playsuit; you can get quite long ones, like bermudas. Or cycle shorts. No one'll know.' She looked at Emma. 'How long have you been doing it?'

'Three years.' Emma thought about pinching herself. Laura hadn't pushed her away or shrieked with disgust. 'I'm bulimic as well.'

'Thought you might be.'

'Why?' Emma stared.

'Couple of things,' Laura said. 'My auntie had it.'

Emma felt dizzy. 'Did she?'

'She's all right now. Still frets a bit about her weight, but she's not chucking up all the time.'

'And self-harm?'

'Nah. She never did that. Why do you do it?'

'I don't know.' Emma blew her nose, laughed awkwardly. 'It helps.'

'Helps what?'

Emma couldn't say. The thing too big, too compli-cated, a shifting shape. 'I don't know.'

209

'Maybe you should find out,' Laura said gently.

'Don't tell them?' Emma begged.

'Course not.' Laura smiled. 'You'd better fix your face, you look like a Goth.'

Emma glanced in the mirror; her mascara had run.

'So the holiday's on, yeah? We'll work something out.'

Emma nodded. She felt peculiar. Like there was a bubble billowing in her chest, big and light. She cleaned her face and put on fresh make-up. She checked her purse and worked out she still had enough money to buy Simon a drink if he hadn't gone yet. Just a drink. She wouldn't lead him on, but it was nice to talk to him. She could tell him about the holiday, see where he had travelled.

Louise

There had been a visit from DC Illingworth in the week after the arrests to go over the details of the prosecution. Conrad Quinn was pleading guilty to wounding Luke and had agreed to testify against the others. They would face charges of murder and attempted murder. The detective stressed that although Quinn's evidence would be a great help to the prosecution, it did not automatically mean that the others would be found guilty.

Louise thought of the faces in the paper, the smudged images from the CCTV. 'What about the bus driver?' she asked. 'Have you spoken to him?'

'He's off sick,' the officer said, 'with stress.'

Louise stared at her, didn't know whether to laugh or cry.

* * *

Luke was moved to a high-dependency unit in Fallow-field at the beginning of March. It was closer to Louise's than the hospital had been, and easier to park.

It was a twilight world, she thought, with several other patients in various states of limited capability. People suspended between life and death, lives riven by sudden, wrenching tragedy. She had no complaints about the staff, and the place didn't smell, which was always a good sign.

She had further meetings with Dr Liu in the process of sorting out the referral and transfer. Louise shut her ears, her mind, to any talk of decisions about life support. Luke continued to be fed via a tube in his stomach.

Louise borrowed Deanne's laptop while the kids were visiting their dad (Ruby had taken her machine to drama college) and began to do more research into the condition. Some of the information she came upon was unpalatable, and she avoided the medical sites where the talk was of studies and statistics and averages. Their savage facts made her stomach churn, threatened to snare her in a place of cold despair. Instead she sought out the personal stories of people who had 'woken up' against all the odds. The young mother hurt in a car crash who had regained consciousness after four months, the man in the US who'd woken after five years with a single dose of a drug, the child who had come round minutes before her feeding tube was withdrawn. Louise held fast to hope because it was all she had and it was all that sustained her. She didn't believe in God or prayer or even miracles, though she knew what she was hoping for would be classed as a miracle. She would not give up, she would never give up.

'What about Luke?' Dr Liu had asked at the last meeting. 'What would he want? Would he choose to live like this for the rest of his life?'

Louise thought of him: restless, always moving, climbing, running. Ducking and diving through his short life. Turning cartwheels, handstands in the park. Squealing with delight as Eddie chased him or tickled his tummy. 'I can't answer that,' she said.

'When you can, you will know what to do,' the doctor replied. Implying that Louise was selfish. But she was doing this for Luke; he needed more time, more of a chance.

She could not contemplate it. Would not talk about it, even with her closest friends. Deanne asked her one day how long Luke could go on at the nursing home.

'Indefinitely,' Louise said.

Deanne's eyes had clouded and she'd asked, 'Till he's old?' And Louise had heard the revulsion and pity in her voice and said, 'I don't want to talk about it.'

She dreamt about it often, dreams where he was hurt and crying and she had him in her arms, carrying him, running for help, her legs burning with cramp, heart slamming in her chest and the terror tearing inside, and then in the dream he would be fine. Just like that. He would be better and at home, just doing something mundane, sprawled on the sofa or sticking a bowl of beans in the microwave, and she'd feel relief like cool water flowing through her, waves of joy. Then she would wake up and the elation would shrivel to fresh disappointment.

She read some of the miracle stories with a pang of unease as the tales of a brother or mother opening their eyes or moving a finger unrolled to describe years of infinitesimally small progress. Even where recovery had been substantial and astonishing, relatives spoke of adjusting to altered personalities, and having to accept that their loved ones would never be the same again. They had gone. There was grief to be borne along with gratitude. So many prospects she shied away from; even as she stubbornly willed his recovery, she would admit no realistic picture of what that might mean: Luke paraplegic and incontinent, drooling; or dumb with depression; or dull and thick with lethargy. I just want him back, was the drumbeat of her hope, my Luke, the same.

The staff at the home told her about support groups she could join, and she smiled and thanked them and said she'd think about it: a tactic she had learnt over the years from some of her clients. Resist and people become persistent, evangelical; promise to consider a change, a new venture, and they'll let you be.

People still asked after him: Angie and Sian, Omar, her friends, people she barely knew as well, when she ran into them at the supermarket. And sometimes they asked about the court case, in a hopeful sort of way, as though that would somehow make things better.

You'd see that on the television, the victims' families talking about justice and how it would allow them to move on. Of course she wanted the people who had hurt Luke to be punished – she remembered arguing with Andrew Barnes, and the depth of her rage that he might mess up the police inquiry – but still she didn't see how that would change anything for her. It was an ordeal to be got through and on the other side things would continue as they were. For her. For Luke. In limbo.

CHAPTER FOURTEEN

Andrew

He ran into her at the bank one Saturday. A fine June morning with the sky stretched high and blue and the trees in blossom and the local high street thronging with shoppers, some savouring coffees and pastries in the pavement cafés.

Andrew came through the automatic door, his paying-in book in hand, and almost collided with her. 'Louise.'

She blinked, nodded. A faint colour crept into her cheeks. He sensed her about to move aside and spoke quickly. 'How are you? How's Luke?'

'He's the same,' she said. 'He's in a residential place now.'

'Right.' He couldn't think what else to say. But he didn't want to leave it at that. 'We could get a coffee,' he suggested.

She drew her head back, preparing to refuse. 'Half an hour,' he said. Almost added 'please', but that would sound too desperate.

She hesitated, then gave a little shrug.

'I'll just pay this in.' He held his bank book up.

Two mothers with babies in strollers were just leaving a table outside the deli, so they sat there. It was in full sun, and Louise put her sunglasses on. It made it harder for him to see her expression. 'About before—' Andrew wanted to apologize for the night he'd gone to Garrington's house, but she cut him off.

'It's all right. No harm done.'

'Thanks to you.'

'How have you been?' she asked.

He puffed out his cheeks, exhaled heavily. 'Hard to say. Not great.' His stomach muscles cramped.

'It's not something you get over, is it?' she said. 'It will always be with you.'

He swallowed, nodded. He was relieved to be interrupted by the waiter taking their order.

'And Luke,' he said, when they had chosen their drinks, 'the place he's in, it's okay?'

'Fine, yeah. The staff are great.'

'And the chances of him coming round?'

He saw her lips tighten, the muscle in her jaw tense. She raised a hand to her mouth.

'Sorry,' he said; he'd put his foot in it.

'The other day,' she made a little huffing sound, 'someone at work I don't know well, she said how awful it must be for him, trapped like that.'

Andrew groaned in sympathy.

'How can I know? How can anyone know?' Louise said. 'He might be dancing or he might be screaming.' She pulled a tissue from her bag, dabbed beneath her glasses.

'Louise . . .'

'The longer it goes on, the more uncertain I feel.'

'About what?'

'Whether I'm right.' Her voice shook. He waited, attentive, while she lit a cigarette, took a drag. He felt the sun warm on his back and his head, but a chill inside. She smoked some more. 'I can't talk about it,' she said brusquely, lowering her head.

'Yes you can.'

She looked at him.

Their drinks arrived. He stirred his, waiting until they were alone again. 'It's only words,' he told her.

215

She turned her head away, looked across the street. He watched a bus rumble past and a sports car with the top down, more cars. At the next table a toddler began to shriek.

'They say there's nothing going on, no brain activity. No response to pain. The feeding tube, it keeps him alive. If I . . . stop hoping . . .' She could barely string a sentence together.

'But it's your decision.'

'How can I choose that?' she asked him. She shuddered, her shoulders moving.

Tentatively he reached out, touched the back of her hand. He tried to put himself in her situation, imagine it was Jason. Failed. No knowing what he'd do. And Val. Would they even agree? He squeezed her hand, then withdrew his. He saw her arm was tanned, her face too. She was lovely, dark hair, an attractive face: heart-shaped, almond eyes, a dusting of freckles. He wondered what it might be like to hold her, to kiss her.

'What if he is suffering?' she asked him.

'Has anyone suggested that?'

'No.'

'They'd be able to tell,' he said, fragments of his training coming back. 'Raised cortisol levels, that sort of thing.'

'They would?' She stubbed out her cigarette.

'Yes,' he reassured her.

She nodded. 'I didn't mean to lay it all on you.' She picked up her drink. Her nails were short, painted a deep crimson.

'It's fine. And your daughter?'

'Ruby. She's great. She's going to a performing arts school, over in Liverpool. She loves it.' She smiled; he felt the warmth of it. Saw the dimples either side of her mouth. 'She's doing so well.'

'Bit of a hike.'

'She stays during the week.'

'You're on your own,' he said.

Her face seemed to sharpen. Perhaps she had a partner now, or a boyfriend. What did he know?

'I go to Luke's most evenings. Watch telly there with him. Ruby's back at the weekends.' She glanced at her watch. 'I let her lie in.'

'The trial,' he said. 'We were told the middle of October.'

She nodded. 'Ruby wants to go.'

'We're witnesses, Val and I.'

'Oh God,' she said.

He cleared his throat. The toddler wrenched away from his mother and careened into Andrew's thigh. 'Hello,' said Andrew. The child was plump, red-faced, a blob of snot bubbling in one nostril. Andrew recalled the weight of Jason at that age: piggybacking him once his legs got tired, Jason's hands wrapped around his neck, burbling in Andrew's ear, his breath sweet and moist. Andrew's back growing warm and damp where Jason clung to him.

'Grandad.' The toddler stopped wailing, stared at Andrew. God, Andrew thought, he'd never be that now. No children in his life. It wasn't like he could borrow his nephew and niece or suddenly change the family dynamics to play a greater role in their lives.

'Sorry.' The mother prised the child away. 'That's not your grandad,' she said to the toddler.

'Someone asked me if I had any kids the other day, a patient,' Andrew said, sorrow coursing deep and slow within him. 'I didn't know how to answer.' Jason in his crocodile wellies and Batman suit in the garden, a compass in his hand. Turning slowly, then faster, spinning like the needle, spinning round the world.

Louise sucked in a breath.

'It's a beautiful day,' he said. They were harder – the glorious light and fine blue skies a savage counterpoint to the brooding, choking burden of grief.

'We're on to the weather now?' Louise said wryly.

He laughed.

She checked her watch once more.

'We could do this again,' he said. His guts tightened.

She picked up her cigarettes.

'Just coffee, talk,' he said.

'Why?' She tilted her head. He saw himself reflected in her glasses. His hair was receding.

'No one else understands,' he said.

He watched her consider this. A couple sailed past, riding a tandem. Then a car, its windows down, the heavy bass of music pulsing through the air.

'Just coffee,' he said, trying to persuade her.

'I preferred the pub,' she said.

He grinned, nodded, ridiculously grateful.

'I'll ring you,' she said. She hitched her bag on to her shoulder as she stood. She was soon lost from sight. Andrew sat there, reliving the conversation and feeling lighter, younger, more alive than he had for weeks.

Emma

It was the best time of her whole life. Even the annoying bits – the delay to the outbound flight, the shower conking out and the mosquito bites – didn't really bother her. Or Little Kim and Laura arguing about where to go for cocktails or whether to meet up with the Geordie lads who had been flirting at the pool.

The week unspooled in the golden glow of chatter

and preparation. Most of their time was spent getting ready: ready for the beach, ready for lunch, ready for a trip into town to hit the shops, ready for dinner and the nightclubs. Emma let the chatter, the gossip and plots, the jokes and anecdotes flow around her. She happily played the role of judge as one Kim or the other or Laura modelled options for what to wear or how to have their hair. She had brought a novel to read but barely opened it; even at the beach or lounging around the pool it was easier to close her eyes and listen to the others. Blonde Kim could talk for England; she even talked in her sleep, Little Kim said.

Emma's playsuit was in mock denim. She felt a bit self-conscious, didn't like the way her bum looked, but she got a couple of sarongs and used those like skirts tied over it to walk about in. The Kims assumed she wore it instead of a bikini because she was a bit overweight, so that was okay.

One night they were eating on a rooftop terrace. They had shared a mixed platter and were having kebabs and salad when a couple of older men who had finished their meal came over.

'Fancy a nightcap, girls?' the taller one asked. He was muscly and tanned and wore a gold chain. His friend had a shaved head and tattoos all over his arms.

'No,' said Laura. 'Not aiming for bed any time soon.'

Blonde Kim giggled.

'Shame, that,' the man said. He had a hard look in his eyes like he didn't like them even though he had stopped to talk. He reminded Emma of her dad. 'And here's us at a loose end. Mate of ours runs the Blue Dolphin, get a real good discount.'

'Tequila slammers half-price,' said his sidekick.

'Ta, no,' said Laura. 'We've plans.'

Emma saw the first man swallow, his Adam's apple

bobbing in his throat. 'What about you?' He spoke directly to Emma. She felt her face catch fire.

'We've all got plans,' Laura said.

'All right, gobby!' The bloke turned on Laura.

Emma was back on the bus, the same ripple of terror driving through her, the tone and the language signalling violence.

'Fuck off, leave her alone,' said Little Kim.

The man glared at them, then snorted, shook his head, sneering to his companion. 'Leave it, Tony, load of lezzers, in't they.' And he stalked away, his friend hurrying after him.

'Good night, Grandad,' Laura yelled after them, and Blonde Kim hooted. Emma felt herself relax, felt the tension ease away. If she'd been on her own . . . but she hadn't. She was with her mates. Her mates!

Laura caught her eye and winked, and Emma laughed, masking the tears that had threatened.

'Here come the girls!' announced Laura, and raised her arm. Emma and the other two touched palms with her, a joint high-five. Emma thought she would burst with happiness.

She sent postcards home, to Mum and Dad and Gran, and she got Mum and Dad a really nice vase, in the local style, to take back.

They blew all the money they had left on their last night. Cocktails and dinner at the fish place and then Club Dionysus. There was a Dutch DJ playing dance music. The bass was so strong that Emma could feel it going right through her, thundering in her chest and her belly, shuddering with each beat.

The place was packed, but there were loads of bar staff on and Emma was served really quickly. When she got back with the spritzers, the Kims and Laura were talking to a boy dressed like a sailor, who moved away.

'Who was that?' Emma asked Laura.

'The candy man,' Laura laughed. She opened her palm. Emma saw four small pills, each with a little lollipop picture on. She felt a bit weird. She had never taken Ecstasy.

Laura plucked one up and swigged it back. The Kims each reached out in turn. Emma bit her lip. What if she had a bad reaction, collapsed and died on her holiday?

'It's really nice,' Laura said in her ear. 'Get all loved up.'

The music changed and a whoop went up from the crowd. A sea of arms rose in the air. Emma picked up the pill, took it.

It was the best night of her life.

At five in the morning, she and Laura watched the stars fade and the sun rise over the sea, their feet in the wavelets at the edge of the bay, watching the lacy foam patterns in the sand appear and disappear. Emma rubbed at the bites on her arm. Flashes of the night flickered through her mind: laughing with Little Kim, dancing till she was breathless, telling Laura she loved her.

'Why do we have to go back?' she said.

Laura laughed. 'So we can raise the dosh to come again next year.'

The prospect kindled a ray of hope in Emma, but it was soon quenched when she thought of what lay ahead in the months before then. What she'd been able to forget about for the last seven days. Now it lurked, large and squat and cold, ominous, waiting to devour her. The court case.

Andrew

The summer was fading, the air already cooler as September approached. The first conkers littered the pavement outside the house. He saw a bat flit zigzag between the houses as he let himself in.

'I thought you were at Colin's. Where were you?'

Andrew froze, tried to think.

Val was sitting on the stairs; she got to her feet.

'You should have tried my mobile,' he said.

'Where were you?'

'With a friend.'

'What friend?' She spat the word out like it was unpalatable.

He rubbed his forehead. 'What does it matter, Val? She's just a friend.' He set his car keys down on the little table by the phone.

Val came down the stairs. 'Who is she?' Her face was taut with emotion, her eyes glittering.

'Why do you care? You see your friends, don't you? Sheena and Sue, you spend more time socializing with them than you do with me these days.'

It was true; she barely seemed to notice him, still off work, still slower, duller from the medication, resistant to his attempts to involve her in anything. He'd given up trying to get her to try counselling. He had been in to their GP, explained how worried he was, how Val flatly refused to consider either bereavement or relationship counselling. The GP heard him out but more or less told him to give it time and tend to his own needs.

He'd tried suggesting other things: a meal out, a weekend away, a trip to the theatre. All declined with the same flat delivery.

There were times when he felt she blamed him for

Jason's death, that if he'd got downstairs sooner, or arrived home a little later, he could have intervened himself. Prevented it – or taken the blow instead.

Even his attempts to share memories of Jason were thwarted. She always changed the subject, or even questioned the veracity of his recall. 'I don't remember that,' or, 'I think you've got that wrong.' Or even worse, she'd not say anything at all. And his anecdotes, about Jason, the little moment he had shared with her, would hang neglected, discarded between them like something shameful.

'Who is she?' Val said again.

He looked back at her, irritated, then resigned himself to honesty. And damn the consequences. 'Louise,' he said. 'Louise Murray.'

Val recoiled as if he'd slapped her. 'Is that some sort of sick joke?' she said.

'We meet for a drink now and then; sometimes I visit Luke.'

Val flew at him, her fists on his chest, then smacking his face, shrieking, 'You bastard! You fucking bastard.'

He caught her arms, restrained her. 'Stop it,' he shouted. Though part of him thought that this – her rage, her reaction – was healthier than her numb indifference.

'You Judas. How could you?' She spat at him. He flinched as the spittle caught his chin.

'I can talk to her,' he said. 'It's a bit of company.'

Val's face seemed to shrink; she was quaking, her lips drawn back in a grimace. 'That scum, if it hadn't been for him—'

'I'm not listening to this.' He let go of her wrists. He wiped his face on the back of his arm.

'Why not!' she yelled. 'You're always on at me to talk about it, pick it over like some scab.'

'Not like this,' he said.

'Have you fucked her?'

He was shocked, at the question and her vehemence. He sighed. 'No. Would it matter? You're not interested any more.' He felt bile at the back of his throat.

'I hate you,' she said, shaking her head slowly.

'Val.' He reached out a hand.

'It's a complete betrayal,' she said, 'a travesty. Our son would be alive—'

'Luke didn't kill him,' he yelled, losing any composure he had tried to cling to. 'The people who killed him are in prison, they're up in court in six weeks' time. Charged with murder. *They* killed him. They consigned Luke Murray to a living death.'

'I want you to leave.' Punishing him.

'Oh, for Chrissakes, Val.'

'I mean it.'

'Well I'm not going anywhere. This is our house, I'm not leaving. You're too distressed to make any sensible—'

'Don't tell me how I feel!' she snarled at him.

'I'm not leaving you. I'm not going anywhere. We have the court case to get through; when that's over we can talk. But nothing happens till then.'

'You can sleep in the spare room.'

He groaned. 'This . . .' He was overcome, took a breath. 'We are both devastated.'

'Really?' she said sarcastically. 'I can't think why.'

He didn't know how to reach her, felt unmoored, caught in the slipstream of her bitter grief. 'We can't decide anything in this chaos . . . I haven't done anything wrong, Val.'

'You have no idea,' she said. And she turned and went past him and up the stairs.

Andrew sat outside, cradling a Scotch, taking solace from the peace in the garden, the scents of the night. Watching the moths around the wall lamp (they would have given Jason the heebie-jeebies) and the bat, still patrolling hither and thither, swift and silent in its tumbling flight.

He was tempted to call Louise, but imagined she'd be less than pleased to hear him moaning about Val: all those dreaded clichés, my wife doesn't understand me, our marriage is all but over. And he didn't want to sully their friendship with the mess of his marriage.

Was it over? Him and Val? He tried to see the future, a version where they stayed together and came through it, then an alternative one where they separated, and neither felt real.

Perhaps losing Jason was too much for them. He had been the heart of their relationship, and without him there simply wasn't enough to sustain them.

I'm forty-eight, thought Andrew. I could have another forty years. And the prospect frightened him.

CHAPTER FIFTEEN

Louise

The court was almost full. Louise and Ruby were close to the aisle on the front row of the public gallery. Below them was the dock where Thomas Garrington and his accomplice (co-defendant, as all the lawyers put it) Nicola Healy sat. They had identified her in court but the reporters and everyone else were still instructed not to publish or broadcast her name because of her age. If she was found innocent, her anonymity would be preserved.

Beyond the dock, lower down in the court, were the lawyers, the clerks and court recorder, the jury to the left, the witness box to the right and more places for the press and members of the public. The press benches were crammed with reporters. She wondered if the hacks who had savaged Luke's reputation were among them.

Louise felt tense; her mouth kept filling with saliva as if she was going to be sick. She had been told that the opening address by the prosecution would be followed by a showing of the CCTV tape from the bus. She knew what the tape depicted and she would not stay to watch. The thought of seeing Luke abused, vilified and assaulted, of seeing those last few moments before they had chased him off the bus, on him like a pack of hyenas, was more than she could stomach. Pain studded her heart, the chill of sorrow spread over her skin. And she did not want to let those images into her head, or Ruby's. She did not want Luke's fear to stick, frozen and pixelated in her mind, corroding other memories, other pictures.

As the prosecutor, Mr Sweeney, drew his address to a close, Louise got ready to move.

'And in this courtroom, ladies and gentlemen, we will prove to you beyond any doubt that Thomas Garrington and Nicola Healy attacked Luke Murray with intent to murder, and when Jason Barnes attempted to intervene and stop the attack, he was dealt a fatal wound with a knife wielded by Thomas Garrington. Listen carefully to the witnesses we will bring, consider the evidence and then deliver a verdict as you see fit. Your Honour, we would now like to show the jury CCTV footage taken on the bus.'

Louise nodded her head to Ruby, and the two of them walked up and out of the door at the back of the public gallery. The usher there said she would tell them when that evidence had been dealt with.

The waiting area outside the courtroom ran the width of the building, a long marble-floored hallway with full-length windows that looked out on to Crown Square. There were little clots of people here and there waiting to enter or leave the various trials.

Louise hadn't seen Andrew here yet. He had told her he was a witness and would only be able to sit in court once he had given his testimony. The same with his wife. Louise guessed some of the people in the public gallery were other members of the Barnes family, and some would be the parents of Conrad Quinn and Nicola Healy and Thomas Garrington.

The lad looked nothing like she had imagined him, nothing like the glimpse she'd seen on Declan's phone camera. Here, he just looked like a kid who had messed up and was out of his depth. Nothing in his appearance or his demeanour screamed racist or killer. And the girl, skinny as a rake, biting her nails, looked scared to death.

Even as she thought this, there was a well of hatred in her for what they had done. What they had taken. Louise had made an impact statement, which would be taken into account if they were convicted and would affect sentencing. How could you put it into words? It was like something physical, something pulled from your guts, sucked from the marrow of your bones. Shards lodged in your heart. Like losing sight or hearing, like the light going dim and the future reduced to a feat of endurance.

Down the hall, a young man in a tracksuit was crying, wiping at his face with the heel of his hand. An older man beside him patted him on the back, talking quietly.

Out of the window, Louise saw a child, four or so, run after a balloon that skittered along the ground then bounced and rose in the breeze. Louise's mother used to do a number with balloons, she suddenly remembered, but couldn't recall the song she sang. The balloons were swirly metallic colours. She had given Louise one and Louise had tied it up next to her wardrobe. They'd used it for a game of keepsie-upsie. Was it Christmas time?

'Mum.' Ruby nudged her. The usher had come out of the court. It was time to go back in. Louise fought the ripple of apprehension, the urge to turn and go the other way, ignored the roiling in her stomach and followed her daughter.

Emma

The woman said, 'It's time now,' and Emma felt the ground tilt and her vision darken.

'You'll be fine,' said Laura.

Emma tried to smile but her face was beyond her control.

Laura gave her a quick hug. 'Good luck. I'll be watching.'

Laura had found her sobbing in the toilets at work a fortnight ago, almost gibbering with terror at the prospect of appearing in court. She had got another letter telling her when to come to court, and a phone call offering her a visit in advance to have a look round. She hadn't slept. Her leg hurt.

'You can bring a friend,' Laura told her, after she had stopped crying. Laura was looking at the leaflet that had come with the letter. 'I'll come.'

'Will you?'

'Yeah, course,' Laura said.

'What if I say the wrong thing?'

'You won't. Just tell them what you saw, that's all. Stick to your guns.'

Now Emma followed the usher into the court and took her place in the witness box. She swore on the Bible to tell the truth. The judge told her to speak up. She felt inadequate already.

Out of the corner of her eye she saw Laura take a seat in the public gallery. There they were, the two defendants, in the dock. Emma looked away, but she had already noticed that he wore a suit and shirt and tie and the girl next to him wore a plain dark dress. He looked tired, the big eyes duller than Emma remembered.

Mr Sweeney, the barrister for the prosecution, was talking to her. Asking her easy questions: her name, where she lived, how she travelled to and from work. But even answering those she could feel her tongue thick and clumsy, her breathing out of sync. Mr Sweeney explained that the jury had seen CCTV footage of events on the bus, on the seventeenth of December 2010. They had also seen that Emma had the seat across the aisle from Luke Murray and close to the defendants.

'In your witness statement you recall the defendants making abusive comments to Luke Murray. Can you tell us what those were?'

Emma swallowed. 'They said he was a wog boy and a dirty nigger and a black bastard.' Her face burned.

'Anything else?'

'A dickhead and a knobhead.' People laughed. Emma felt awful swearing in front of everyone, even though she knew she had to say it exactly as it had been.

'Who actually said wog boy?'

'Thomas Garrington,' she said.

'And dirty nigger?'

'Thomas Garrington.'

'And black bastard?'

'Nicola Healy.' Her throat felt parched.

'And dickhead?'

Embarrassment scalded her skin, her gullet. 'Thomas Garrington.'

'And knobhead?' The word sounded ridiculous coming from the smart lawyer.

'Thomas Garrington, just before he hit him.' She saw the lunge the bully had made in her mind's eye. The sickening noise when Luke's head hit the window.

'Did you hear Thomas Garrington threaten Luke with a knife?'

'Yes,' Emma said.

'Can you remember his exact words?'

'Yes, he said, "I'll do you, I'll have you, I've got a knife."'

'Was anything else said about the knife?'

'Yes, he told the other two to tell Luke. And Conrad Quinn said, "He has, he'll shank you."'

'Did you know what that meant?'

Emma coughed. 'I guessed it meant he'd stab him but I hadn't heard it before.'

'It wasn't a term you were familiar with?'

'No.'

'Was there any more talk about the knife at that point?'

'Nicola Healy said, "He'll cut you."'

'How did Luke react?'

'He ignored them as much as he could; he was looking out of the window.'

'Then Jason Barnes came downstairs. What happened then?'

'Thomas Garrington punched Luke in the head.' She tripped over the words, carried on. 'His head hit the window and Jason came closer and said, "Leave him alone."' Emma remembered the fear, like acid searing through her, and how she had wanted to escape, to disappear. 'Thomas Garrington told Jason to fuck off. And then Jason said "Just leave it."'

'Did you hear Luke speak at any point?'

'No,' she said.

'You saw Luke once he was off the bus?'

'Yes, he was running.'

'Did you see him provoke anyone? See him shout or offer any physical violence?'

'No, he was running away, they were chasing after him.'

'And that was the last you saw?'

She nodded. The lawyer waited and she remembered she had to speak. 'Yes.'

'And where was Jason?'

'He was behind them all, trying to catch up.'

Mr Sweeney nodded and thanked her.

Shaky with relief, Emma turned to go, but the usher put her hand out to stop her.

'Please wait,' the judge said. 'The barristers for the defendants now have the opportunity to cross-examine you.'

Someone sniggered. She was mortified. She stepped back into place.

Mrs Patel came forward; she was defending Thomas Garrington. She wore her hair up in clips at the back of her head and the barrister's wig perched on top. When she spoke she had a southern accent, clipped tones and long vowels.

'I'd like to take you back to the bus, to the point at which someone said, "I've got a knife." Where were you looking then?'

'What?' Emma had the buzzing in her head, the blank static.

'Were you watching my client?'

'No.' She hadn't dared look; she had studied her hands in her lap, the snow outside.

'Where were you looking?'

'Nowhere.'

'So you heard the expression but did not see who said it.'

'I heard it,' Emma said, unnerved.

'And how could you tell who said it?'

'From the voice.'

'From the voice?' Mrs Patel made her sound demented. 'Would it be fair to describe the scene on the bus as chaotic?'

'Yes,' Emma said.

'Things happened quickly?'

'Yes.'

'You did not know any of the people involved?'

'No,' Emma admitted freely.

'Were either of the defendants or Conrad Quinn facing you?'

'No.' And she had prayed that they would not do so; she'd done all she could to make herself invisible, irrelevant.

'Yet you claim to be able to tell who said what in a heated exchange when you were gazing elsewhere? How so?'

The gazing was a cheap shot, as if she hadn't cared about what was happening. She had. But she had been so uncertain, so frightened. 'They sounded different,' Emma said. Her heart was banging in her chest.

'In what way?'

Emma tried to find the words. Her hands were shaking. Everyone could see her hands were shaking. Then Mrs Patel was waiting, her head angled to the side, her eyebrows raised. And Emma couldn't remember what she had been asked. She pressed her knuckles to her mouth.

'Shall I repeat the question?' Mrs Patel asked.

Emma nodded.

'In what way did the defendants sound different from each other?'

'Conrad Quinn sounded squeakier.'

People in the gallery laughed. Emma blinked. She scanned the seats. Found Laura. Laura wasn't looking fed up with her or embarrassed but alert, and she looked straight at Emma and gave a small tip of her head.

'Squeakier?'

'Yes, like he had a cold, and he giggled a lot after he spoke, like he was a bit nervous.'

'Thank you,' Mrs Patel said quickly, and Emma felt a bit better because it made sense, what she'd said, and she saw one of the people in the jury nod his head.

'You claim Conrad Quinn said, "He'll shank you."
How would you describe his manner?'

'He was mean, aggressive, they all were.'

'Please only answer the question as put to you,' the
judge said.

'Sorry.' Emma was awkward. She was hot, could feel
sweat between her breasts, on the back of her neck.

'Mr Quinn appeared aggressive and mean?' Mrs
Patel asked.

'Yes.'

'Did he at any point object to what the defendants
were saying?'

'No,' Emma said. She didn't understand why she was
asking this.

'He didn't try and stop them threatening Luke
Murray?'

'No, he joined in.' Emma knew Conrad Quinn had
pleaded guilty to wounding Luke. He had admitted to
the police his part in everything.

'Did you hear anyone coerce him?'

'No,' Emma said.

'And when Jason Barnes remonstrated with Thomas
Garrington, what did Conrad Quinn do?'

'He jeered at him.'

'Jeered?'

'Yes, he jeered.'

'What did he say?'

'I can't remember.'

'Really?' The lawyer's eyes sharpened and Emma felt
a twist inside her. She looked down.

'You can't remember? But you've had perfect recall
up until now; why can't you remember?'

'I don't know,' Emma stammered.

'Perhaps some of what you've already told us is less
than accurate?'

'No, it's all true—' Emma started to say, but Mrs Patel cut her off. 'Can you really be one hundred per cent certain that it was Thomas Garrington who said "I've got a knife"? In the commotion of the encounter, with people jumping on seats and yelling, surely you could be mistaken?'

Emma felt caught, blinded in the spotlight, everyone looking, her head a blur again. 'No,' she said.

'Please speak up.' The judge sounded irritated with her.

Cat got your tongue? Dozy Dora, Whispering Winnie.

'No,' she said; her throat hurt. 'I'm right.'

'Can you be absolutely certain that Thomas Garrington didn't say, "He's got a knife"?' Emma felt a swing of doubt. She steadied herself, replayed the memory. 'No, I'm certain, he said "I've got a knife."'

She waited for the blow, the ridicule, the murmurs to drown her, but nothing happened. The barrister thanked her, invited the judge to ask questions then handed over to Mr Floyd. Mr Floyd was quite young; he had dark hair and looked a bit like an actor in a spy show on the telly. He was Welsh.

'In your statement you said you thought the defendants knew Luke Murray? Why was that?'

'They called him Pukey Luke.'

'Please be precise; who used that name?'

'Erm . . . Thomas Garrington.'

'Did you see my client, Nicola Healy, touch Luke at any point?'

'No.'

'Did you see her touch Jason Barnes?'

'No.'

'Did you see her touch either Luke Murray or Jason Barnes after they got off the bus?'

'No.'

'And you didn't say anything on the bus when the alleged threats were made?'

'No.' Emma bit her cheek. Felt the fizz of static in her head.

'You didn't say anything when Luke Murray was pushed?'

'No.' Emma was shrinking, her breath getting thinner.

'Perhaps you thought it was just horseplay? Is that the case?'

'Erm . . . I wondered . . . Because they knew him and no one else—'

'Did you think it might be horseplay? Yes or no?'

'At first,' Emma said. But then there had been danger in the atmosphere, the violence thick in the air, which had raised every hair on her body, shrivelled her stomach, shredded her nerves. 'But then I didn't.'

'But you still said nothing?'

'I thought . . . I wasn't sure what was happening . . . Nobody else—'

'I'm not asking anybody else,' the barrister said firmly. 'I'm asking you. You weren't sure what was happening? This could have been high jinks getting out of hand? Is that fair?'

'Yes. Perhaps,' she said.

'It might have all calmed down?'

'Yes,' she agreed.

'You didn't want to make a fool of yourself?'

Emma felt herself redden. How did he know? She hadn't said that in her statement.

'Because at that point it was far from clear whether this was a group of youngsters messing about or something more serious. Is that true?'

'I don't know.' She was lost again. In a maze and all the tunnels the same. 'I'm not sure. I was scared.' Her mouth trembled.

'Miss Curtis,' the judge snapped, 'please stick to the questions.'

Mr Floyd spoke. 'I suggest to you that it was far from clear what the relationships were between my client and the other people accompanying her and Luke Murray, and that's why you didn't intervene?'

'No. I was just scared really,' Emma said. She looked at the public gallery, at Laura, at the woman and the girl, and the other group who she thought might be relatives of Jason. 'I'm sorry,' she said. There was a catch in her voice and she fought not to break down, but she couldn't control the way she shook.

'Thank you,' said Mr Floyd. 'No further questions.'

Laura met her in the foyer and hugged her and told her she was bloody brave.

'I'm not,' said Emma, crying a little. 'I'm a coward. I sat there and—'

'Hey, I'd have been the same,' Laura said. 'But you came here. The way they talked to you! Outrageous. I wanted to slap that Patel biddy.'

Emma giggled in spite of herself. The laugh dangerously close to sobbing. There must have been a break then, because the people poured out of the court and milled about.

Mr Sweeney came up. 'Well done,' he said. She wiped her eyes. 'Bit of a rough ride but you did very well.' He moved away, walking swiftly across the concourse. They were all being nice to her and she didn't deserve it.

The teenager she had seen in the public gallery, a beautiful girl who looked a bit like Luke, came over. 'Luke's my brother,' she said; her eyes were soft and hurt. Emma's heart lurched. 'Why didn't you . . .' The girl began to cry.

Emma was smarting, the guilt splintering inside. She

couldn't bring herself to speak; she kept shaking her head by way of apology.

'Ruby.' A woman came, her face drawn; she pulled the girl away.

Emma closed her eyes. She wanted to lie down and die.

'Oh God,' Laura sighed, 'let's go.'

'I'm going to stay.'

'You don't have to.'

'I do,' she said.

'What – and beat yourself up some more?'

For a moment she considered going with Laura, pleasing her friend, escaping, but the tendril of resolve quickened and blossomed. She shrugged. 'I'm going to stay and watch the rest of it. I owe them that.' With her eyes burning, she went back and found a seat in the public gallery.

CHAPTER SIXTEEN

Louise

L ouise had seen pictures of Val Barnes in the papers. One in particular she remembered: Val and Andrew beside the hearse at the cemetery. Val had been wearing a hat with a veil; she was almost as tall as Andrew, willowy.

In person, in the witness stand, she was thin as a rake. She'd fine blonde hair that fell straight to her shoulders, a striking, angular face.

Andrew rarely spoke of her, although he had told Louise that she had been off work with depression and also that she had refused to go see anyone to talk about it, though she was on tablets from the doctor.

Val's voice was firm, cool, as she answered the initial questions. Yes, she was the mother of Jason Barnes. Jason had been out with friends that evening; he was home from university for Christmas. She described being alerted by shouts outside; she went and looked out of their lounge window. She could see figures in the garden. Her husband was upstairs in the shower.

Ruby edged closer to Louise and Louise grasped her hand.

Val described opening the door. 'There was someone on the ground, three others kicking him.'

Louise set her jaw, tried not to go where the words threatened to take her, fought to skim over the surface of them.

'I saw Jason running in through the gate. He was

shouting, "Get off him, leave him." He pulled one of them off, Thomas Garrington. But he pushed Jason back, knocked him over.' She stopped abruptly. Louise watched her steady herself, raise her jaw and then continue. 'I shouted at Jason to stop, to come in. I shouted that I was ringing the police.'

'Did Jason come inside then?' Mr Sweeney, the prosecutor, asked.

'No.' Her voice broke but she went on speaking. 'He . . . erm . . . he picked up this garden lantern, he hit Thomas Garrington on the back. That's when I went in and rang the police and fetched Andrew.'

'What were the others doing?'

'They were still kicking.'

Louise felt something come loose inside her; she arched her neck, breathed through her mouth.

'Were they are all actively involved?'

'Yes,' Val said.

'Can you please describe where the three people were in relation to Luke, and how Luke was lying?'

Ruby squeezed Louise's hand. Louise turned to her, mouthed 'You okay?' prepared to leave if Ruby needed to. Ruby nodded, her mouth pinched with misery, blinking fast. Louise passed her a tissue.

'Thomas Garrington was near his feet. Luke was on his left side facing away from the house; he had his arms over his head, his knees were bent.'

'A foetal position?'

'Yes,' Val said.

He slept like that, Louise thought. And now he can't even do that any more. Instead he lies stretched out, and when they turn him, to avoid bedsores, they never curl his limbs close to his body. She remembered him as an infant coiled like a comma on her grandad's lap. A little sea horse.

'Please carry on,' said Mr Sweeney.

'Conrad Quinn was by his head, near his shoulders.'

'And Nicola Healy?'

Louise saw the girl in the dock look down, studying her hands.

'She was the other side of Luke, near his middle,' said Val.

'And you clearly saw them all kick Luke?'

'Oh yes.' Her tone firm.

'What happened when you returned?'

'I was on the phone in the hall, the door was still open. Andrew ran outside. Thomas Garrington was at the gate, and Nicola Healy too. Jason had his hands on Conrad Quinn, on his shoulders, pulling him away. As Andrew went out, he pulled away from Jason and ran off as well. And Andrew went after them.'

The courtroom was almost silent, tight with concentration. Louise felt brittle; her pulse was thrumming hard.

'I went to Jason, to try and get him to come in, but he was worried about Luke. Andrew came back then, and Jason shouted to get an ambulance.'

'At this stage, did Jason appear to be hurt?'

'No,' Val said quietly.

Louise looked up at the ceiling, at the fine plaster mouldings and the pendulum lights. Ruby wiped her eyes. Louise heard someone in the rows behind her stifle a sob.

'Andrew sent Jason in. We could hear the ambulance coming and Andrew waited outside for them. Jason was trembling.' She swallowed.

Louise felt the hairs on the back of her neck rise.

'Then the police came in,' said Val, 'and Andrew too. He said he thought Jason was in shock and he'd make a hot drink.' Val stopped talking abruptly. She pressed her fist to her mouth and closed her eyes.

'Mrs Barnes?' the barrister enquired softly. Val raised her head, moved her hand to grip at the necklace she wore. She was shivering now, her face quaking, her voice uneven as she spoke. 'Then . . . erm . . . Andrew saw . . . Jason looked so pale . . . He fell forward, he was sitting down and he fell forward, and then . . . he was hurt, there was blood on his coat, on the chair.' Louise's neck tingled; her heart felt too big, swollen in sympathy.

'Jason was taken to hospital then?'

'Yes.'

'And he was declared dead on arrival?'

Val nodded vigorously, tears spilling. 'Yes, but we didn't know for a while.'

'And you were told that he died as a result of a stab wound in the back?'

'Yes,' she said simply. She was amazing, thought Louise. The strength in her as she relived that dreadful night. Her dignity.

The barrister thanked her and the judge ordered a recess before cross-examination.

'You okay?' Louise asked Ruby as they filed out.

Ruby nodded.

'Hungry?'

'Always,' she said wryly.

'We'll grab a sandwich.'

The area near the courts had a spooky, science-fiction feel, Louise thought. Skyscrapers, gleaming in the pale sun and windy open spaces between. Most of the people wore formal work suits. They fitted the setting: polished and glossy, expensive. Louise felt out of place by comparison, and dazed, emptied by the strain of the trial.

When they got back to court, Val was already being questioned by the defence barrister. A current of mutual dislike seemed to crackle between the two women as Mrs Patel tried to undermine Val's account. Val appeared to grow stronger, surer under the barrage. Asserting again, clearly and confidently, what she had seen. Never wavering. Then Mrs Patel focused in on some of the detail.

'When Jason hit Thomas Garrington with a cast-iron lantern, what position was Thomas Garrington in?'

'He was by Luke Murray, by his feet, kicking him.'

'His back to Jason?'

'Yes.'

'So Thomas Garrington was not expecting the blow?'

'No,' said Val.

'He wouldn't have seen it coming?'

'No,' she said.

'Did you see anyone produce a knife?'

The sudden change of topic startled Louise and she sensed the same reaction in Val as Val's head jerked up and she blinked before she replied. 'No.'

'Did you see anyone use a knife?'

'No.'

'Did you hear anyone speak of a knife?' Mrs Patel asked.

'No.'

'You saw Jason arrive in the garden when you first went to the door. You observed everything up until he assaulted Thomas Garrington with the lantern?'

Val hesitated. Louise knew it was the word assaulted. There like an obscenity in that context. Laying blame on Jason. The same way the papers had smeared Luke.

'Yes,' Val replied in a steely tone.

'Did Jason appear to be sober?'

Val blinked. 'I don't know.'

'Was his speech slurred? Was he weaving about?' said Mrs Patel.

'There was a fight going on,' Val protested.

'He had been out drinking with his friends?'

'Yes,' Val said briskly.

'For several hours?' the barrister added.

'Yes. He wasn't drunk,' Val said.

'How could you tell?' Mrs Patel said. Val didn't reply.

'And when you came back to the doorway, only Conrad Quinn was still fighting Jason?'

'Yes,' Val said.

'Mr Quinn was the last to leave the garden?'

'Yes.'

'How did he appear? Mr Quinn?'

'Erm ... out of control, enraged, like a madman. They all did.'

'Mrs Barnes,' the judge said, 'please restrict your replies to the particular question. Members of the jury, please disregard that last reply.'

'Mr Quinn appeared enraged? Did he seem at all frightened?'

'No,' Val said.

'Or upset, or anxious?'

Louise saw that Mrs Patel was shifting attention from her client on to Conrad Quinn, casting him as the real villain. He *was* a villain; he had after all confessed to wounding Luke, but what his role had been in the murder was in dispute.

When Nicola Healy's barrister began, he concentrated on trying to get Val muddled up about Nicola's role in hurting Luke. How many times had Nicola kicked Luke? Which foot had she used? Where had she kicked him?

Again Louise barricaded herself against the tide of images, substituted a rag doll, a mannequin for Luke, refused to contemplate the visceral terror her son must

244

have suffered. Distancing herself from the details, the jagged facts that were all the more horrible for the steady, workaday way in which they were laid out for the court.

Some of the questions were impossible to answer, and Val glared as she gave her replies, aware that the barrister was succeeding in inducing some doubt into the proceedings. Louise knew that it was all they needed. Enough doubt, enough uncertainty and the defendants would walk away scot free.

The final question for Val was about the weapon. 'Did you see Nicola Healy with a knife at any point?'

'No,' Val answered, as everyone knew she would, and closed her eyes.

Louise understood that establishing who had stabbed Jason was crucial to the murder case; that the only people who had seen the fight, Andrew and Val, had no idea a knife had been used. That left the three attackers as the only witnesses. One of them had stabbed Jason. Conrad Quinn claimed he was innocent of that, and Thomas Garrington and Nicola Healy, too, were pleading not guilty. Someone was lying, one of the three was the killer, and Louise felt a wash of unease at how uncertain the outcome now felt.

Andrew

Val came back into the witness suite and sat beside him, looking shattered. She accepted the offer of a cup of tea from one of the volunteers.

'How was it?' Andrew said. 'You okay?'

'They were there,' she said, 'looking like butter wouldn't melt. All scrubbed up.'

They had both been advised not to discuss their

evidence, which seemed preposterous to him, given that they were man and wife and must have relived the events they had seen together many times in the months since it happened. Even so, Andrew asked her what it was like.

'His barrister's a right bitch.' Val gave a swift shake of her head. 'You know what she said?'

The volunteer returned with her drink and Andrew warned Val with a look. Val got the message and kept quiet. The woman told Andrew that he'd probably be called after lunch now. When she'd gone, Val said quietly through gritted teeth, 'She had the audacity to suggest that Jason assaulted one of them. Jason!'

'What?'

'Because he hit Thomas Garrington with the lantern.' She gave a humourless laugh. 'The bloody gall of it.' Her anger twisted into sadness and she pressed her fist to her mouth, squeezed her eyes shut. Andrew put his arm around her, hoping she'd accept the comfort, lean into him, but she was stiff, unyielding. He could smell her hair, her perfume. He reached his hand to cover hers, stroking her fingers, her wedding ring.

Val straightened up, leant forward for her drink. He moved his arm. 'She's there,' she said.

'Who?'

'Louise Murray. I assume it's her, at the front, with a teenage daughter.'

'Of course she'd be here.' He didn't know what Val expected him to say. Any further discussion was prevented by the arrival of three elderly women, witnesses in another case.

After the stifling wait over lunch, it was his turn to go into the witness box. Val left to find a seat in the public gallery.

He took in the court with a sweep of his eyes as he entered the box, feeling slightly giddy. The place looked full. In the public gallery he could see his parents, Val with Colin and Izzie, and Louise and Ruby in front of them. Other families too. The glimpse he got of Garrington in the dock sent a spike of adrenalin through him. He and the girl looked ridiculously young. Callow was the word. They *were* young; she was younger than Jason, he a few months older.

He turned to face ahead – to face the jury – and was sworn in. It was bearable at first, describing Val hammering on the shower door, and chasing them away. Less so as he related Jason's desperate pleas about Luke: 'I think they've killed him. Get an ambulance!' Tasted again the raw desperation in Jason's voice.

Andrew could hear the tremor in his own voice as he spoke about Luke. 'His face, you couldn't really make the features out, there was a lot of blood but he was still breathing.'

'Did you notice the lantern?'

'No.'

'And then Jason went inside?'

'Yes, there was a policeman who wanted to speak to Val. Jason . . . I could see something was wrong, the way he looked.' Andrew took a breath. His hands clasped together rigid. If he'd known Jason was wounded at that point? If he'd got the paramedics to stop the bleeding straight away, could he have been saved? The treacherous thought, torturous, slithered through him.

'Then he collapsed.' Andrew clenched his jaw, damming the tide of emotion that threatened to engulf him. He cleared his throat, answered the remaining questions about the hospital, the death with short, practical replies, in a dry, flat tone.

Mrs Patel began with an expression of sympathy for his loss and a comment about how difficult this must be.

On his guard after what Val had said, Andrew didn't trust a word of it. She confirmed that he had given identifying information to assist in the drawing up of the e-fits.

'You didn't see the beginning of the altercation?' she asked.

'No, I was upstairs.'

'You didn't see Jason hit Thomas Garrington with a cast-iron lantern?'

'No, but Val told me—'

'Hearsay,' she barked, and the judge asked him to confine his testimony to those things he had witnessed directly.

'You didn't see anyone use a knife?'

'No,' he said.

'When you went into the garden, where were the defendants?'

'By the gate, near the pavement.'

'And Conrad Quinn?'

'He was with Jason, Jason was pushing him.' The figures in the spiralling snow.

'Pushing or pulling?'

'Erm . . .' Andrew pictured the scene. 'Pushing, pushing him away.'

'You're certain?'

'I think so,' he said.

'You're not sure?'

His stomach flipped. 'That's how it looked,' he said. But he felt she had scored a point. He had to be clear, he knew that; he had to be convincing, rock solid, not waver, allowing different interpretations.

'What were Thomas Garrington and Nicola Healy doing at that time?'

'Shouting.'

'What were they shouting?'

'I don't know, I think—'

'We don't want your thoughts, Mr Barnes, we want the facts.'

'Right.' He ground his teeth together. He could feel sweat on his palms, on the sides of his chest. He was here to tell them what had happened to Jason, but it was a trap, a false trail. She was leading him down it, away into marsh and bog, places where the sun didn't shine, where shadows lurked and shifted shape. And he was stuck. Sinking sand. He blinked, his eyes losing focus; saw Jason, just leaving the courtroom, slipping out and glancing back but distracted. Distracted and not seeing Andrew.

'Mr Barnes.'

'Sorry?'

'Shall I repeat the question?'

He couldn't do it. He had come here for justice, to bear witness, and he couldn't even do that properly. He was diminished. 'I'm sorry,' he said again. He dared not speak; his jaw ached with the tension, his heart felt as if it would burst. The usher stepped towards the witness box. But he would not give in. He held up one hand. 'I'm fine,' he said. 'I want to carry on,' but he couldn't control the way his hand trembled.

'Very well,' said the judge.

Mrs Patel resumed her questioning. 'What was Thomas Garrington shouting as he stood at the other side of the fence?'

'I don't know,' he said.

'So he may well have been remonstrating with Conrad Quinn?'

He stared at her. 'It didn't look like that, it looked like—'

'But you've just told the court you don't know—'

'Their body language,' he interrupted. 'They were

excited, high, wild. Ready to run. They were waiting for him.'

'Speculation,' she rapped.

'That's what I saw.'

'Your Honour ...' There was an interchange between the lawyer and the judge. Andrew took a sip of water. He could do this, he had to do this. It was all that was left to him.

Mrs Patel resumed her cross-examination and he answered her few remaining questions with as much clarity as he could muster.

Mr Floyd, the barrister for Nicola Healy, appeared to take up the same thread. Implying that Nicola Healy and Thomas Garrington had fled the scene and wanted Conrad to come too. 'Conrad Quinn was still struggling with Jason, am I right?' he asked.

Andrew agreed.

'Conrad Quinn had persisted even when his friends had run off?'

'Only for a moment,' Andrew said.

'A moment?' Mr Floyd scowled. Could he be more precise? 'One second, two seconds, five?'

Andrew counted in his head. 'Three, no more.'

'How long would you say you were outside in all? Until you returned after the chase?'

'It's difficult to say. It was all very quick.'

'When you first came out of the house, was Conrad Quinn kicking Luke Barnes?'

'No, he was struggling with Jason.' They kept coming back to Conrad, to what he was doing, but Conrad wasn't up there in the dock, the other two were.

'Did you see Nicola Healy touch Jason at any point?'

'No,' Andrew said.

'Did you see Nicola Healy kick Luke Murray?'

'No.'

'Did you see anyone kick Luke Murray?'

'No.'

'Would it be true to say that the only violence you witnessed that night came from Conrad Quinn and was directed at your son Jason?'

He felt a swell of irritation. It wasn't a fair question. It ignored everything else: what had happened on the bus, then what Val had seen. 'Yes, but—'

'Thank you. No further questions.'

Andrew walked back down into the pit of the building, numbly following the volunteer to the witness suite. He felt a flame of anger growing steadily inside him. For the first time he grasped that they might not win, that the defendants might possibly be acquitted, and he knew then that he would spend the rest of his life trying to bring them to justice if that was the case. He felt his fury cooling and hardening into something solid as stone. He would never give up, never let it go.

CHAPTER SEVENTEEN

Louise

The second day of the trial opened with Conrad Quinn in the witness box. Before he was called, the judge announced that if there was any disturbance in court, he would clear the gallery.

Louise heard the whispers behind her – liar, grass, scum – as he came up the steps into the dock. He was accompanied by a uniformed guard, a reminder to everyone that he had come from prison, where he was on remand awaiting sentencing.

She fixed her eyes on him. He was wiry, short; he looked undernourished, ill fed. He had a cheap-looking suit on. It was too big for him, shoulders sagging, the sleeves drowning his hands. He had a tattoo on his neck, barbed wire. His hair was so short you could see the pale scalp beneath, and marks here and there as if he'd shaved it himself and nicked the skin. This was the boy who had destroyed Luke, the one who had kicked him in the head until—

Her hurt, her rage trembled beneath her skin. She took him in, drank him in, avid.

Mr Sweeney cut straight to the chase. 'Conrad, you pleaded guilty to charges of Section 18 wounding in the case of Luke Murray, is that correct?'

'Yes, sir,' he said.

The sir made Louise want to weep. As if showing respect for authority now would help him. Or perhaps he had to say it in prison and had got into the habit.

'You just answer the questions; no "sir" needed.'

The boy nodded.

'And have you given a full and truthful account of the incident to the police?'

'Yes.'

Someone hissed. The judge didn't appear to notice.

'In order to appreciate the sequence of events that led to the affray, I would like you to tell the court about an incident that occurred on the thirty-first of October 2010. At a house party. When Luke Murray and Thomas Garrington exchanged words.'

Louise braced herself. Ruby gave her a look; she knew what was coming too.

'We was at this party and Gazza was—'

'Mr Garrington?'

Conrad Quinn shuffled uneasily, gave an embarrassed smirk. 'Yes, he was having a go at this girl, ragging her, you know. Like putting her down. And Luke tells him to do one.'

What might have happened if Luke had kept his mouth shut, not said anything and left the party then? No run-in with Garrington, no deadly encounter on the bus. He'd still be coming home, heading straight for the microwave, then the Xbox. Still learning his trade as an electrician, a bit of money in his pocket, growing in confidence, more settled, happier. Maybe meeting a girl, someone bright and funny; he was a looker, after all. Getting a job, married, babies.

'"Do one"; that means to leave, to stop?' Mr Sweeney clarified.

'Yeah. And Gazza didn't like it, he swings for him and he misses. Luke trips him up and he hits the deck and he's fuming. Really racked off. Then Luke's got his phone out filming. Then they went.'

'They?'

'Luke and his mate.'

Oh Luke. Again the petty spite of filming and then circulating the footage of Garrington on the floor, looking stupid, threatened to unravel her. A moment's meanness that had led to such a bitter end.

'What became of this video clip?'

'They posted it on the web,' said Conrad Quinn.

'Did Thomas Garrington and Luke Murray know each other prior to this?' Mr Sweeney asked.

'No.' Conrad Quinn rubbed the underneath of his nose to and fro with the back of his index finger.

'And after that?'

'Gazza swore he'd get even.'

Louise blinked hard, felt her throat close. This was important: that Thomas Garrington had made threats. All those days between Halloween and December the seventeenth and Luke had been a marked man. Had he known? Had he any idea that Garrington would come after him? Did he think he'd get away with it?

'And did Thomas Garrington see Luke Murray before the night of the seventeenth of December?'

'No.'

'That evening you were with Thomas Garrington and Nicola Healy. Can you tell us what you had been doing prior to boarding the bus?'

'Hangin' out at Nicola's.'

'Doing what?'

'Just hangin' out, drinking and that.'

'What were you drinking?'

'Baileys.'

There was a ripple of laughter at this. The image of the cream liqueur, the Christmas drink popular with mums and grandmas, was at odds with that of kids getting rat-arsed. Louise hated them for laughing.

'It was her mum's,' he added, by way of excuse.

Louise saw Nicola wriggle; as though this pathetic misdemeanour could in any way compare to what had followed.

'And did you consume any drugs?' said Mr Sweeney.

'Just some coke.'

'Cocaine?'

'Yeah. Then her mum kicked us out, so we went to get the bus to Gazza's. Luke was on the bus. It all kicked off. Gazza went for him, ranting he was, and he hit him.'

'What were you doing?'

'I didn't hit him,' Conrad Quinn said defiantly. 'Not then.'

'Did you verbally abuse Luke Murray?' asked Mr Sweeney.

'Yeah.' At least he had the grace to look ashamed, thought Louise.

'What did you call him?'

As the litany rang out, Louise felt the punch of each one, set her teeth against imagining Luke's feelings as they harangued him.

'And when Jason Barnes intervened and Luke ran off the bus, you gave chase?'

'Yeah.'

'Tell us in your own words what happened then?'

Louise felt nausea rising, a burning beneath her breastbone.

'I ran and Luke went into this front garden but Gazza grabbed him before he could get to the door.'

'Why d'you think he was going to the door?'

Conrad Quinn shrugged. 'Made sense, try and get some help.'

And if he had? If Val had got there sooner and let him in? Or Andrew? Just a few moments and things would have been so different.

'Carry on, please,' said Mr Sweeney.

'Gazza pushed him over. It was snowing and he was on the floor. We give him a kicking.'

The affectless tone he used chilled Louise's blood, turned her skin cold.

'Who kicked him?'

'All of us.' Dots danced in her eyes. She tried to swallow the knot in her throat, to hang on and not be dragged under by the awful questions and answers.

'More than once?'

'Oh yes.' He gave a jerky nod, almost eager. She hated him; waves of fury rode through her. She wanted to slap at his face, claw at him, shake him, show him the depth of her hurt. How had he ended up like this, this scrappy kid? Had he been restless, unsettled, struggling with school like Luke, and then what? Masked his lack of power, his low self-esteem with aggression? Had he grown up confusing violence with attention, where a slap was as likely as a smile? Or had he simply been weak, lost, following Thomas Garrington wherever that might lead?

'Continue, please.'

'Then Jason Barnes grabbed Gazza and Gazza slung him off. This woman opened the door, she was calling out. Then Jason Barnes hit Gazza on the back, knocked him to his knees.'

'What did he use?'

'I didn't see, I thought it was a metal pipe or summat, but I didn't see it. Gazza was screaming, he got up and he went after Jason. Jason was coming towards me. Then Gazza got his knife out.'

'Where from?'

'He kept it in his boot. And he sticks Jason with it, real fast. Then he runs off and Nicola with him.'

'Where was the knife at this point?' said Mr Sweeney.

'Gazza still had it. He said later he put it in his pocket.'

'Let's stick with what you witnessed. You knew he was carrying a knife?'

'Yes, he always has one.'

'Liar!' a woman yelled. 'You bloody liar.' There was a hubbub in response, people shuffling around to see who had called out, others echoing the sentiments. Louise saw a woman towards the back, her face bright red, mouth tight. The skin of her neck loose, like one of Louise's elderly clients. Her hair puffy and dry, a dandelion halo of an indeterminate shade.

'Silence!' ordered the judge. 'I will not tolerate interjections in my court. If there is any more disruption, those responsible will be held in contempt and the gallery cleared.'

The woman wrenched herself away from the man beside her. Louise thought she'd walk out, but instead she set her face and folded her arms. Louise wondered whose mother she was. Garrington's, she guessed. She thought the ones behind them, the overweight woman and her two daughters, were Nicola's family. The girls looked like Nicola, but she was the prettiest.

'Did you expect Thomas Garrington to use the knife?' said Mr Sweeney.

'No, never. I wouldn't have hung around if I'd known.'

Just for the kicking, then? Louise thought bitterly. This is my son: the one on the ground, the one bleeding in the snow. The reckless one, the live wire, the one who always had to push it that bit too far and was lucky to survive. Lucky? There's a thought to conjure with. The sarcasm was a prop, something sharp and hard to cling to. She would not break down here, she would not. Her nose stung, her teeth were aching, jaw clamped so tight she thought they might shatter.

'You ran from the scene?'

'Yes, soon as I realized what Gazza had done.'

'You didn't remain to continue fighting with Jason Barnes?'

'No, he was just in the way. I was trying to get out of there.'

'Then what happened?' asked Mr Sweeney.

'We ran into the estate until we were sure no one was following us. Gazza said split up. Nicola was like, "What have you done, man? You'll get us all banged up." And I'm the same.'

'And how did Gazza react?'

'He said to stop shittin' ourselves and to separate. Said if anyone asked we're to say we'd been in town after we left Nicola's – where they have the ice rink. Hangin' out there till midnight.'

'When did you find out what had happened to Jason Barnes and Luke Murray?' said Mr Sweeney.

'The next day. Gazza rang us. He said to lie low and that. Not to blab.'

'He was warning you not to say anything about the incident?'

Louise was sick of the term 'incident'. It wasn't a freaking incident; it was murder and attempted murder.

'Yes, he was,' said Conrad Quinn.

The boy continued to answer questions about the appeal and seeing their pictures in the paper.

'In all this time did it ever occur to you to come forward and give yourself up?'

'No,' he said.

'Why not?'

''Cos I didn't want to go to prison,' he said. People muttered at this, a ripple of sound. Louise caught Andrew's eye. His gaze was unguarded, naked. She would have liked to have been sitting next to him, she realized. Or going for coffee in the breaks between witnesses. Dissecting the evidence with him, sharing outrage and confusion and indignation. Over the months, she had come to appreciate his company. The tragedy that linked them put them on special ground, a unique tribe in a ghastly place that only those who'd lived through similar experiences could comprehend.

'But once you were arrested and charged, you turned Queen's evidence, pleading guilty to Section 18 wounding, a very serious charge that carries a lengthy sentence. When you could have pleaded not guilty along with the defendants and possibly been acquitted. Why didn't you do that?'

'Because I know what I've done and what I 'aven't and it seemed best to tell the truth. I never meant to kill anyone, and I never did. I never had any intent. And if I lied and pleaded not guilty and then if it went the wrong way, the trial I mean, I'd get life for something I never did.'

'One final question,' Mr Sweeney said. He paused and the room stilled. 'Please consider your answer very carefully and remember you are under oath.'

The boy nodded, made the same nervous gesture wiping at his nose.

'Did you clearly see Thomas Garrington stab Jason Barnes with a knife?'

'Yes, I did. I did. He did it.'

Andrew

If Andrew thought his own cross-examination was tough, it was a walk in the park compared to the savaging that Conrad Quinn received. At one point, the judge admonished Mrs Patel for harassing the witness.

The stress told on the lad, who began to rock, obviously a subconscious reaction, tilting up on the balls of his feet and back, wiping repeatedly at his nose and getting less and less articulate as the gruelling interrogation went on.

The gist of the defence was to portray Conrad Quinn as a violent young thug who was out to save his own skin at the expense of his mates.

'Have you ever carried a knife?' Mrs Patel demanded.

When Conrad Quinn hesitated before answering, she swept in with, 'It's not a difficult question, is it? Yes or no?'

'Yes,' he said.

'Regularly?'

'I suppose.'

'You suppose. And where was your knife on the seventeenth of December?'

'In my sock.'

He sounded pathetic, thought Andrew.

'Handy enough to pull out when Jason Barnes came at you.'

'I never!' he said.

'What happened to your knife?' asked Mrs Patel.

'What?' said Conrad Quinn dully.

'Where is it? Where was it when the police searched your house?'

'I got rid of it,' he said.

Andrew groaned inwardly. It looked so incriminating.

'Why?'

'Because of what happened.'

'Because you stabbed Jason Barnes?'

'No!' Conrad Quinn protested, still for a brief moment. His face and his neck, with the unfortunate tattoo, flushed dark red. 'No, because my knife was a bit like Gazza's and they might think it was the one what had been used.'

'Was there any blood on your knife?'

'No,' he said. 'But they could say I'd cleaned it. Bleached it and that.'

'Did you?'

'No. No.' He sounded panicky now, and Andrew caught an intake of breath in the seats behind, where the other families were. What must it be like to be his parents? he wondered. To watch this, to see him there, clumsy and frightened, already baldly admitting to having kicked Luke hard enough to crush his skull and damage his brain.

'Where did you get rid of it?'

'In the river.'

'I'd like to suggest a different version of events. It was you that stabbed Jason, wasn't it? It was your knife, wasn't it?'

'No.'

'You were still there with him when Thomas Garrington and Nicola Healy had run out of the garden. They had seen you get out your knife and they wanted to put as much distance as possible between themselves and you. But you were intent—'

'I did nothing!' Conrad Quinn objected.

'Is there a question?' Mr Sweeney had risen to his feet.

'Did you stab Jason Barnes?' Mrs Patel had her eyes pinned on him.

'No. I never. I never.' Andrew didn't know whether to believe him or not. And if he didn't, how would the jury know? He continued to watch the boy falter and bluster and struggle with Mrs Patel and then with the girl's barrister. Any decorum or composure long gone.

Mr Floyd finished with a flourish, 'It might be easier for this court to believe your account if you had gone to the police in the weeks between the murder and the date of your arrest. Yet you only saw fit to assist in the investigation once you were yourself at risk of being charged with murder. I put it to you that the account you have given was invented afterwards to fit the facts and save your skin. To make Thomas Garrington and Nicola Healy pay for the murder that you actually committed. Isn't that the truth?'

'No. That's a lie. That's a lie!'

'I'd say you know a fair bit about lies,' Mr Floyd said, 'and I put it to you that you are lying to this court.'

'No.' Conrad Quinn swiped at his face.

Andrew rubbed his own forehead. Closed his eyes while the final thrusts and parries were made. It felt like he was watching someone poke a caged animal.

They made their way through the clot of reporters outside in the square, past the cameras and the news vans. Mr Sweeney had advised them not to answer any questions. They would be able to give a statement to the press at the end of the trial, once the verdicts were in. Andrew couldn't second-guess the result any more.

When they reached the car park, he stopped Val and handed her the car keys; he'd go and pay. She didn't even look at him as she took them, didn't speak. Everything about her remote, withdrawn.

Colin shuffled from foot to foot as they waited in line by the pay-station machine. 'You and Val . . .' he began.

'Don't,' Andrew said.

'It's not just the trial, is it?'

Andrew sighed.

The queue moved closer.

'Mum and Dad are—'

'Val's depressed, they know that. And she doesn't

want my help.' Andrew realized he sounded churlish, self-serving.

'She was phenomenal in there,' Colin said. 'Just watching her go through that. She was so strong, and it was . . . everybody was moved. It must have been so hard for her.'

Andrew could imagine it. That grit inside Val, that unbending determination to do what had to be done, to bear witness, to cleave to the truth, to defy any challenge. He closed his eyes. 'She thinks I've betrayed her,' he said.

Colin's eyes widened.

'Not like that. Not exactly. Val blames Luke Murray for everything that happened.'

Colin nodded. 'It's fair to say he provoked the guy.'

'Six weeks prior to the attack. C'mon, Colin. Not exactly provocation. Anyway, I ran into Luke's mother, Louise. We met up.'

Colin stared.

'Just friends,' said Andrew. They moved closer to the machine.

'You idiot.' Colin shook his head and exhaled noisily. He put his ticket in the slot, fed the machine coins.

'There was nothing in it.' Andrew put his ticket in. 'Just for coffee,' he said.

'That hardly matters,' Colin said. 'She's still going to see it as a betrayal, isn't she?'

'Let's just leave it,' Andrew said. 'It's nobody's business but ours.' He could feel Colin's disapproval, great waves of it. But he didn't feel guilty about his friendship with Louise and he wasn't going to pretend to for Colin's sake.

'She's your wife,' Colin said sharply as they climbed the concrete stairwell. Andrew could smell the damp stone, and the fumes of petrol and oil from the cars.

He stopped on the landing and turned to his brother. 'We sit next to each other in court, we sleep under the same roof, we have a joint bank account. That's all there is now. That's the extent of my marriage.'

'Well, a tragedy like this—'

'Don't you bloody dare.' Anger crackled through him, a surge of static. 'Don't you dare lecture me about what a tragedy like this does or doesn't do.' He wanted to hit Colin, shove him down the stairs. Colin was always bossing him about, big brother knows best. Well this was one time when Andrew knew better. He walked quickly up the stairs and pushed through the door to the cars. Colin caught up with him, put a hand on his shoulder. 'Andrew.'

'Just fuck off.' Andrew wheeled away, raising his hands, palms open. 'We'll see you tomorrow,' he said curtly.

He got in the car. He thought Val might ask him what was up with Colin, but she said nothing. He was shattered, his bones and muscles aching as though he'd been beaten up. He hadn't the energy to try and communicate with her. They travelled home in silence, through the mild evening air.

CHAPTER EIGHTEEN

Emma

Emma had been to Gavin to ask for the rest of the week off work to attend the trial. She had not expected him to agree, but when she told him she had some annual leave left and she could use that, he said yes.

On the third day, most of the evidence was from doctors of one sort or another. There was a doctor who had been on duty at the A&E department describing what efforts had been made to revive Jason Barnes. Then the pathologist who performed the post-mortem. He explained Jason's injury and that the massive loss of blood had led to his death. After him they heard from the doctor who had treated Luke Murray and the consultant neurologist who had overseen his care while he was in the infirmary. There were only a couple of points where either of the defence lawyers cross-examined. Mrs Patel asked the pathologist whether he had recorded Jason's blood alcohol level. At this Emma heard a sharp gasp from Mrs Barnes, who was sitting with her husband. The pathologist told them that Jason's blood alcohol level was raised. He gave a figure and explained that it was just over the drink-drive limit.

'So Jason would have been intoxicated?'

'It's impossible to know what his tolerance level was,' the pathologist said. 'Individuals are affected very differently.'

'But he'd be unfit to drive?'

'Legally, yes.'

And the same barrister asked if the position of the wound gave any indication as to who had used the weapon, whether for example it was someone left-handed or right-handed.

Emma glanced at the defendants in the box, wondering if this was an important issue. But the pathologist said no such thing could be inferred, not even whether the person had struck from behind, or had been facing Jason and reached around him.

There was a sense of disappointment in the courtroom. Emma knew that if this had been on television, the person on the stand would have been able to tell all sorts of things just from the wound that would help them identify the culprit once and for all.

When she was listening to the evidence, Emma didn't feel so awkward, but in between, when there were breaks and everyone went out, she could feel the girl, Luke's sister, glaring at her. Despising her. She imagined other people sharing the same thoughts, whispering about it: *She's the one from the bus. Just sat there. Could see them getting violent, did nothing.*

The last witness for the prosecution was the police inspector in charge of the investigation. He described the sequence of events up to arresting the defendants. He explained that there was no forensic evidence to prove who had used the knife and the weapon had never been recovered in spite of exhaustive searches of the suspects' homes. He also described how Conrad Quinn had confessed and pleaded guilty to a lesser charge.

The defence barristers made a meal of that. Mr Floyd, representing Nicola Healy, focused on how Conrad had tried to evade the police up until his arrest and would probably have remained at large if a member of the public had not helped identify the suspects. Going on about how he only began to co-operate when he faced the most serious of charges. And the other barrister, Mrs Patel, kept repeating that Conrad Quinn was playing the system to save his own skin.

Emma grew tense again, her stomach churning, their hectoring reminding her of the way the lawyers had grilled her about who said what on the bus and how she could possibly tell.

Even the inspector got ruffled, raising his voice a couple of times as they kept on trying to make out that Conrad Quinn was unreliable and an opportunist who had fooled the police.

Finally Mr Sweeney announced that there were no more witnesses for the prosecution, and the judge said the defence case would open in the morning.

On the way to the train, Emma saw the newspaper sandwich board: JASON TRIAL: FULL COVER-AGE. On Monday, the trial had been headline news everywhere. And she had been mentioned. *Fellow passenger Emma Curtis, 23, told the court that Garrington had bragged about having a knife before punching the teenager. At which point Jason Barnes first intervened.*

It had been in the *Express*; her mum had texted her and then rung after tea. 'Your dad saw it before I did. And it was on the six o'clock news too.' She sounded thrilled, as if Emma had done something clever. She heard her mother mumble, 'Just a minute, Roger.' Listened to the rustling as he took the phone, and his voice: '"Visibly shaken", that's what it says here. I can just see it, hah hah! "Claims adviser", it says. Must be in a sorry state to let you advise anyone. Eh, Emma? Cat got your tongue? Here, I'll get no sense out of her.'

Malice delivered, she heard him return the phone to her mum.

'You'll have to tell us all about it,' her mum said.

You must be joking, Emma thought. Was she on another planet? Had she not just heard him?

'When are you home again?'

'I'm not sure,' Emma said.

'Okay. Bye for now. Byeee.'

Emma stared at the fish in her aquarium very hard. She watched a little tetra winnow through the weed in the corner, past the conch shell. She stared and stared but the hot, angry lump in her chest would not melt away.

Andrew

The defence case began with Thomas Garrington taking the stand. He swore on the Bible. Andrew had worked out by now that the couple who always sat near the back were his parents. He was a huge man, bald, with the look of a boxer, the broken nose. She was tiny, nervy, red-faced.

As Thomas Garrington gave his account, prompted by questions from Mrs Patel, Andrew quickly realized that he was contradicting all the salient facts of Conrad's story. According to Thomas, it was Conrad who drew the knife, Conrad who first kicked Luke, Conrad who stabbed Jason. Garrington admitted to calling Luke names and pushing him on the bus. 'I didn't punch him, I just pushed him.'

And when he realized Conrad Quinn had used the knife?

'I got out of there, I couldn't believe it. We didn't even know the guy.'

'How would you describe Jason's actions in the garden?' Mrs Patel asked.

'Well he was really pumped up, you know, screaming. I think he was drunk. He hit me from behind with something, broke my rib.'

Andrew was stunned; he heard Val gasp. He could see the image they were trying to construct: Jason raving and pissed, wielding a weapon. A million miles away from the boy he was.

'We'd like to show the court the exhibit,' said the barrister. The judge agreed. A still photograph was projected on to the screens. It was dated four days after the murder and showed Thomas Garrington stripped to the waist, a bruise the size of a plate on his lower back. Someone murmured in sympathy; Val made a sound of disgust. Andrew sucked in a breath, could hardly believe the cheek of it.

'This is the injury you sustained?'

'Yes.'

Val shook her head, made to move. Andrew feared she'd shout out, risk the judge's displeasure and get the public gallery cleared. He put out his hand to restrain her. She turned to him, her face alive with outrage. He nodded; he understood.

'And you visited the GP with this?'

'Yes. He said it was a broken rib,' said Garrington.

'Why do you think Conrad used the knife?'

'Speculation,' protested Mr Sweeney.

'Trying to establish cause,' Mrs Patel said.

'Rephrase the question,' decided the judge.

'Did Conrad tell you why he used the knife?'

'He'd seen Jason hit me; he thought he had a knife an' all. He wanted to defend himself,' said Garrington.

'Did Conrad Quinn believe he was in danger from Jason Barnes?' said Mrs Patel.

'Yeah, the way he was carrying on: like he was off his head.'

This from someone who'd been drinking, snorting coke and had chased down Luke Murray to deliver a beating, thought Andrew.

'You refer to Jason Barnes?'

'Yeah.'

Andrew heard Val groan, and the judge looked across at the public gallery.

Thomas Garrington went on parroting Conrad's evidence, but in his version it was Conrad who had thrown the knife in the river and Conrad who had sworn them to silence.

'What do you say to the allegations Conrad Quinn made in this court that you had a knife and that you stabbed Jason?' Mrs Patel sounded stern, unsympathetic as she put the question.

'It's not true.' His eyes were big and blue and it looked like he was close to tears.

'Can I remind you that you have sworn an oath to tell the truth and only the truth. Who stabbed Jason?'

'Conrad did.'

'Is there anything else, Thomas?' she said quietly.

'I'm sorry. I'm sorry I didn't tell the police. But Conrad was a mate and well ... I knew he'd done wrong but I couldn't turn him in.'

During the break, he and Val were waiting by the windows overlooking Crown Square, going over and over the bare-faced cheek, the audacity of Garrington's story, decrying the exploitative shock value of the photo, all in hushed whispers.

'What if they fall for it?' she said. 'The jury. Think Jason was the aggressor.'

'They won't,' he said. 'They're intelligent people.'

Val baulked, 'We don't know that.'

'They'll believe you, Val,' he said, 'what you say happened, not this garbage.'

She pulled a face. Still worried. 'I'll just go to the loo before they start back.'

He nodded.

A couple of minutes later, he saw Louise and Ruby coming up the nearby stairs.

'Louise,' Andrew said as she reached the hallway. She stopped. She nodded, polite, a little guarded.

'You remember Ruby.'

'Hello,' he said. Bizarre, the stilted introductions, when they had sat in court only a few feet away from each other hearing about their sons, sharing the aftershocks from that terrible night all over again.

He was going to carry on, talk about Garrington's testimony, then he sensed rather than saw Val returning. He twisted round: she was standing across the foyer; she shot a look of such loathing their way that Andrew almost recoiled. He felt she would misinterpret this, weave it into whatever false picture she was composing of his relationship with Louise. He noticed Louise follow his glance. Then Val pivoted on her heels and stalked towards the court.

Louise stood there, red spots of colour blooming on her cheeks.

'I'm sorry,' Andrew said, heartsick and hurting. 'I'd better go.'

He wanted to reassure Val, to explain, to make her believe that Louise was no more than a friend, but then perhaps being just a friend was too much for Val to take. She still blamed Luke, clung to her belief that he was the bogeyman, that he deserved no pity or concern and that by extension his family was to be shunned. Even after all they had heard in court.

Sometimes he thought Val's strength, her conviction, was a flaw rather than a virtue.

Louise

Mr Sweeney got up; he looked grim. 'You called Luke "wog boy", is that right?' he said to Thomas Garrington.

Louise felt apprehension wash through her again. She glanced at Ruby, wishing she could shield her from the abuse, from a world where strangers hurled insults and blows because of a person's skin colour. Ruby raised her head, a gesture of pride and defiance, and Louise's heart rose with love for her.

'I can't remember.'

'You called him "dickhead", yes?'

'Yes,' Garrington said.

'You called him a "dirty nigger"?' said Mr Sweeney. Louise flinched.

'Can't remember,' Garrington said.

'You called him a "knobhead"?' said Mr Sweeney.

'I can't remember.'

'You hit him, forcing his head against the window?'

'I pushed him,' Garrington quibbled.

'And he hit his head against the window?'

'Yes,' Garrington said.

Louise deliberately let her vision blur, gazing into the middle distance. 'Look at me, Mum.' The first time Luke had scaled the sycamore outside the house. Her heart had swooped with fear for him. He must have been forty foot up, legs astride a bough. 'Trust him,' her grandad always said when Luke was tiny. 'Most kids know what they are capable of.' Luke in the tree, burnished by the late autumn sun. King of all he surveyed. The joy of him, the thrill of him. She had crowed with delight. She wrenched her mind back to the here and now.

'You had a knife in your boot?'

'No I never.'

'You had a knife,' Mr Sweeney insisted, 'and Nicola Healy was heard to say, "He'll shank you."'

'She meant Conrad.' The boy's face was stark with anxiety.

'An independent witness, with no vested interest in the outcome of this case, swears that Nicola Healy was referring to you. That it was you who boasted about having a knife.'

'She's wrong, then,' said Garrington.

'Are you asking the jury to take your word over that of an innocent bystander?'

'Yes, 'cos it's true.'

'You had taken cocaine and been drinking alcohol earlier that evening?'

'Yeah.'

'How does it make you feel, cocaine?'

'High.' Someone laughed. Garrington betrayed the trace of a smirk. He was forgetting to play the penitent. Louise felt irritation whip through her.

'Hyped up, aggressive?' Mr Sweeney suggested.

'No.'

'Perhaps the mixture of alcohol and cocaine prompted you to seek out a confrontation, to become violent?'

'No.'

'You kicked Luke Murray?'

'Yes,' Garrington said.

'Where?'

'In the garden.' People laughed. Louise felt a rush of hatred, dizzying, almost robbing her of control. She balled her fists, bit her tongue.

'Where on his body?' Mr Sweeney said quietly.

'His legs.'

'How many times?'

'Don't know.' Garrington chewed at his lip.

'Ten, or twenty?'

'Not that many,' he said.

'How many?'

'Maybe four.'

'You wanted to hurt him. And when Jason Barnes tried to stop the abuse, you pulled a knife. I think you're lying to me, to the jury, to Jason Barnes' parents. You're lying to save your neck.'

'I'm not! Conrad had the knife.'

'Luke Murray had humiliated you, hadn't he? The picture he had taken on your birthday at the house party, he had posted it on the internet, made a fool out of you. You were humiliated, is that fair to say?'

Garrington hesitated. 'Yeah.'

Louise heard Ruby beside her give a little sigh.

'So you wanted revenge, and when Jason Barnes tried to prevent you, you were prepared to do anything to stop him.'

'No.'

'This is a pack of lies, isn't it?' said Mr Sweeney.

'No.'

'Where did you get rid of the knife?'

'I didn't have a knife,' Garrington said.

'You usually carry one.'

'No.' He was red-faced now, frowning.

'You expect us to believe that as a habitual carrier of knives, you chose that particular night to leave your knife at home. The night when you were involved in a hate crime that led to a fatal stabbing?'

'It's true,' he said.

'I don't think so,' said Mr Sweeney. 'I'll tell you

what I think happened. You were kicking Luke; you and Conrad and Nicola. Nicola was near his stomach, Conrad at his head, you were by his legs, closest to the gate.'

Louise, her heart thumping like a drum, her stomach cold and aching, concentrated on taking a steady breath in and out.

'Jason Barnes reached you first; he pulled you away, but you were enjoying yourself by then. Your blood was up and you were relishing the savage attack on Luke Murray. You knocked Jason down and returned to Luke. Jason hit you on the back and you fell down; he moved round you to reach Conrad Quinn, and you pulled out your knife.'

Garrington shook his head continuously, protesting repeatedly, 'No. No. No,' as the barrister continued. 'Jason Barnes had his back to you when you drove the knife into him, pulled it out and ran. That's really what happened, isn't it?'

'No way.' His face contorted, spittle at the corners of his mouth. 'No way. Conrad did it. Not me. I never did it.' He was shouting, his panic and anxiety overridden by a virulent anger.

Louise got a taste of the aggression in the man and understood that he had the wherewithal to kill. She thought he was lying. She believed Conrad Quinn, pathetic though he was. Garrington was a bully. He had been bullying the girl when Luke first ran into him at the house party, and everything Emma Curtis had heard on the bus went against him. Louise looked at the jury, praying that they shared her instincts.

Louise ran into Emma Curtis in the ladies' toilets. She felt a twist of embarrassment and went to leave, then thought better of it. 'My daughter,' Louise said, 'I'm

275

sorry. Things can be very black and white at that age.'

'I'm sorry,' Emma said. She was hugging her upper arms, worry etched on her face. 'I wish I could go back, do something different.'

Louise pressed her tongue to the roof of her mouth. Gathered herself. 'We've all been there,' she said, 'on the train, at the bus stop, in the park. Seen someone needing help, someone outnumbered, someone being hurt. A bloke slapping his girl or a racist hurling abuse. We've all been there and wanted to disappear: if I ignore it, it'll go away.'

'I was scared, and no one else . . .' Emma stopped. Her cheeks were bright red. She looked away.

'My girl, Ruby,' Louise said, 'would I want her to do something in the same situation? With my heart in my mouth, yes. But if she was beaten as a result? Killed?' Louise's voice shook. 'How could I?'

There was a silence. Emma's face was mobile, struggling with emotion.

'But thank you for coming here, that was very brave,' Louise said.

'No. I just wish—'

'You can't go back,' she said. 'It's what you do next, what you do in the future, that matters now.'

Emma gave a brief nod. Louise returned to the foyer, grinding her teeth together and fighting tears.

CHAPTER NINETEEN

Andrew

Nicola Healy's testimony was almost word for word the same as Thomas Garrington's. She accused Conrad Quinn of carrying the knife and of using it. She kept her answers short and shorn of detail or elaboration until she got agitated. She blinked with nerves and often bit her thumbnail, a habit that made her appear even younger than seventeen. When Mr Sweeney began cross-examination, he challenged her about her comments on the bus. 'You said, "He'll cut you." Referring to Thomas Garrington.'

'No, that was Conrad I meant.'

'Not according to an independent witness.'

'Yeah, but she didn't know, did she? I know what I said.'

'Had Gazza told you he was not carrying a knife?'

'No.'

'But you knew he often did carry one?'

'Yeah,' she said.

'So it would be fair to assume that Thomas Garrington did have the knife on him that evening?'

'But he didn't.'

'You didn't know that, though, did you?'

She stalled, her mouth working. 'You're mixing me up,' she complained. She bit at her thumb.

'Both Conrad Quinn and Thomas Garrington could have been carrying knives that evening. They were both habitual carriers of knives. Yet you claim only Conrad had one?'

'Yes.'

'Why wasn't Thomas Garrington carrying his?'

'I don't know. That's just how it was.'

'Do you deny that Thomas Garrington said, "I'll do you. I'll have you. I've got a knife"?'

'Conrad said that.'

'Did Conrad say, "He'll shank you"?'

'No, he said, "I'll shank you."'

'I don't think you're being entirely truthful, Miss Healy. In fact I don't think you're being truthful at all. I think you've twisted the truth to point blame at Conrad Quinn, haven't you?'

'No.'

'Had you met Luke Murray before?'

'No.'

'You knew Thomas Garrington had a score to settle with Luke?'

'Yeah,' she said.

'So the brutal way you attacked him, that was done on Thomas Garrington's behalf, was it?'

'Not really.'

'Why then?'

'He was disrespecting us, wasn't he?' Andrew saw Louise shift in her seat. He imagined her anger at the warped justification.

'How exactly?'

'He told us to fuck off,' she said.

'After you began intimidating him?'

'He should have had more respect, but we never meant for him to get hurt bad, he just needed a bit of a slap.'

'How many times did you kick Luke Murray?' said Mr Sweeney.

'A couple.'

'Mrs Barnes described it as a frenzied attack. Isn't that the truth?'

'No. Just kicked him to scare him a bit. Just a couple of kicks. I never meant to hurt him, but Conrad went mental. Kicking his head over and over.'

'And you say you saw Conrad Quinn stab Jason Barnes?'

'Yes.'

'And Jason was facing Conrad at the time?' said Mr Sweeney.

'Yes, and Conrad had the knife out,' she said.

'Could Jason see the knife?'

'I don't know.' Her answer chimed with an objection of 'Speculation!' from Mr Floyd.

'Was the knife you allege Conrad Quinn to have produced visible to you before Jason touched Conrad?'

'Yes.'

'There was a space between them, and Conrad had the knife?'

'Yes.' She sniffed.

'Jason reached Conrad and grabbed him?'

'Yes.'

'Let's be completely clear about this. Jason Barnes, an unarmed man, advanced towards Conrad Quinn, who had a knife pointed at him?'

'Yeah, I said so.' She sounded defensive, petulant.

'And you're telling us that as Jason moved towards him, Conrad just stood there, did not raise the knife to strike at an open target?'

'Yeah.'

'And then as Jason got close enough, Conrad Quinn reached around and stabbed him in the back?'

'Yeah.'

'Which hand did Conrad use?'

Nicola Healy faltered, opened her mouth and closed it again. Blinked several times. 'I can't remember,' she said. Andrew thought she sensed a trap.

'Everything else is crystal clear, but this particular detail is gone?'

'I don't know, I can't remember,' she said.

'Luke was prone on the floor; you were by his side, his stomach, facing the house. Conrad and Jason would have been just to your right. Just the other side of Luke, a couple of feet away, if that. Was it his left hand, the hand nearest to you, or his right, the one furthest away, that Conrad had the knife in?'

'I can't remember,' she said. Her eyes darting about.

Andrew felt a glow of hope. She was lying. And the last exchange made it clear. He leant forward and rubbed his face, caught movement from along the row, Louise catching Ruby's hand and squeezing it. She knew it too.

Louise

After lunch came the closing speeches. Louise watched the jury as Mr Sweeney began. Most of the jurors were impassive, though one or two nodded on occasion and she thought it was a hopeful sign that almost all of them looked at Mr Sweeney as he spoke, rather than avoiding him. They were prepared to consider what he was telling them. Eye contact mattered; for truth, for lying.

When Luke had told her fibs, she had often been able to tell: the way his eyes slid away, or his elaborate blinking and scratching at the back of his neck. Distraction techniques.

'Look at me,' she'd say. Able to discern in the flicker of his eyes and the expression there whether he was being honest. He got wise to that eventually, would stare at her, eyes bold and bare, unblinking. A mask to fake the truth – at least some of the time. What she'd give for a look like that from him now. For those sweet brown eyes to fly open and brim with life.

She caught up with what Mr Sweeney was saying. 'Two young men with their lives before them, loved by their families and full of promise, cut down by the vicious unprovoked attacks carried out by the defendants. At the beginning of this trial you heard from an independent witness, Emma Curtis. Miss Curtis told you clearly that it was Thomas Garrington who led the attack on Luke Murray and Thomas Garrington who boasted about using his knife. Conrad Quinn witnessed that fatal knife attack on Jason Barnes and has told you what he saw. Make no mistake: in pleading guilty to Section 18 wounding, Conrad Quinn may yet face a life sentence. That was not an easy option; it was an honest option. It was not a selfish choice but a moral choice. In giving evidence, Conrad Quinn has helped those here today who grieve for Jason Barnes, those who face a life sentence caring for Luke Murray; he has helped them pursue justice. Luke Murray did not provoke his attackers on that December night. Luke Murray, an apprentice electrician . . .'

Louise remembered the first thing he had fixed, when he'd replaced an overloaded extension cable with a pair of new wall sockets and she'd dared to hope that he'd stick to the training.

'. . . had completed his end-of-year modules. He had been out to celebrate with his classmates. Luke had discovered his vocation. He was sitting quietly on the bus when he was terrorized by Thomas Garrington, Conrad Quinn and Nicola Healy. Just a few days before Christmas, Luke Murray was kicked so badly that he suffered a fractured skull and serious brain damage. He will never recover.'

Louise tensed at the stark finality of the pronouncement.

'His family will never recover. All three of his attackers are culpable. Only Conrad Quinn has had the guts to own up to his part in this most savage attack.'

He was right, she thought: for all that she hated the boy because of what he had done to Luke, he had confessed. That was brave of him.

'Jason Barnes had started university in September; he was a promising student and a popular one. Home for the holidays, he was on the same bus as Luke. He'd been out for couple of drinks with his friends from school. When Jason saw Luke being racially abused and physically threatened, he did not hesitate. Without thought for his own safety, he tried to defend Luke Murray. Not just on the bus, but afterwards as the trio chased Luke into Jason's own front garden, as they set about their cowardly attack.

'We have heard conflicting accounts of how Jason Barnes was stabbed. I ask you to consider the evidence. On the one hand we have the testimony about the threats on the bus from Emma Curtis, a witness who has no vested interest in the outcome of this trial and who clearly heard Thomas Garrington threaten to use a knife. This is supported by the statement sworn by Conrad Quinn, who stated fully his role in the dreadful attack on Luke Murray and went on to describe the murder. Conrad Quinn described how Thomas Garrington, already crazed with seeking revenge on Luke Murray, his rage fuelled by a cocktail of cocaine and liquor, drew his knife immediately after Jason Barnes hit him with the garden lantern. Thomas Garrington rose up behind Jason and stabbed him. Then weigh that against the bizarre claims of the defendants and ask yourselves these questions. Is it credible that Thomas Garrington did not have a knife on that night of all nights? Is it credible that Emma Curtis did not hear those threats on the bus, made by people only inches from where she was sitting? Is it credible that Jason Barnes launched himself forward towards someone holding a knife? Is it credible that rather than thrust that knife into Jason from the front, the attacker then grabbed him in some sort of bear hug and stabbed him in his back?

'Thomas Garrington and Nicola Healy have attempted to mislead this court, fabricating an account that is not borne out by independent witnesses. Nicola Healy, less than two feet away from Jason, could not even tell you which hand Conrad supposedly held the knife in. There is a simple explanation as to why she could not remember – because Conrad Quinn did not draw a knife and attack Jason Barnes that night; that was the work of Thomas Garrington. Thomas Garrington was at the gate. Ask yourselves why – because he had already used the knife and wanted to make good his escape. It was Thomas Garrington who had the grudge against Luke Murray, it was Thomas Garrington who led the cowardly attack on the bus and it was Thomas Garrington who murdered Jason Barnes. That, members of the jury, is what the evidence tells us.

'Luke Murray did not deserve to be beaten senseless, confined to being fed by a tube for the rest of his days. Jason Barnes, the only child of his loving parents, did not deserve to have his life cut short for trying to help someone in distress. What they both do deserve is justice. They deserve the truth. They and their families deserve to see these callous perpetrators convicted of the charges before you: murder and attempted murder.

Jason Barnes stood up for Luke Murray; members of the jury, I ask you to honour his name by standing up for him in turn.'

Someone was weeping. Ruby too. Louise swallowed, breathed hard, her pulse choppy. There was a moment's silence, then the judge invited Mrs Patel to close for the defence on behalf of Thomas Garrington.

Andrew

Andrew sat tight, though a thousand objections came to him as Mrs Patel's speech unfolded. Her performance was electrifying. Her delivery crisp, perfectly timed.

'Members of the jury, the charges against the defendant are the most grave in the land. Murder and attempted murder. In evidence we have heard confusing, indeed conflicting, accounts of the events of that December night: an altercation that got out of hand and ended in an appalling tragedy. But Thomas Garrington was not the person responsible for kicking Luke Murray in the head. That was Conrad Quinn, a fact confirmed by Conrad Quinn himself and by Mr and Mrs Barnes. It was Conrad Quinn who delivered those brutal blows, Conrad Quinn who left Luke Murray with a fractured skull and serious head injuries that mean he still lies in a coma today.

'Thomas Garrington was not carrying a weapon of any sort that night, but Conrad Quinn was. And when Jason Barnes, rightly incensed by the attack on Luke Murray, and remember, under the influence of alcohol, first battered my client, with such force that he broke one of his ribs, then lunged at Conrad Quinn, it was Conrad Quinn who drew a knife. Conrad Quinn used that knife. He ignored police appeals to come forward and threatened Thomas Garrington and Nicola Healy, warning them not to speak out.'

Battered! Lunged! Andrew felt a swell of rage. Beside him Val twitched, made a little plosive sound of outrage. Jason had had a few beers at the pub and the barrister was implying he was drunk and violent.

'You have heard Conrad Quinn admit to throwing his knife in the river. Is that the action of an innocent man? We have heard no plausible explanation for this action. But if you accept, as I put it to you, that his knife was the murder weapon, then his actions make perfect sense. Conrad Quinn is attempting to fool you, ladies and gentlemen, pleading to a lesser charge – and it is a lesser charge – and falsely accusing my client Thomas Garrington of murder. Don't be fooled. Trust the evidence.'

Why had he thrown his knife away? Andrew thought. If only he'd kept it, he might have been exonerated; they could have proved it was not the weapon that had killed Jason.

'There is no forensic evidence to support Conrad Quinn's reckless allegations. The only witnesses to the knife attack were the defendants and Conrad Quinn. Conrad Quinn blames Thomas Garrington, but both Thomas Garrington and his co-defendant Nicola Healy have told you repeatedly, under oath, that it was Conrad Quinn himself who stabbed Jason Barnes. The burden is on the prosecution to prove beyond all reasonable doubt that the defendants committed the crimes as charged. I say to you that there are many serious doubts about the prosecution case. It falls far, far short of the unshakeable evidence that would be required to convict. The evidence is flimsy, circumstantial, unsound, paltry. Remember, there is not one shred of forensic evidence to support the prosecution case.'

Andrew thought of the snow on the lawn, footprints smeared in the mêlée, obscured by a fresh fall, the snow near Luke sorbet pink.

'The case for the prosecution turns on a few shouted comments heard by a traumatized young woman on a bus and the self-serving account given by the witness who was the most vicious assailant on Luke Murray. A witness who, I caution you, has every reason to evade the full force of the law. I ask you to use your minds as much as your hearts, ladies and gentlemen, and you will find Thomas Garrington not guilty on all counts.'

Andrew ached again for Jason. Even after so many months. In fact it grew harder. How would he cope if they got off? He understood obsession now, tales of campaigning parents, stuck forever in the mire of appeals and hearings. Life limited and defined by the quest for justice. Could he and Val get the authorities to pursue a civil case if a criminal one failed? What if there weren't strong enough grounds? There had to be a reckoning; he had to know who had taken Jason's life. Otherwise he would go mad.

Emma

It was the turn of Mr Floyd, Nicola Healy's lawyer. 'On the seventeenth of December, my client got caught up in events that will haunt her for the rest of her days. She had no idea that a spat between teenagers on a bus would spiral out of control.'

A spat? Emma recalled the atmosphere, the ugly menace. But to be fair, she had tried to persuade herself at the time that it was just kids messing about, hadn't she? Though her gut, the tension in the air, told a different truth.

'Nicola Healy has sworn on oath to tell the whole truth here today, and that is what she has done.'

Emma could see the girl in the dock, her head bent over, a tremor across her shoulders. Was she crying?

'She has sworn on oath that it was Conrad Quinn who threatened Luke with a knife, Conrad Quinn who dealt the most devastating blows once Luke Murray was defenceless on the ground and Conrad Quinn who, drunk on bloodlust, drew his weapon and stabbed Jason Barnes. My client is not guilty. And she chose to fight her case here in court so you might judge her. She has nothing to hide. Nicola Healy never touched Jason Barnes. She did not lay a finger on him. Nor did she encourage anyone else to. The murder of Jason Barnes was an appalling crime, but it was a crime in which Nicola Healy played no part.

'On the charge of attempted murder, my client pleads not guilty too. There is a whole world of difference between a kick that splits someone's skull, as admitted by Conrad Quinn, and one that barely marks the skin. Nicola was horrified to see Conrad Quinn begin the assault with such ferocity. There had been no plan to the events of that evening, no plot to find and hurt Luke Murray. A random encounter on a bus escalated beyond all proportion and spiralled out of control, driven by the savagery of Conrad Quinn. My learned colleague is correct: these are the most serious charges in the land, and the prosecution must prove their case beyond all reasonable doubt. In the case of my client, they have singularly failed to do so. Nicola Healy found herself in a nightmare that still plagues her. But she is innocent, innocent of murder and of attempted murder. Please consider all the evidence you have heard, and if you do so, ladies and gentlemen, I am assured that you will find that you can reach only one conclusion: Nicola Healy is innocent.'

The judge summed up after the break. He told the jury they must decide whether the prosecution had proved that the defendants were guilty as charged. Any uncertainty and a guilty charge could not be agreed. He began to define the laws of murder, and Emma's concentration drifted. She made her way out of the court as quietly as she could. Thomas Garrington's mother gave her an acid look, quick so that no one else could see, and Emma felt sick inside. She couldn't stop thinking about what Luke's mother had said: 'It's what you do now that matters.'

She thought of her life, her job, Laura and the Kims, her flat – less lonely since the holiday. She had the girls round for nights now and again. She thought of the bingeing and the cutting. Her mum and dad. Luke's mum was right. She had been brave, but that was like penance really. Most of the time she wasn't brave and she wasn't happy and it just went on and on. She let it go on and on. Like she was stuck on a travelator going nowhere. Or a luggage carousel, the last bag that no one claimed, going round and round for ever. And she was sick of it all.

Andrew

When they failed to reach agreement in the couple of hours left at the end of the afternoon, the jury was sent home for the night. Andrew's parents had invited him and Val to eat with them that evening. Colin and Izzie would be there, and the kids.

Andrew was ready to leave; he called up to Val, 'We should go.'

She came to the top of the stairs. 'My head's killing me. I'm going to go to bed.'

'Do you want me to stay?' he said.

'No, I'm going to try and sleep.'

'Val, if this is about Louise Murray, I'm so sorry . . .'
He began to climb the stairs.

'It's not,' she said.

'What then?'

'I told you, I've got a headache.'

He reached the top step, leant against the railing on
the landing. 'No. You're still freezing me out. I want to
help. Tell me what's going on.'

'I can't do this now, Andrew. I can't even think about
it. Not while twelve people out there are deciding on the
verdict. I haven't got space in my head.' She looked
harrowed, her eyes burning. 'That's all I can cope with
at the moment.'

'Okay.' He understood. 'But afterwards.' He looked
at her. 'I love you,' he said. 'You know, everybody said
you were amazing on the stand. I wish I could have seen
you. And they'll remember that, the jury.'

'You weren't so bad yourself.' She choked off a little
sob.

He put his palm against her cheek. 'We'll be all right,'
he told her. 'It's nearly over.' He gave her a hug.

'Tell them I'm sorry,' she whispered. 'I really just
need to lie down.'

'Okay.'

They drew apart and he went back downstairs. He
accepted that all the energy she had was focused on the
outcome of the trial. Once they'd got beyond that, then
there'd be a chance to pick up the pieces. To work out
how they could salvage their relationship. He wanted
her back. He would listen to what she needed, and do
all he could to make things right between them. She was
weakened by the depression and it had felt like she was
holding out on him deliberately, being cold and

unresponsive, pushing him away almost as if she was forcing him to give up on her. Well, he wouldn't. He wouldn't throw away twenty-five years. He would be stronger than that, strong enough for both of them if necessary. And his resolution would give them firm ground on which to build their future.

His mother had made a chicken casserole and creamy mashed potatoes. Comfort food, he thought. They were all eager to discuss the court case, the minutiae of replies and rejoinders. The manoeuvrings of the defence. Speculating on who had been lying, who they believed. The spirited debate was a complete contrast to the absence of interaction in his own house. We're living in a mausoleum, he thought, buried alive with our dead son.

He told them what he thought of doing if they lost the case, and they all agreed to back him. Colin said he'd need legal advice about whether they had grounds to bring a civil suit.

'I can ask Mr Sweeney,' said Andrew.

'You won't need to,' his mother said, setting down a cut-glass bowl of fruit salad in the middle of the table. 'Any fool could tell they were guilty as sin.'

'But they can only convict on the evidence,' Andrew pointed out. 'Gut feelings, instinct – they don't count.'

'The evidence is there,' Izzie insisted. 'The girl on the bus for a start.' The chatter went on, and Andrew thought back to the haze of days after it had happened, to the numbness that had enveloped him. The way he had felt there was a veil between himself and the rest of them.

On his way out, his mother contrived to catch him on his own. 'You and Val are having problems?'

'Colin been shooting his mouth off, has he?' He felt a scratch of irritation.

'I have eyes in my head, Andrew,' she said wryly.

'I have tried to help. It's tough. And please don't quote "in sickness and in health" at me.'

'She's still off work?'

'Yes.' He pulled his coat on, grabbed his scarf from the hook on the wall.

'Does she still see her friends?'

'Yes, not as much, but yes.' He paused, collecting his thoughts. 'I know losing Jason, the strain, something's bound to give, but I don't want to lose her too.' His eyes ached.

If he lost Val, he would lose so much more. The joint experiences they had shared, not just with Jason, but everything that had come before: the lost babies, the hardware store, burying her parents, her brother's sudden departure for a monastic life. And their marriage: how they'd discovered each other's charms and irritants, the way they had grown together, the intimacies no one else had knowledge of. And their love: the way his heart used to leap at the sight of her, his senses quicken at her scent. Then at last the wonder of parenthood: the ins and outs of vaccinations, parents' evening, holidays, as well as all the little domestic rituals the three of them developed, the familiarities, like bedtimes spent checking the room for moths. Learning Jason's foibles: the way he got carsick, his inability to sit through a meal without knocking something over, the sound of him singing, his voice fluting like clear water. And always Jason, at the centre, the sun they orbited.

His mother moved to hug him. 'We're here,' she said, 'always.'

'I know,' he said. Moved by her understanding. Grateful to her for not coming out with advice or platitudes.

It was late, but Andrew wasn't ready to go straight home. He rang Louise. 'You okay?'

'Not really,' she said.

'Fancy some company?'

'I don't think so – Ruby's here. It's not a great time.'

'Of course, another day then.' He was disappointed.

'Yeah, thanks for ringing. Andrew?' she said quickly, before he could finish the call. 'It's going to be okay.'

He assumed she meant the verdicts. 'You think?'

'I do. We just have to wait.'

CHAPTER TWENTY

Andrew

The call came late on the second day of deliber-
ations. Val answered it; something quickened in
her eyes and he knew.

'The jury's back,' she said.

He held his hand out for the phone. 'I'll ring the
others.'

'Andrew.' It was a plea. He saw the fear lancing
through her eyes, her face blanched white.

'Oh Val.' He reached her, held her.

'I can't bear it.' She was weeping. He could feel the
bones in her shoulders, the span of her ribs. She was
skeletal.

'I know,' he murmured. 'I know. We'll go together,
we'll be together.' And he heard the prayer in his words.

There was a bizarre, slow-motion quality to the next
hour. The agonizing crawl through the school-run
traffic; parking. Weaving through the press pack
already assembled: people rigging up cameras and
lighting, running cables, setting up ladders.

Then the security checks. Going through the scanner.

Jason on the way to Sardinia, his arms akimbo,
calling to Andrew, 'Can they see all my bones, Dad?'
Putting his trainers back on the wrong feet.

A few years later, aged fourteen, he had made his
jaw-dropping announcement that he would never fly
again; it was the worst thing you could do for the planet.

'What about holidays?' Val had asked Andrew.

'Butlins?' he'd teased her. 'Camping in Wales?'

Now Andrew collected his mobile phone and car keys from the tray and joined Val. As they took their seats, he tried to ignore the nausea that swirled in his stomach. The jury were filing into court, the clerks were in place. The lawyers exchanging pleasantries. The other families settled in their places. There was a steady hum of conversation, a buzz of anticipation that quietened as the usher instructed everyone to stand for the judge.

The clerk got up. 'Would the jury foreman please stand.'

One of the jurors rose to his feet. He dipped his head to swallow; he clasped his hands in front of him.

The clerk spoke. 'In the case of Thomas Garrington, on the count of murder, have you reached a verdict upon which you are all agreed?'

Andrew felt febrile, hot and cold all at once, skin too thin. Val reached over and put her hand on his arm, gripping him tight. I don't care, part of him howled, I don't want this, any of this! I just want him back. Please. I just want my boy back.

'Yes, we have,' the foreman replied.

'What is your verdict?'

Guilty, Andrew prayed. Guilty, guilty, guilty. Val's hand was a vice on his forearm.

'Guilty,' came the foreman's answer.

Andrew's stomach turned over, his heart pounded. He saw Thomas Garrington jolt, his hands go to his head, heard a woman cry out. Val fell against him. He embraced her, shut his eyes.

The clerk asked for silence.

Louise

Louise looked over to Andrew. His face was taut, his mouth clenched tight, a frown scored his forehead. He was cradling Val, her hair over her face, and he had his eyes closed. He looked close to weeping. Louise's heart stumbled. Her head felt muzzy; she heard the wash of blood in her ears.

She and Ruby had come straight here from Luke's bedside. Each evening after the court had finished business they'd told Luke everything they could remember about the day's proceedings. But this afternoon they had simply been filling time until they were summoned. Louise had felt brittle and on edge; she had been smoking too much and her mouth was peppery and dry, her lungs tired.

She had not been able to sleep the night before. So she had sat sewing Luke's quilt. The final edging: a strip of navy drill cotton cut on the bias. The only fabric she had to actually go and buy. The quilt was warm on her knees. As she worked, her eyes roamed over the different hexagons, prompting memories associated with the swatches. The stripy Babygro that Deanne had passed on to her for Ruby. A patch of one of her grandma's summer skirts, sprigs of jasmine on powder blue; as a child nestled on her lap, Louise had tried to count the flowers. A portion from her mother's trousseau, cherry silk; Louise had hesitated before using it, her feelings for her mother still muddled, found wanting even after all this time. She'd spoken to Andrew about it once, briefly. 'I was so cross when she died; that seemed to be my main reaction, and I was cross with her when she was alive. She was always leaving. It was as if I never really had her.' A piece of one of Eddie's flannel shirts. Jamaicans were meant to be natty dressers, but Eddie was a slob. He dressed like a lumberjack. Blue jeans and check shirts, pork-pie hat on occasion. Scrubbed up well enough for their wedding. He made the effort when he had to.

She'd finished the quilt last night and taken it in to Luke today. She'd lined it with a very soft cotton sheet, which would be gentle enough for his skin.

In his room, Ruby had practised her solo for the school's performance of *Chicago*, and Louise had massaged Luke, washed and shaved his head. 'I could leave it, let you grow an Afro,' she teased him, 'but you'd never forgive me, would you?'

The court fell quiet. Louise's stomach contracted. Ruby looked at her, biting her lip, panic and tension just below the surface. Louise nodded, trying to reassure her.

'On the count of attempted murder, have you reached a verdict upon which you are all agreed?'

'Yes.'

'Do you find the defendant Thomas Garrington guilty or not guilty?'

Of trying to kill Luke, chasing him down and . . . Her thoughts were like a mad chatter, splinters inside, teeth sharpened, nails like talons. The horror, feeding on the cold misery of her grief.

'Guilty.'

Louise's heart stammered, robbed her of breath.

'Yes!' Ruby bent forward, collapsing with relief, and Louise put her arms around her.

Andrew

It wasn't over yet. They still had to deliver the verdict on Nicola Healy. She was only a few years older than his niece, thought Andrew. He pictured her as he had first seen her, standing near the gate, in her white fur-trimmed jacket. Screaming along with Garrington. Her eyes wild, her beauty made terrible by the expression on her face and the tableau between them: the body on the floor, Jason and Conrad tugging at each other. The violence acrid in the air.

The clerk asked the defendant to rise. Nicola stood up. Beside Andrew, Val straightened, using a tissue to wipe her eyes and nose.

'In the case of Nicola Healy, on the count of murder, have you reached a verdict upon which you are all agreed?'

'Yes,' the jury foreman said.

'What is your verdict?'

'Not guilty.'

'Yes!' a woman called out, and Nicola turned, looking up at her family, her face pale, raw with hope.

Andrew felt the lurch of disappointment. Then heard shock ripple through the courtroom as people absorbed the verdict. Val shook her head, turned to him with glittering eyes. He took her hand. Held it between his. Rubbed his thumb over her wedding ring.

It's all right, he told himself. Garrington had been found guilty. The jury had given them an answer. Someone to blame, someone who would pay, who would be punished for taking Jason's life. That was what today was about. Justice. Truth. He didn't know what would await them, Garrington and Quinn, how many years they would get. Did not even know if it would do them any good. Everything he had read in the papers over the years seemed to say prison did not rehabilitate. People came out worse than when they went in, with no greater education, insight or understanding and with fewer prospects. Work, accommodation, opportunities even scarcer.

There was cold comfort in the verdicts. He had thought there might more of a sense of peace or resolution. He accepted it was crucial to go through the process, that without the trial, without the ritual of apportioning guilt, he and Val would have been left in limbo. Tearing themselves apart. Even more damaged than they already were. Maybe he'd feel different in time, once he had absorbed it all. Then maybe he'd feel the release he craved.

Louise

Not guilty of murder! Louise froze. Was Nicola going to be freed? She had been there, she had egged them on, she had kicked Luke. It was Nicola who'd called him a black bastard.

Andrew was leaning back looking drained, his eyes bloodshot. She saw his shoulders move as he exhaled, the slight shake of his head. He turned and met her gaze, shared a rueful smile. She wondered what would become of them now. Andrew and his wife. And Andrew and Louise? Would the awkward friendship they had built be broken off? Would either of them want to sustain something rooted in these bloody events? Wouldn't it just be salt in the wound as time went by? Wouldn't they be haunted by the stark facts: that his son had died trying to save hers?

She would miss him. He was a good man.

'On the count of attempted murder, have you reached a verdict upon which you are all agreed?' asked the clerk.

'Yes,' the foreman said.

'Do you find the defendant Nicola Healy guilty or not guilty?'

Nicola, who had kicked him in the belly, the soft part. Surely if Garrington was guilty on both counts, then the jury must have accepted that he and Nicola had lied, had conspired to blame Conrad Quinn for everything. Yet they had cleared the girl of murder. Louise wondered if they had argued, the jury. If any of them had believed Nicola Healy; if they had debated which of the boys was telling the truth.

Louise's breath caught, her head spun. The silence arched across the space; she was suspended, rigid, petrified.

'Guilty.'

Louise felt relief tumbling through her, something loosen inside, and she was weeping, for her boy, for Jason, for herself. For the inhumanity of it all.

'No!' Nicola screamed. 'I never, I never. It's not fair.' The guard made her sit down; she was weeping noisily.

Louise felt a swell of gratitude for Mr Sweeney, the man who had fought for her son's right to justice, who had made them see that he was just an ordinary boy who should have been able to walk the streets without fear. A beloved boy who was cherished and missed.

While the judge spoke, Louise stroked Ruby's back and closed her eyes. She longed for rest and sleep and some semblance of control again. A life not strained to breaking point as hers had been since last December. She felt close to collapsing. The blood scraping through her veins too fast, the surface of her skin, her scalp tender, sensitive, as if she'd been sunburnt or scalded. She was so very tired.

Andrew

After handshakes and good wishes from Mr Sweeney and his team, and the relief of a hot drink, they had to perform for the public.

Mr Sweeney had a prepared statement to read out, and Andrew would speak next. Louise declined; she didn't trust them, the press. Not surprising.

'I'd like to say something.' Ruby spoke up.

Louise looked startled. Ruby handed a piece of paper to her mother. 'I wrote it last night.'

Louise scanned it, blinked rapidly, nodded, mute. She passed it to Mr Sweeney. He read it, smiled at Ruby. 'That's excellent,' he said.

It was sunny outside, a golden autumn afternoon. A warm breeze sent dust motes dancing in the air. But Andrew felt cold to the bone, shivery, edgy in spite of the guilty verdict.

He closed his eyes, saw the warm red of his eyelids. The setting sun flooding Jason's room flaming red. 'And that's the west, the sun always sets there. And the other way is east, where it rises.'

'How does it get there?'

'I'll show you.'

Felt loss tumble through him again. Oh my boy, my love.

There was an atmosphere of victory, of triumph. News crews were asking for comments. Mr Sweeney stood between Val and Andrew, Louise and Ruby as he spoke. Andrew's parents and Colin and Izzie waited behind them with others from the legal team and the police.

'I would like to thank the jury, the witnesses and the families for their dedication and service in an extremely distressing case. The verdict today is all we hoped for and justice has been done. Thank you. Now Mr Barnes would like to address you.'

Andrew shivered, cleared his throat. 'Jason was our wonderful child. A young man with everything ahead of him. And we will never come to terms with losing him.' He faltered, focused on Jason giggling; Jason strumming his guitar; Jason scuffing his feet on the ground, his laces trailing; Jason bent over a map, drawing shark fins in the sea. 'Nothing can bring Jason back,' Andrew said, 'but the people who took him from us have been caught and convicted. For that we are grateful. He will live forever in our hearts.'

Mr Sweeney introduced Ruby, and there was another battery of flashes as the photographers set to work. Ruby raised her piece of paper and read: 'I miss my brother Luke every day. Sometimes you don't know how important a person is until they are gone. Luke is still in a coma; he will probably never wake up. I'm glad the people who did it will be punished, but I wish it had never happened. I wish he was still here, and all right. I love him so much – and my mum. And I want to say thank you to Jason, who tried to protect Luke, and I'm sorry that he lost his life trying to help.'

Val had her eyes cast down, hiding from the sentiments, Andrew guessed. He sniffed hard and focused on the trees that edged the square, the leaves beginning to turn. Mr Sweeney thanked the press, shook hands with the families again, and the group began to split up.

'What would you say to other people, Mr Barnes?' one of the reporters shouted. 'Should they have a go or walk away?' The question hung in the air, echoing round the square as Andrew and Val, their family and Louise and Ruby walked down the steps and through the crowd.

Emma

Emma rang her mum that evening. 'Did you see the news?' she asked her.

'Of course,' her mum said. 'They got what they deserved. A case like that, you wish they'd bring back the death penalty.'

Emma gritted her teeth, closed her eyes. As if more killing would make anything better.

'What train are you getting on Friday?' her mum said.

Emma's mouth went dry. 'I'm not coming.'

'Why? What's happened?'

'It's Dad. I'm sick of him making nasty comments.' Emma got to her feet, walked to the window. There was a train pulling in. She turned back into the room.

'Oh Emma, it's just his way,' her mum wheedled.

'Listen to me,' she said, 'please. I'm not going to put up with it any more.' Her skin felt peculiar, like it was covered in a prickly mesh. Her heart was running fast.

'It's only—'

'Let me talk!' she shouted. There was a shocked silence at the other end of the phone. 'I don't want to see him again. Ever. I don't want to hear from him or about him.' Her voice shook, but she kept going. 'I'd love to see you, Mum, but I'm not coming to the house. Not when he's there.'

'That's ridiculous, Emma,' her mother snapped.

'We can meet in town sometime, or you can come here, but I mean it, Mum.' Emma quelled the fear and the tears that brimmed just below the surface. She had hoped stupidly that her mum might understand, might even have some sympathy.

'You're upset,' her mum cajoled.

'Yes, and he's the reason why. I don't want him in

my life.' She was trembling, her breath hard to catch. She imagined him ranting at her, dragging her home and making her feel sick and stupid.

'He's your father, Emma.'

'I mean it, Mum. I'm going now.'

'Well what shall I tell him?' Her mother's voice rose, shrill with exasperation.

'Whatever you like,' Emma said. 'Bye.' She set down her phone, then ran around the room making mewling noises, half petrified and half elated. Waving her hands at her sides.

After she'd calmed down a bit, she fed the fish and had a Thai green curry ready-meal. And a bowl of rice pudding. Then she texted Laura and Simon: *Anything on @ weekend? Letz party.*

And she sang in the shower.

Andrew

Andrew slept well that night. When he woke, Val's side of the bed was empty. There was a calm within him, reminding him of the sensation after a long hill walk, or an arduous journey: the feeling of achievement, the respite of reaching the final destination. An ordeal completed and the body and mind able to let go.

He showered and dressed. Downstairs he made coffee and toast and took it into the conservatory. He wondered where Val was. Perhaps she'd gone shopping; perhaps the conclusion of the trial, the landmark of the verdict, had released her from the worst of her depression and she had made a new start. Maybe she was out there, busy, practical. The old Val was coming back.

The day was washed in gold. Outside, wasps and hornets hovered among the flowers. He should start some winter crops in the polytunnels. A day doing something relaxing before going back to work.

He heard the door bang, and called out, 'I'm in here.'

His good mood shrivelled when he saw her: she looked beaten down, weakened. 'Would you like coffee?' he asked her. 'Some toast?'

She hesitated, then said, 'Coffee.' She sat on one of the wicker sofas.

'Where've you been?'

'To get my prescription,' she said.

'Right.'

When he returned with their drinks, she was looking out of the windows, her fingers encircling her wrist like a bracelet, twisting to and fro.

'Coffee,' he said, setting it down.

She turned, and he saw that her face was streaked with tears. He felt a punch to his guts. 'Val?' He sat beside her. 'What is it?'

'I can't do it, Andrew. I can't go on like this.'

His chest felt tight, his heart swollen. 'Hey, it'll be all right. You'll get better and we'll find a way . . .'

She shook her head.

'We have to try,' he said. 'We can't just give up. That's not you, not the real you.'

She gave a shivery breath, put her hands over her face and rocked forward.

'It's hard to know where to start,' he said, his throat dry, 'and maybe we need help. After all we've been through, it's no wonder, is it?'

Outside, a butterfly, a small white, danced over the fence. Not a moth. Why were butterflies all right but moths so scary?

'I can't,' she said. She lifted her hands and held them as if in prayer, fingers steepled against her lips.

He was lost again; he had to find his way back, make

her see sense. 'I love you, Val, that's all that matters. I love you and we'll make it work. It might not be easy, but I'm here.'

She looked at him, her nose reddening, eyes spilling tears, her mouth drawn back in anguish. 'I don't know what I feel any more,' she said. 'I'm sorry.' She cried helplessly. 'I think we need some time apart.'

He felt something plummet inside him; vertigo was darkening his vision, filling his head with bees. 'Val, no,' he managed.

She swept at her tears and spoke on, the words coming at him in small bites. 'Sheena's got space. I just need some time.'

'Why?' He couldn't understand. He needed her here. They had made it this far; they had to stick together now. Rebuild their lives. 'Is this because of Jason?'

'No. I don't know,' she said. 'I'm so sorry.'

Anger and panic were swirling within him. 'Don't go.' He looked at her, his eyes blurring. She might never come back. Didn't she love him any more?

'Oh Val,' he said. And then they were embracing and weeping and he felt the future trickling through his fingers, evaporating, changing. The course tilting and altered, the route obscured. He kept hugging her – what else was there to do – until their breathing settled and the tears dried, salt on their cheeks.

EPILOGUE

'Another?' Louise raised the bottle, and Andrew nodded.

'Are we getting drunk?'

'Speak for yourself,' Louise said as she poured the wine. 'I can hold my liquor.' She spilt some, and he laughed.

'Looks like it.'

A fine May evening and they were on her patio; she had lit citronella torches to keep the midges off, and they cast a yellow glow over the table. The rest of the garden was illuminated by the fat white moon that hung above them.

The anniversary of Jason's death had come and gone. Andrew knew that Christmas would always be tainted by the memories. Conrad Quinn had been sentenced. The bus driver had been fired. His claim that work-related stress had made him incapable of acting on the night of the attacks had been thrown out. At the cemetery, Jason's rowan tree was heavy with creamy white flowers. When Andrew had visited at the week-end, there were blue tits flitting among the slender branches, bees buzzing round the blooms.

'How's Val?' Louise said.

He shrugged. 'Still at Sheena's; phased return to work.' But no return to him. Phased withdrawal more like; it felt as though Val was leaving him in stages. Stretching it out, wearing him down. Perhaps she thought it would be too brutal to just put an end to the marriage in one fell swoop. So now they were living apart and he'd had someone come and value the house. He'd asked her about it the last time they had spoken on the phone.

'If you're not coming back—' he'd begun, anger at the prospect simmering beneath his skin, hidden in his voice.

'Andrew, I don't know,' she interrupted.

'Then we might need to sell.'

Silence. He heard her breath, a sip in, then the sound as she swallowed.

'I can get a valuation at least.' He knew part of him was saying this to force a decision from her. He had waited months, giving her time, giving her space. He was frustrated at not being able to reach her. As though he was looking at her through the wrong end of a telescope: remote, miniaturized.

'Okay,' she said dully.

His stomach clenched when she agreed. He'd hoped she would protest, argue with him, give him some sign that the house still had a role to play, would be a home for them again. Allow him to dream of a time when she'd be back there with him.

'I love you,' he said quickly.

'I know,' Val had answered. And said goodbye and hung up.

He had feared for his sanity in the weeks after she left. Times when he got drunk and cursed her and threw things about. Behaving like a child. Still sick with grief for his son, he mourned the marriage. He missed her day and night. It was as if the intimacies they had shared, parenting their lovely boy with his messy ways and his foibles and his sweet smile, had been taken from him. He'd lost access to those joint experiences along with his marriage partner. It made him think that the marriage must have been weakened long before the murder. And the events of that ghastly night had only served to widen the fault lines. But he'd had no inkling. They were his world: Val and Jason.

There would never be enough tears for Jason.

The prospect of permanent separation, of divorce, plagued him. Like an open wound he probed it time and again. Leaving the house would be the final wrench, severing the connection to Jason, to their little family, to the marriage. But he couldn't hang on there alone if Val wasn't coming back. Everything that had made it a home, a sanctuary, was gone now. All we have in the end is memory, he thought, his skin tingling. The shrine was no longer there; he had cleared it away, storing the remnants. Perhaps one day he and Val would have to share them out, along with the family photos; apportion the record of their lives together.

Eventually he had decided that if he was to win her back, he needed to stay strong, retain his dignity and self-respect. He threw himself into his work, gaining satisfaction from the small victories there: people rediscovering speech, overcoming the legacies of illness or accident. Smiles and handshakes and the occasional tears of gratitude.

And he started volunteering. Helping on an orienteering course for hard-to-manage teenagers. Showing them that sat nav wasn't the only system for finding your way. He filled the hours, the long, empty evenings, the wastelands of the weekends. He kept busy. Like Val, the old Val. But he was marking time, too. Treading water. Almost drowning.

Louise lit a cigarette.

'Thought you'd given up?'

'I had.' She shrugged. Her phone chirruped. She picked it up, read the message, smiled. 'Ruby. They got three standing ovations.' Her daughter had been scouted and was appearing in a musical in the West End. Andrew smiled.

Louise looked down at the table, sombre now.

'What is it?' he asked her.

'Luke. What if I sign the form and let him go when one day he might have woken up?'

He put his glass down. 'You know the statistics.'

'Yeah. And I don't believe in miracles. Opium of the masses.'

'Think that's shopping these days, not religion.' He took a drink. 'If you leave Luke alone, ignore the form, and against all the odds he wakes up. What then? The chances are he'll be locked in, or unable to do more than blink, maybe swallow.'

'I know he'll never come back, the Luke I had.' She groaned and covered her eyes with her hand. 'I go round and round and round. If only he could tell me what he'd want.'

'I think you know what he'd want,' Andrew said.

She looked at him sharply, and he feared he'd gone too far. She turned her face away. 'He could run so—' She stopped. 'And climb,' she said. 'We took him out to Alderley Edge once, me and Eddie. Have you been?'

Andrew nodded. He and Jason at the small stone circle. Lifting Jason on to a low branch, promising to hold him tight.

'Luke was still using a buggy. He'd have been three or so. I was pregnant with Ruby. He went over the edge, the cliff bit, like Spiderman. He met this dog, raced off to play. But how can I starve him? Sit there and watch?'

'If you want, if it's any help, I'll come, I'll be there.'

'It's a big ask,' she said.

'What are friends for?'

'Not that, usually!' she joked.

He laughed, full-throated. She always made him laugh. He took a drink.

She ran a hand through her hair. 'Okay. If it comes to that. Thank you.' She settled back, sat for a few moments, smoking and sipping her wine.

He looked up at the heavens, the pole star flaring phosphorus white. The brilliant orb of the moon, with its tracery of blue from the mountains and craters that sculpted its surface. In a garden close by a cat yowled, and then he heard the spat of a cat fight.

'I'd better be off,' he said, and drained his glass.

'Okay.'

He got up, stretched.

'Don't leave it so long next time,' Louise said.

He nodded. 'And if you need me . . .'

'Thanks,' she said. 'Do you want a cab?'

'No, I'll walk.' He looked up at the sky again. 'It's such a lovely night.' He made his way past the sycamore tree and out into the street, and set off among the black shadows and the soft silver light.

She was sitting on the doorstep as he came into the drive, her hair bright in the moonlight. A jolt ran through him.

'Val?'

She got to her feet, gave a ghostly smile. 'You've been out?'

He tasted the lie, tempted, but swallowed it. He would not lie to her. 'Louise's.'

Val blinked, gave a small nod. 'Just friends?' she said, the faintest tremor in her voice but no sarcasm that he could discern.

'Yes,' he said simply, waiting for her to meet his gaze

and judge he was telling the truth. Holding his breath, tensing in anticipation of her reaction.

'How's Luke?'

'The same,' he said, relieved that she had cared to ask.

'I want to come home,' she said, her face crumpling.

He moved to her, his heart kicking in his chest. 'Val.'

'I don't want to sell the house.'

'No, of course not.' His arms went round her. She burrowed her head in the crook of his neck.

'Jason, his whole life was here, we can't lose that,' she said.

'I know.' Was that the reason she wanted to come back: for Jason, his memory, his history, to keep that close? His fingerprints on every door jamb, his laughter in the paint and plaster. Was that all of it? The house a museum, and Andrew – what, a curator? That wasn't enough for him. He wanted her love, her passion; he needed her to want him just as deeply. Not to cling together because of what they had shared and lost, but to cleave together for what the future held, tomorrow and the next day and the years to come. To grow.

He placed his hand on the crown of her head, felt her silky hair and the heat beneath.

'I want you, Val,' he whispered. 'I want you back here with me.' He felt her convulse, a sob in her shoulders. Then she raised her face to look at him. Tear-streaked. She edged closer, closed her eyes. Kissed him. A lover's kiss. Long and sensuous. Leaving them both breathless.

'Let's go in,' he said, blood singing in his veins. He couldn't take his eyes from her face, her lips.

'I love you,' she said, starting to cry again. 'Oh Andrew, I love you so much.'

He pulled her close, hushing her, kissing and stroking

her hair. He drank in the warm night air and the honeyed scent of wallflowers; he stared up at the luminous disc of the moon, climbing higher now, and felt the peace settle inside him.

Across the street, Jason, arms outstretched, walked along the edge of a tall garden fence to the corner. He stood there, wobbling precariously, and beamed at Andrew. That hundred-watt smile. Then he jumped down and set off along the pavement towards town. Andrew watched until he was out of sight.

Then he took Val's hand and they went in together.